The Complete Adventures of

# Richard Knight

R.K.

Volume 3

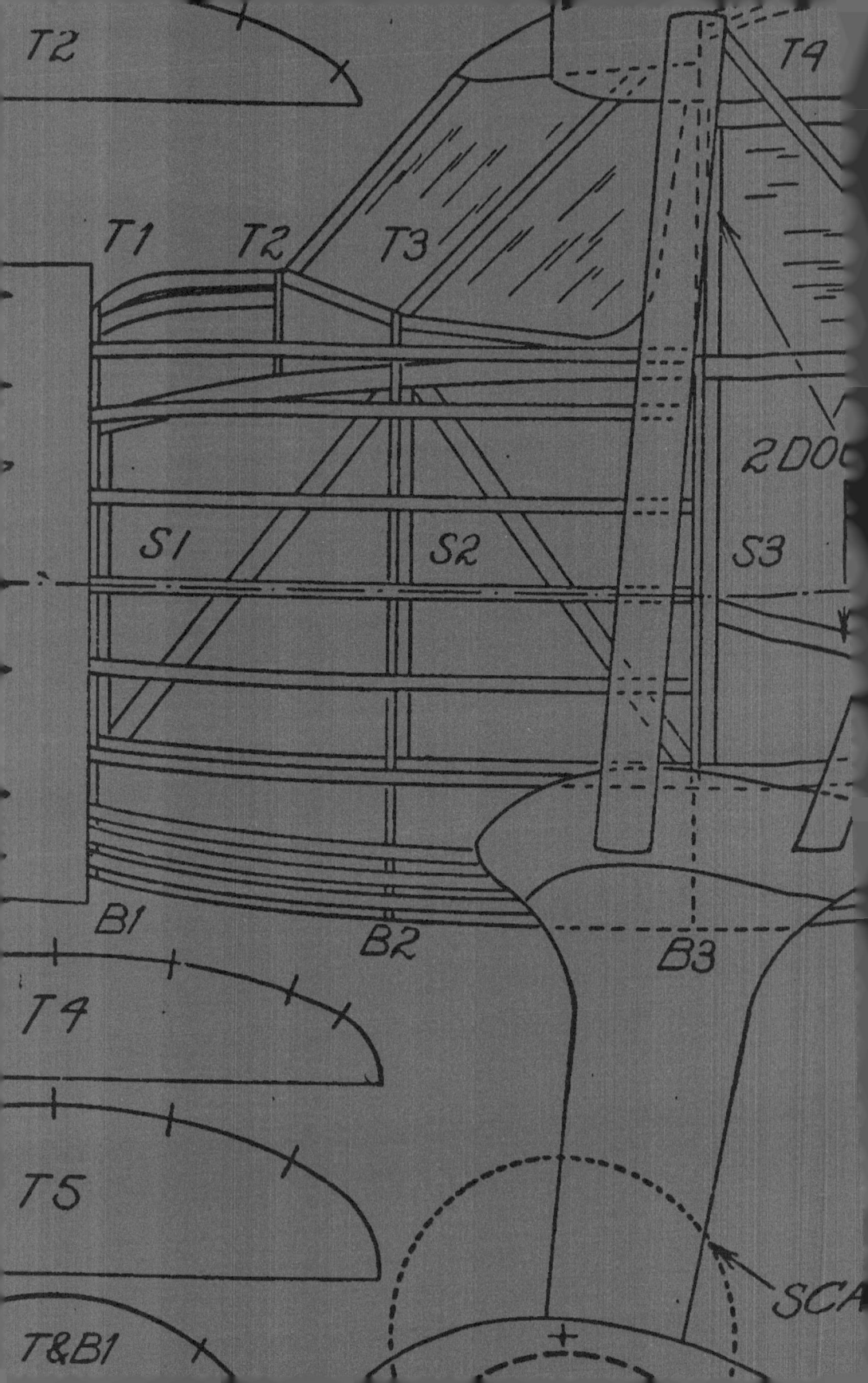

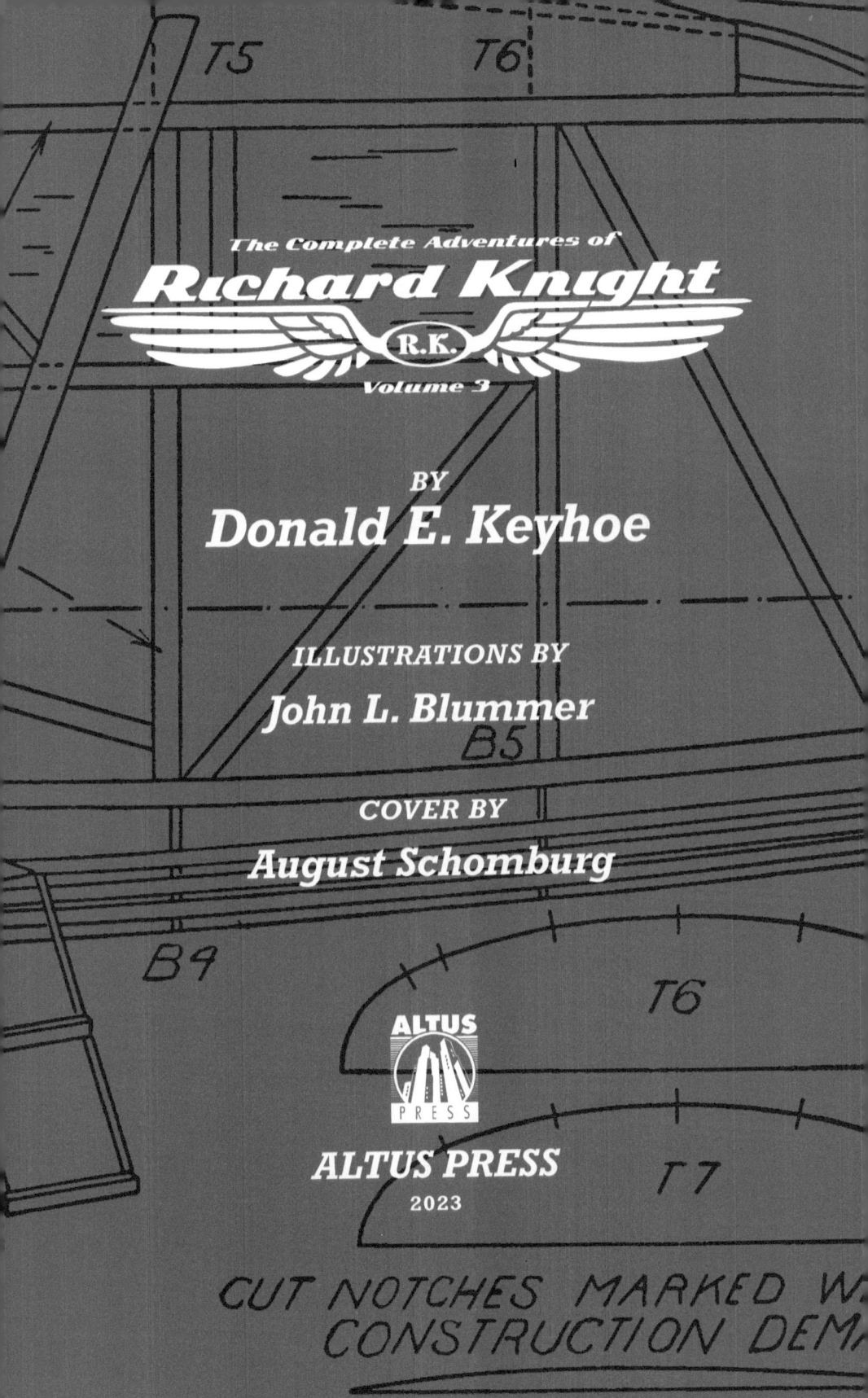

*The Complete Adventures of*

# Richard Knight

**R.K.**

*Volume 3*

BY

# Donald E. Keyhoe

*ILLUSTRATIONS BY*

## John L. Blummer

*COVER BY*

## August Schomburg

**ALTUS PRESS**

2023

PUBLISHING HISTORY

"Hell Hammers Harbin" originally appeared in the March 1938 issue of *Flying Aces* magazine (Vol. 28, No. 4).

"Vultures of Silence" originally appeared in the May 1938 issue of *Flying Aces* magazine (Vol. 29, No. 2).

"Hell's Hangar" originally appeared in the July 1938 issue of *Flying Aces* magazine (Vol. 29, No. 4).

"Sky-Fire Scourge" originally appeared in the August 1938 issue of *Flying Aces* magazine (Vol. 30, No. 1).

Visit *altuspress.com* for more books like this.

# TABLE OF
# *Contents*

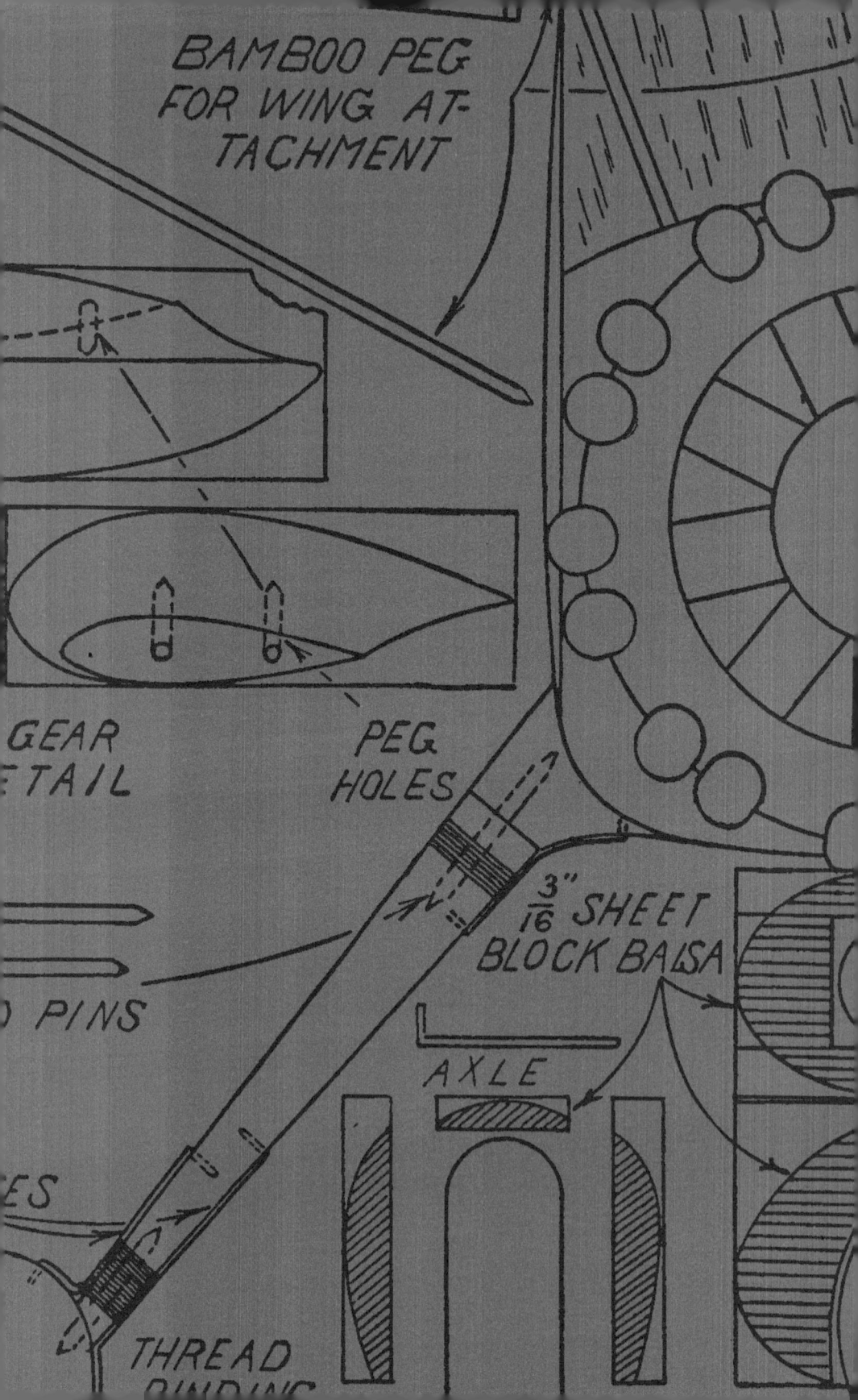

BAMBOO PEG
FOR WING AT-
TACHMENT

GEAR
ETAIL

PEG.
HOLES

PINS

3"/16 SHEET
BLOCK BALSA

AXLE

ES

THREAD

# Hell Hammers Harbin

## CHAPTER I

### White Doom

**F**ROM THE tiny amplifier in the front cockpit of the speeding Northrop, there suddenly came whispered words: *Guam to Q... Guam to Q—Range Three.*

Richard Knight bent over the special high-frequency radio, swiftly pressed a button marked "Three." There was a brief interval as the sealed black stratosphere plane droned on under a frozen moon, then the whispering voice spoke again on the new wave-length.

*Okay, Q... Six, two, one... six, two, one. Five, four, and twenty... Five four, and twenty... That's all for now.*

The bronzed American agent turned, looked back under the double Plexiglas enclosure to where Larry Doyle, former Marine Corps pilot, was fumbling with a map.

"Got that, Lothario? Longitude 126, latitude 45 degrees and twenty minutes."

Doyle grunted, switched on a cockpit light to augment the cheerless moonlight. A broken nose which had healed crookedly gave his homely face a lopsided look. He stared at the map, looked up at Knight.

"That puts us sixty miles southeast of Harbin—just about over the railroad from Mukden. How do you feel?"

Knight smiled a trifle grimly. "There have been times when I've felt better," he admitted.

"Same here," muttered Doyle. "And to think four hours ago I was in the Cathay bar at Shanghai, with a bottle of Scotch and nothin' to worry about."

Knight gazed unseeingly over the wing of the Northrop, and down at the murk of massed clouds which hid the Japanese puppet state of Manchukuo. Then his glance came back to the silent radio.

"If we only knew what it was all about, it wouldn't be so bad. General Brett must be pretty desperate to rush us up here with such sparse information, and especially to send you into a tight spot like this."

Doyle grimaced. "Yeah, I kinda wish I'd learned enough Jap lingo to get by. Nobody'd ever take *me* for a Jap, even if I made up like one. But if I got shoved in front of a firing squad I could tell 'em to go to hell so they'd understand it."

**KNIGHT SWITCHED** off the automatic pilot which, after their take-off from Shanghai, had guided their ship straight over the Yellow Sea and Chosen Bay into the heart of Manchukuo.

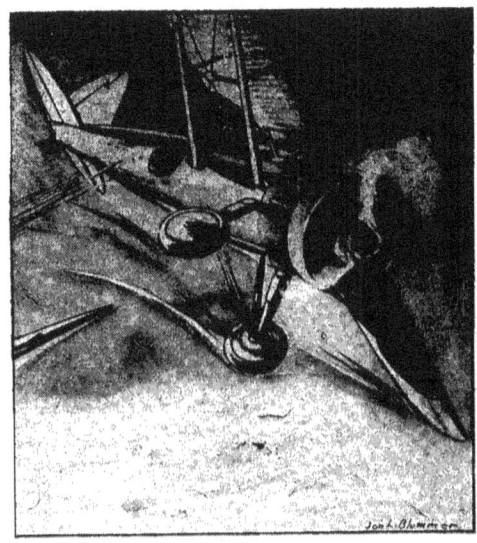

With a swift renversement, Knight hurled the Northrop at the first Nakajima as it plunged past the falling flare. But the other two 91s now charged in diagonally, concentrated a lethal crossfire upon the desperate American airmen.

"If Brett's going to give us those last-minute orders he'd better hurry," he said to Doyle. "We'll be over Harbin in fifteen minutes."

"You sure that G-2 colonel got it straight—the message he gave us at Shanghai?"

"Positive. He said General Brett had rushed to Guam by Clipper with word for us to stand by when we came back from Macao. I saw the Guam message myself both in code and deciphered. It had our secret number, and Brett's the only one who knows it and the two key words before and after it. He said for us to fuel the Northrop to capacity for maximum altitude, to take off for Harbin, and then send 'Q' every ten minutes, alternating on our three high-frequency wave-lengths. He said the Guam station and the flagship at Manila would take bearings. Then Manila would radio their bearings to Guam, and the Guam operator would send us a 'fix' with the latitude and longitude figures backwards. The last sentence was 'Mission desperate, final instructions will be given on Range Two as you near goal; cruise to arrive between nine and nine-thirty.'"

"Arrive where?" growled Doyle. "I suppose we just squat

down on the Harbin airport and tell th' Japs we're th' guys they've got a reward out for."

"Unless we get definite orders—"

Knight broke off as a strained voice sounded from the amplifier:

*B to Q... B to Q!*

"It's the general himself!" exclaimed Doyle. And the voice of the distant Intelligence general went on hastily:

*Do not answer now! Take advice Horace Greeley. Do not settle in city, but follow advice with Seattle twist and discover a Casey Jones line. With speed of three century notes, out from center four M's, then turn right cheek two M's and a very bright emerald will take pilgrims to Plymouth Rock. Prodigal sons take word of apparent Buddha who has their number.*

"Holy smoke—he's gone nuts!" howled Doyle.

"Give me the map!" Knight said tensely. Then, as he was gazing at it under the light, General Brett's voice came again, tense and vibrant:

*B to Q—a repeat. If clear, send number my Washington office. If not, reverse the member.* He went on with a quick and concise repetition of his peculiar message. As he finished, the Q-Agent took up his hand-mike and threw the transmitter switch. He gave the number of Brett's office, switched off the transmitter, and nosed the strato-plane downward.

"Listen, master-mind," said Doyle, "I can unscramble part of that dictionary omelet, but—"

"Remember Horace Greeley's advice, back in the '90s?" Knight interrupted. "He said 'Go West, young man'—and we're going to head West from Harbin. Seattle twist must mean northwest, and a Casey Jones line would be a railroad. There's a railroad running northwest from Harbin, so that fits. At a speed of three hundred, four minutes would cover twenty miles. Then we turn right and fly for ten miles. Either we fire a green Very star, or look for a green light on the ground to show us where to land."

"I got that—the pilgrims landing on Plymouth Rock,"

grunted Doyle. "But what about a Buddha havin' our number. Th' last Buddha idol you monkeyed with turned out to have a bird with a gas-bomb inside it."

"We'll have to figure that out after we land," said Knight. "The main thing is to come in over Harbin without any noise, or we're finished before we start. According to reports, there's a Japanese pursuit squadron stationed at Harbin and the whole place is thick with troops."

"I still think Brett's gone screwy," Doyle said gloomily. "And we were twice as goofy to come up here."

"Switch off your light," said Knight. "We'll be down through those clouds in a few minutes."

**THE TWIN-RADIAL'S** thunder had faded to a muffled drone. Knight watched the altimeter hand sink from 35,000 to 30,000 and then drop steadily as the ship was swallowed up in the solid darkness of the clouds.

The Northrop finally broke through the cloud-masses into snow-filled air. A vague blur of lights appeared ahead and slightly to the right. The Q-Agent swore under his breath. To locate the railroad, they would have to go lower than he had intended. He had not expected snow, but at least it was not heavy.

He closed the throttle completely, and the two-seater descended on faintly-moaning wings. Harbin began to take on shape through the snow flurries. He had visited the city briefly before the Japanese occupation, and now he began to recognize its salient points. The Pristan or wharf district lay almost dead ahead, its well-lighted streets leading up toward the plateau where New Harbin had been built. Holding the ship to its slowest possible glide, he reached for his high-powered field glasses which were held in a clip at one side. He was focussing them on the western part of the Pristan district trying to pick out the northwest railroad, when a queer, faint shriek sounded from up in the night.

He jerked his head back. High and to the north something was flashing down at the speed of a meteorite, leaving a glowing trail behind it. The shriek grew into a terrific screech, all in a second. He shoved the throttle open, whirled the Northrop into a tight renversement. There was a blur of luminous smoke at one side, then a blinding white flame leaped up at the edge of Old Harbin.

In amazement, Knight saw huge fragments of burning wreckage blasted two hundred feet in the air. Above the drone of the engine came a harsh, grinding roar. The weird white flame leaped up, then spread out like a gigantic mushroom. Beyond its edges he could dimly see tiny figures running frenziedly through the streets, away from where other less fortunate ones had been stricken down by the blast.

For an instant, that eerie spectacle held Knight paralyzed. The flaming mushroom was beginning to descend like a vast fountain of liquid fire. As it fell, great white tendrils of flame gushed out, setting nearby houses afire. One blazing tongue licked out for half a block, and a score of those tiny figures vanished in the white glare. Slowly the great tendrils faded, became white smoke, but where the main blast had been a holocaust was raging.

Knight tore his eyes away, stared back at Doyle. The homely ex-Marine was looking down in horror at the scene, and his face had a bloodless look in the ghastly brilliance.

"Dick!" he said hoarsely. "What in Heaven's name did it?"

Knight mutely shook his head. He had pulled up into a climbing turn, and as the shock of that weird disaster lessened he banked the ship westward. Whatever it was, it had increased their peril. The Nipponese were certain to link the catastrophe with the Northrop, which was sure to have been seen as the strange white flame lit up the night. Intent on finding the northwest railroad, Knight held an altitude of about five thousand feet, with the radial at one-third throttle. Out of the maze of buildings and streets, he suddenly located the railroad station. He was swinging parallel with the tracks which led northwest when two anti-aircraft guns abruptly blazed beneath.

The Northrop rocked as one of the shells burst close to the left wing. He chandelled, ruddered back as other shells exploded furiously to his right. Motor now wide open, he zoomed up into the snowy night. The glare from the burning section was two miles behind, and he was nosing down to pick up the railroad again when a parachute flare blossomed out, a thousand feet above the sealed two-seater.

"Japs!" bellowed Doyle. He leaped up, snapping his gun-harness about his waist. Knight had instantly banked as the flare appeared. He shot a hasty glance upward. Three Nakajima 91s were diving steeply at the Northrop!

A half-muffled pounding came from behind him as Doyle flipped the twin 50-caliber guns upward in their airtight turret. The leading Nakajima whipped aside, its tracers smoking into space. Two red lines shot above Knight's head, ended on the left wing-tip. He felt the two-seater vibrate from the impact of the burst. With a swift renversement, he hurled the Northrop upon the first Nakajima as it plunged past the falling flare. His finger closed on the first of three buttons on the stick. Sliding flaps whirled open in the leading edge of the wing, and two hidden Browning .30s clattered into life.

The Japanese pilot cowered over his controls as the high-speed guns riddled his cowl. The Nakajima pitched on down, twisting to the left. Knight roared the Northrop after it, fingers taut on the stick-buttons, but the other two Nipponese fighters now charged in diagonally at the tail, concentrated a lethal crossfire upon the American low-wing. Doyle was swearing savagely as he whirled the rear .50s from side to side.

Knight bent over the stick, eyes glued to the special sights which his first burst had automatically raised from their niche in the cowl. A wing with a rising-sun insignia swam before his eyes. He squeezed a button, and the wing-root .50s, duplicates of Doyle's guns, blasted with a roar. A gaping hole appeared where the rising-sun symbol had been, and the Nipponese pilot frantically tried to bank on the uninjured wing. Knight slammed the two-seater around toward the nearer of the other Nakajimas. His spouting guns were almost centered on the ship when Doyle gave a shout of dismay.

"Watch out—that first Jap!"

**KNIGHT JERKED** around in his seat. The pilot of the crippled ship was trying to ram the Northrop broadside. He snapped the controls back, and the bullet-torn fighter plunged underneath. With a crazy chandelle, the brown-faced pilot cut back. The other Nakajimas spread out hastily, Doyle unloosed a fierce barrage at the one on his right, and the pilot flung into a vertical bank. Knight kicked away from the crippled plane, then went rigid. The third Nakajima had renversed at the same instant, was racing at him head-on!

Thin streaks of fire lanced from the fighter's cowl. Knight booted his rudder. The Northrop skidded to the left, its nose swinging toward the Nakajima. He clamped the top stick-button, and with a roar all four wing-guns flamed.

Like cardboard, the right wing of the fighter sheared off, and the grinding guns ate their way through the uptilted tail. As Knight pitched the two-seater clear, the wrecked ship fell on its side. It plummeted a hundred feet, tore off the other wing, and the pilot was catapulted into the air like a human ball. White silk flapped upward, spread out into a dome—only to collapse as the shattered wing struck it in the center. With chute and wing tangled above him, the doomed Nipponese fell swiftly away and was lost from view.

The drifting flare was by now only a short distance above the battling ships. Knight banked tightly to escape from the lighted space. Doyle's .50s hammered again, and as the two-seater pulled up beyond the flare Knight saw one of the remaining Nakajimas go whirling down in flames. The third Japanese pilot came furiously after the two Americans. Doyle raked the fighter's turtleback, swung his guns for another blast as the Nakajima went into an Immelmann. Knight leveled out with the compass pointing northwest. The two-seater was a mile away from the flare with the Nakajima lost in the snowy gloom, when another weird white flame mushroomed up from a spot near the Harbin airport.

Knight stiffened. Against that uncanny brilliance, six more Nakajimas were silhouetted less than half a mile across the sky. The Japanese planes were flying toward them, and before he could more than start a turn the fighters' guns were pounding, the six ships spreading out to hem them in.

Doyle pumped a fusillade at the first Nakajima, madly spun the gun-turret to rake another Nipponese. Knight stood the two-seater on its tail, and the superior speed of the ship carried it above the storm of leaden death.

With a lightning turn, he now pitched back at the zooming fighters. A fast-climbing Nakajima plunged back with its prop shot off. Knight rocked the rudder pedals, all four guns throbbing. Another Nipponese fighter swerved too late, flew straight into that deadly stream. Its fuselage broke in two, leaving shattered wreckage forward of the cockpit, and the luckless pilot clawed frenziedly to free himself from the smoking front section. Oily smoke enveloped him, became an inferno that further lit up the snow-lined sky.

With a vengeful fury, the rest of the Japanese pilots charged in at the Northrop. Guns from three directions gouged at the two-seater's tail. Knight flung the ship into a fast half-roll, changed direction. Two Nakajimas loomed ahead, diving in from right and left. He kicked to catch one of them under the guns. The other was within sixty yards, and two more Japanese were darting in from the sides. Just then three bullet-nosed Soviet fighters dropped headlong into the battle. One Nakajima spun off with a crumpled wing as the first Red pilot struck. Knight had a swift glimpse of the first Soviet plane. It was a 2KB-19, gray save for the huge red stars on its wings and tail. Two guns were spitting from mounts above the Rolls Royce Kestrel engine, and two more from the wing-stubs.

The other Red fighters pounced on the startled Nipponese,

and another Nakajima went whirling to earth, snowflakes eddying wildly after it. Knight pointed the two-seater for a hole between two ships. The Northrop was almost through the opening when one of the Soviet pilots ruddered alongside.

Under the transparent enclosure, the man's fur-clad figure resembled a crouching bear. Knight saw him lift his right hand, then a cockpit light flashed on. The pilot swiftly threw back the hood of his fur parka, jerked open the heavy garment. Knight started. The man wore the yellow robe and cowl of a Buddhist monk!

## CHAPTER II
## *The Sign of the Four Faces*

*NOW THE* Northrop and the 2KB raced on side by side, leaving the last Japanese to the grim mercies of the other Soviet pilots. The man in the yellow robe flung a look down at his compass, then gazed back at Knight and Doyle. He lifted his hand again, crossed two fingers, hurriedly showed all five, then two.

"X-52!" shouted Doyle. "That's your new code number, Dick!"

Knight nodded hastily to the man in the Russian plane. As quickly as he had given the first code, the pilot gave Doyle's recognition number. Knight stared at the face the cockpit light showed. The man's features were massive, with dark, deep-set eyes under a towering forehead. Heavy black brows met above a huge, hooked nose. And a zigzag scar—white against his left cheek—ran from his temple to his chin.

As the monk-pilot finished Doyle's number he looked anxiously back toward Harbin, then gestured for Knight to swing in behind the fighter. The secret agent eased his throttle, dropped back but kept slightly above to avoid the 2KB's slipstream. He took a swift glance rearward. Searchlights were vainly probing through the falling snow. He could see a whitish glow near the airport, and another glow the color of normal flame where the buildings in Old Harbin were burning. There was no sign of pursuing ships.

He turned back to the controls. The Soviet fighter was nosing down, its lighted cockpit clearly visible against the snowy gloom. In a moment the cockpit light went out and landing-lights near the wing-tips flung two bright beams downward. Knight followed as the 2KB leveled out above a railroad. The rails and ice-covered telegraph poles swept by underneath, then suddenly the mysterious pilot waggled his wings and banked to the right. In less than two minutes a crescent-shaped clearing in the heart of the birch and larch woods became visible under the fighter's tilted lights. Knight switched on his own landing-lights, made a wider circle as the Soviet plane started to land.

At first he saw only the icy desolation of a Manchukuan woodland, then back under the trees on one side he glimpsed a log hut. Smoke came from its chimney. The 2KB side-slipped over the trees on the opposite side from the hut, leveled off, then came to a quick stop on the snow-covered ground.

Knight looked back at Doyle. "Here go the prodigal sons, Lothario. Sit down and fasten your belt—I don't like the looks of that field."

"And I don't like any of this business," Doyle retorted. "Who the devil do you suppose that bird is?"

"He's the Buddha who's got our number," Knight said drily, as he lowered the landing-gear.

"Yeah—and maybe those Japs back there have got it, too."

"They couldn't see where we went," replied Knight. "Anyway, we have enough fuel left to reach Vladivostok if things get too hot."

He dipped the Northrop into a forward slip, and the ship moaned down over the trees. Through the slanting lines of snow he saw a number of wheel-tracks in the white crust below. They were only half obliterated by the falling flakes. He looked around quickly for another ship, but he saw none. The tracks curved back toward the hut, then out again. Carefully, he brought the nose up and held the two-seater clear until he was exactly over the spot where the 2KB had landed. The Northrop rumbled across a hummock, bounced, slowed to a stop with a flurry of prop-whirled snow. He stood on one brake, taxied in beside the Soviet fighter, and pivoted to swing the ship around into a take-off postion.

Then he unlocked the gear which kept the cockpit sealed, and Doyle slid the Plexiglas dome back. A blast of icy air blew into the cockpit. Just as Knight cut off the engine the pilot of the 2KB reached the side of the Northrop.

"Switch off your lights," he said in English. His voice was deep, unhurried. "One of those Japs might still be looking for us."

Knight turned on his shielded cockpit light before switching off the others. The faint rays shone on the upturned face in the parka hood. At close range, the man's features proved even larger than they had seemed at first, and Knight knew that some glandular disorder must have brought about that strange abnormal growth.

The man's dark eyes flicked to Doyle, then back to the senior agent.

"You are Richard Knight?"

Knight nodded guardedly.

The monk-pilot smiled. "All this must seem very peculiar, I know. I'm John Creele, of British Military Intelligence. My government has instructed me to place myself at your service. But I'll explain inside—you're probably half-frozen."

"No, the cockpit was heated," said Knight, "but I'll admit you've some chilly air up here."

"Come into the hut," said Creele. "Better cover over your pit—it looks like a blizzard coming on."

**AFTER LOCKING** the ignition circuit, Knight turned off the light and slid the Plexiglas shut. Doyle had introduced himself, and he and Creele were talking as Knight jumped down.

"Why, no," he heard the pseudo-monk say in a tone of surprise. "I thought you might enlighten me on that. I supposed they might in some way be connected with your mission up here."

"What's this?" asked Knight.

"I was asking about those queer explosions we saw," grunted Doyle. "I thought they were incendiary shells."

"They couldn't have been shells," said Creele as he led the way to the hut. "It's two hundred and fifty miles to the nearest border, and I don't know of any long-range gun that could send projectiles half that distance."

"What about the possibility of Soviet bombers?" queried Knight.

Creele shook his massive head. "I think I'd have known about that. I've been working closely with the Red air force lately, as you may have guessed from seeing my ship and the other 2KB's."

They had reached the hut, and now Creele lifted the heavy wooden bar which held the door closed. The wind sent snow-flurries in after them, then the hooded agent leaned against the door and dropped an inner bar in place.

Knight turned, shot a glance about the hut as he unfastened his flying-coat. A log was smoldering in the fireplace, and its dim embers cast a faint, fitful glow through the room. It was scantily furnished with a crude table, a bed, and two chairs. A tarnished gilt image of Buddha stood on the table, beside some greasy dishes. A large, dirty bearskin rug covered most of the floor.

"Pardon the filth," rumbled the false monk. "All this is necessary—in case the Japs should get inquisitive. I'm supposed to be a White Russian who became disgusted with life after the revolution and became a follower of Buddha. I've been playing the part for a long time, but even yet they watch me occasionally," he said as he lit a candle and went over to toss another log on the fire.

Knight waited until he turned, then spoke up. "I don't understand your connection with General Brett. Is he working through Britain?"

Creele's heavy black brows went up with an astonished expression. "But that's just what I was going to ask you!" he replied. "I've been wondering about the meaning of my orders to cooperate with you."

"Then you don't know why we were sent here?" exclaimed Knight.

"No," said Creele blankly. "Don't you?"

"I haven't the slightest idea," said Knight. He and the

pseudo-monk stared at each other. Doyle broke the silence with a groan.

"I knew it was screwy all the time. We've been framed!"

Consternation came into Creele's scarred face.

"Then they must be onto me, too! But how—"

"Wait," Knight said with a forced calmness, "we'll have to figure this out. When did you first hear about our coming here, and how did you get word?"

Creele hesitated, a look of vague suspicion in his eyes. Then he shook his huge head.

"London vouched for you—so you must be all right." He unbarred the door, peered out, shut the door again and kicked back the bearskin rug. A neatly fitting trapdoor was revealed. He pulled at the recessed handle and lifted the trap. Warm air came up from the dark space below. He took the candle, motioned the two Americans to follow. A basement twice the size of the hut became visible, fitted with a comfortable bed, a well-provisioned food locker, book-shelves, a large wardrobe cabinet, and other furnishings in decided contrast to the room above. A cheerful fire was crackling on a hearth directly below the fireplace in the hut. Knight saw an air duct from outside. It opened near the fireplace so that the draft would draw fresh air into the basement. At the opposite end of the chamber was a radio receiving set operated from a storage battery. A chart on the wall indicated various hours for listening-in on London, Singapore, Hong Kong and other official British short-wave stations.

"That's how I received word about you," said Creele. "It was relayed through our Hong Kong station," he added as he lighted a gasoline-pressure lamp and blew out the candle.

"This is some layout," said Doyle.

The other man laughed with a trace of harshness.

"And it might put me in front of a firing-squad if the Japs ever saw it. But I've prepared for escape, if it ever comes to that." He pointed to the food locker. "It's hinged against the wall, and there's a passage behind it leading to a hidden exit in the woods. At least I'd have a fighting chance."

"It must have been a job, doing all this alone," said Knight, his gaze traversing the room.

"I had two Russians helping me at first," replied Creele. "But that was several years ago. I've gone it alone since then, except when Soviet pilots dropped in here or one of my spies brought me a new battery or supplies."

**THE AMERICAN** agent lighted a cigarette, stood with his back to the fireplace. "We'd better get on to our problem. Exactly what do you know about our coming here?"

Creele tossed his parka on the bed, threw back the cowl of his yellow robe. His huge fingers absently rubbed his shaved head as he answered.

"The first message came early this morning. It was from the senior British Intelligence officer at Hong Kong, from whom I've received orders ever since the Japs seized Manchukuo. He said that the United States had asked secret assistance on a matter of vital importance and that Moscow was also cooperating since the move was considered to be advantageous to Soviet interests. Both of you were named and described and your recognition numbers given. Your ship was also described, and the message stated you would be flying from Shanghai with orders from General Brett, chief of American Army Intelligence."

"Then you haven't heard from Brett directly?" interrupted Knight.

"No, though there's a chance he may have called me while I was across the border at the Soviet squadron south of Lake Khanka. That's where the second message directed me to go, so a Russian two-seater was over for me just after dusk. I haven't dared keep a ship near here, though I was trained originally for air intelligence. But when I arrived across the border, I found that my chief at Hong Kong had arranged for me to borrow a 2KB and be ready to escort you on your mission. Those two fighters you saw with me were sent to distract attention from me and cover up the sound of my motor when I circled down to land here. It was purely a coincidence that we arrived over Harbin during that battle. When I recognized your ship from the description, I signaled the Soviet pilots to help me drive off the Japs."

"For which we're thankful," said Knight. "But this leaves us in a bad spot. General Brett wouldn't have appealed to your government unless a grave emergency had arisen. Also, he wouldn't have been so careful to mask his instructions about finding this place, unless he thought that some one would be combing the airways even up in the ultra high-frequency bands we've developed for espionage work. It may be that he's waiting to be sure we've had time to land here before he sends his final orders."

"I'm due to listen in for Hong Kong in about forty minutes," said Creele. "But we might as well have a bit of dinner while we're waiting. I'm hungry, and you chaps must be starved."

Knight shook his head.

"Count me in," said Doyle. "Better change your mind, Dick. This may be the last call this side of a prison-camp."

"Not now," said Knight. He glanced absently at the ward-robe cabinet, watched Creele carry a bottle of wine and some food from the locker to the table. "About those strange explo-sions, have you any theories at all?"

"They looked like chemical fire the way they mushroomed up," the false monk answered. "But where could the stuff have come from? And who beside the Soviet could have done it? The Chinese up here are powerless."

"How much information do you get on things beyond Harbin?" asked Knight. "And how close are you cooperating with the Soviet? They could be doing a lot of things under cover."

"I get reports from a hundred sources in Manchukuo," Creele said firmly. "As for Russia, we've been working with them a lot more than is generally known. If it comes to a war, we'll probably be allied with her against Japan and Germany; that's my main reason for being here, to help strike against the Japs when the time comes."

Knight heard only part of the answer. His eyes were fixed on the handle of the wardrobe cabinet, and now he was sure. The handle had been turned, a fraction of an inch at a time, until now it was almost straight up and down. He slid his hand inside his coat, grasped the butt of his automatic. As he drew out the weapon, Creele halted, staring.

"Why the gun, Knight?"

**ABRUPTLY THERE** was a muffled sound from inside the wardrobe cabinet. Knight leaped aside just as the door flew open. An arm flashed up, and the lamp-light shone on blued steel. Knight fired twice, so swiftly that the roar of the other man's gun made the three reports seem like one. Creele stood paralyzed as a yellow-faced figure tumbled out head-long onto the floor.

Knight kicked a smoking pistol from the fingers of the man he had shot. The dying Oriental tried to lift himself up, collapsed. For a moment longer, as a red stain widened on his left side, he glared up with a look of hate that encompassed all three white men. Then suddenly his tortured gasps ended, and the fury in his eyes became a glassy stare.

"Good Lord!" Doyle said hoarsely. "And to think that devil was in there the whole time. How'd you ever spot him, Dick?"

"Saw the door-handle move." Knight looked at Creele, lowered his voice. "Your hut door was barred on the outside— so there's only one way he could have got in here."

The stupefied look faded from Creele's eyes. He whirled toward the food locker.

But Knight caught his arm. "Don't open it! If there's anyone in the passage, he might blast us from the dark before we could see him. And those shots probably scared away anyone who might have been in there."

"Yes, but it means they've discovered the secret exit!" muttered Creele. "We'll have to escape while we've still time."

"Hold on," said Knight. "This man is not a Jap. He's Chinese. Search him, Doyle, and see if there's anything on him to give us a lead."

"Even if he *is* Chinese," grated the pseudo-monk, "he's undoubtedly working with the Japs! We'd better get over the border before it's too late. Even now—" he hesitated. "What's the matter?"

Doyle had stopped his hasty search, had jerked back one sleeve of the dead Oriental's coat.

"Look, Dick!" he whispered. "The sign of the Four Faces!"

Creele and Knight stared down at the arm of the corpse. Four faces had been tattooed so that they encircled the forearm. All four were identical. All four had the same expression of grim, brooding menace.

"So they're back of this," Knight said half to himself.

Creele looked at him with a blank expression. "I don't understand. What does that tattooing mean?"

"Then you've never heard of the Four Faces?" said Knight.

"The name strikes a vague memory," Creele answered. "But I can't recall—"

"It's the name of a huge criminal organization headed by four unknown men," Knight broke in tersely. "I've a strong suspicion that one of the four is Lowenstein, the rich Belgian who was supposed to have fallen from his private cabin-ship over the English Channel. And I've never been satisfied as to the stories of Stavisky's death or that of Kreuger, the Swedish match king. I believe those three and some other supposedly dead financier have built up the Four Faces in a quest for world power. We've tangled with them several times, and they've reason to hate us."

"You mean this organization also exists in America?" said Creele.

"All over the world," replied Knight. "Its members include men and women all the way from court circles down to the gutter. A great many are undoubtedly forced to serve the Four Faces by blackmail, or threat of death, though the original members seem to have been mainly from the under-world."

"But what could they want of me?" Creele demanded.

"Probably information you've picked up about Japan or the Soviet. Or they may intend to use you in some way. They have forced more than one foreign agent into their ranks, you know, and we've had proof they're interested in munitions and war supplies. I think they operate through dummy corporations headed by some of their members."

Doyle stood up, shook his head.

"Nothing on him but a little money and an extra clip for the gun."

"I didn't expect much," said Knight. "The 'killer' agents are seldom entrusted with important papers."

He glanced into the wardrobe cabinet, looked back at Creele, who was bending over the dead Oriental.

"Are all the members of the Four Faces tattooed like that?" muttered the false monk.

Knight gave him an odd smile.

"Suppose," he said softly, *"you* tell us."

## CHAPTER III
## *Question in Red*

**F**OR A moment the only sound was the crackling of the fire on the hearth. The man in the Buddhist robe stared at him with a look of complete amazement, and Doyle stood open-mouthed.

"I don't understand," the pseudo-monk finally broke the silence.

Knight's eyes were on the other man's now-nervous hands.

"I wouldn't try anything," he said calmly. "Doyle, come around on the left side and search him. Watch out for those sleeves—I think he has a gun up in one of them."

"You mean he's a phony?" Doyle said incredulously.

"Knight, you're out of your mind!" rasped the robed pilot. "If I'd have wanted to kill you, I could have done it half an hour ago."

"It's no use," replied Knight. "I suspected you even before your friend tried to help you capture us. And one look in that wardrobe proves you're a liar. Those clothes were made for a man half your size."

Dark blood rushed into the other man's face, and his white scar stood out like a streak of lightning.

"Very clever!" he snarled. "But it will do you no good. You're trapped, and you may as well give in now."

Knight smiled grimly.

"At least we understand each other—and don't make any mistake about this gun. I've nothing to lose by shooting you."

A glare of fury came into the captive's eyes, but he stood motionless while Doyle yanked up his voluminous sleeves. A Russian-made Nagarre revolver in a small holster hung upside-down on his left arm, with a flap to hold the gun in place.

"Nice set-up, Buddha," Doyle grunted. "Too bad you didn't have the nerve to reach for it."

"I think he's been ordered to take us alive," Knight interrupted. "Hurry up—the others may try to rush us at any minute."

Doyle ripped open the yellow robe, and a heavy flying-suit became visible. He jerked the zipper, carefully keeping to one side as he searched the prisoner's pockets in order that Knight's aim would not be blocked. The false monk's lips had set in an icy, mirthless smile, but his eyes narrowed when Doyle extracted a folded map from an inner pocket. Knight took the map in his left hand, spread it on the table as Doyle finished the search and stepped back with his pistol lifted.

It was a map of northern Asia showing eastern Siberia, Manchukuo, and the upper half of China. Well above the northern border of Manchukuo a large question mark had been drawn in red crayon. Knight turned the map over, but there was nothing on the other side.

"Any dope?" asked Doyle.

"Nothing here but a question mark," returned Knight.

The pseudo-monk gave him a sneering grin. "Shall I tell you the answer, my smart Mr. Q-Agent?"

Knight eyed him thoughtfully as he put the map inside his flying-coat.

"I wonder what you did with the real Mr. Creele. You didn't have much time to work here, or you'd have been more familiar with the food locker."

"Creele is dead," the other man said viciously. "And you'll be, too, if you don't agree to my terms."

"Which are—?" Knight queried.

"That you drop your guns and march upstairs with your hands in the air," came the reply.

"And after that, you take us to some headquarters of the Four Faces? That must mean more ships are coming here—at least one other two-seater."

Doyle looked uneasily toward the opened trap-door.

"We'd better get moving, then."

"You haven't a chance," grated the robed pilot. "There are a dozen men outside, all armed."

"Nice of you to warn us," said Knight. He motioned for Doyle to cover the prisoner carefully, then stepped to the food locker and silently began to clear the middle shelf. The false monk opened his mouth, shut it at a savage thrust from Doyle's gun. Knight stepped back, leveled his automatic, and squeezed the trigger.

The report roared through the confines of the basement, and a muffled howl instantly sounded on the other side of the cabinet. Knight had jumped aside the instant after he fired. A gun blasted, inside the passage, and wood splintered beside the hole his bullet had made. He fired again, low, and a screech of agony followed. At the same instant, a furious pounding sounded from up at the entrance to the hut.

"Pull back the locker!" Knight shouted at Doyle. "I'll cover him."

**DOYLE LEAPED** forward, but Knight stopped him with a hasty signal. Three shots crashed from the other side of the cabinet, and a crooked hole the size of a man's fist appeared in the back. A dim light shone on the other side, and Knight caught a flash of some one running into the passage.

"It's clear now!" he flung at Doyle. The ex-Marine sprang to the locker and tugged to pull it open. Knight backed toward the pressure-lamp, his eyes riveted on the tense face of their prisoner. The blows on the hut-door had redoubled in force.

"Tell them we've escaped by the tunnel!" Knight said fiercely.

The man's lips twitched into a snarl, but he did not speak. Knight's finger tightened on his gun trigger, and an ashen color spread over the prisoner's misshapen features.

"The passage—the Americans are escaping!" he cried out frantically.

Doyle swung the locker open on its hinges as he spoke, and a narrow passage was revealed. A young Japanese lay dying with a bullet through his stomach. There was no one else in sight, and the tunnel led straight ahead for a hundred feet or more.

"We'd better try the passage," Knight hastily told Doyle. "Go ahead!" He gestured at the false monk with his gun. "You're next!"

Hands lifted, the prisoner started forward. He was half-way to the passage when the hut-door crashed open. A violent draft blew down into the basement and through the tunnel. The lamp flickered wildly, almost went out. In the sudden gloom, the captive made a frenzied dive for the dead assassin's weapon. Knight fired, missed in the crazily flickering light. Before he could aim again, a gun blazed from the top of the steps. He whirled, pumped a shot toward the trap-door, then sprang backward into the passage.

The pseudo-monk had snatched the dead Oriental's pistol, rolled to one side. Knight jerked the cabinet half-shut, dashed into the tunnel. Doyle was crouching a few yards away, trying to aim through the crevice. He jumped up, and they raced for the turn in the passage. Light abruptly streamed from the basement. Knight whirled, triggered two shots. A smallish figure tumbled to the ground, and at the second shot the gasoline lamp went out.

"Slade!" a voice cried shrilly. "Don't shoot—it might start a fire!"

"Get above and cover that exit, you fool!" came the furious response of the scarred pilot. "I'll take care of this end!"

Knight bumped against Doyle, held onto the other man's arm as they hurried into the dark passage.

"I knew he was lying—we'll have only one or two men to contend with."

"Why not duck back through the hut?" Doyle said hoarsely.

"I think our friend's going to block that way," muttered Knight. "And it can't be far to the exit."

They had passed the bend in the passage and were starting up an incline when a dull roar sounded behind them and the red glare of flames showed dimly around the curve. Doyle swore.

"The dirty rat! Now we've got to get out this way."

"Look out!" whispered Knight. "There's the end."

A wooden trap similar to the one in the hut had been left open, and by the faint glow reflected around the bend in the tunnel he could see trees and falling snow. He jerked off his helmet, raised it on the muzzle of his gun. A shot roared, and he saw a spurt of flame by a tree at the right. The flame disclosed a fur-clad figure, and Doyle instantly fired. The man dropped his gun, slid to his knees without a sound and lay with his face buried in the snow.

"Good shot," said Knight. Then he jumped up and helped Doyle onto the level ground. A flashlight was probing back and forth, two hundred feet away, as some one fled through the trees toward the clearing. The two agents followed as fast as they could, tripping now and then over tangled brush or rocks frozen into the ground. They were within a short distance of the field when one side of the hut blazed up. The fire in the basement had quickly reached the upper floor.

Two men in fur parkas were dashing toward their Northrop. Knight took careful aim, eased the trigger back. His gun jetted flame, and one of the men stumbled. The other wheeled, flung two shots into the woods. A bullet chipped bark from a tree beside Knight. He fired again, and the other man ran desperately for the 2KB-19.

"It's Slade!" fumed Doyle.

"We've got to stop him!" rapped Knight. "He'll strafe us if he gets off!"

**THEY CHARGED** for the clearing. Slade scrambled into the cockpit of the fighter, and the starter whined. The motor caught almost instantly. Both Knight and Doyle blasted shots at the unblocked ship as it lurched forward, but the pilot rammed open the throttle and was swiftly out of range.

"Come on!" Knight said tautly. They ran to the Northrop, and in another moment he was fumbling for the key to the locked circuit. He switched on the twin-radial, pressed the inertia starter button. To his consternation, nothing happened.

"They've cut the starter wires!" he shouted at Doyle. "See if you can swing the prop!"

Doyle tumbled out, raced to the nose of the ship. He was about to pull the prop when the Soviet fighter came thundering down the field. Knight whirled in his seat. The 2KB was fifteen feet off the ground. Just as he turned, the left wing dropped slightly and the nose of the fighter swerved toward the Northrop. Knight hit the release-gear at the back of his seat, clutched the spade-grip of the rearpit .50s.

As two crimson eyes blinked on the cowl of the Soviet ship, the Q-agent tripped his heavy guns, and tracers interlaced with the fuzzy lines sprang toward the 2KB. Slade hauled back into a tight chandelle, and Knight's tracers drilled into space.

"Switch on!" bellowed Doyle. "Hurry up before that devil tries it again."

"Switch on!" shouted Knight. Doyle lunged at the prop. The engine coughed, died. Before he could swing again, the 2KB came shrieking down in a power dive. Again, Knight whirled to the .50s. Slade's tracers were stabbing into the snow-covered ground three hundred feet away. Frantically, the American jerked the double trigger. The guns tilted swiftly, blasted straight into the right wingtip of the fighter. The 2KB flipped off and dropped on the left wing, and the streaking tracer-lines Slade had poured out missed the Northrop by a scant ten feet.

Knight let up on the trigger, thinking the fighter was doomed. But with an amazing turn Slade recovered and zoomed above the trees. Doyle jerked the prop as Knight spun around to the controls, and this time the engine caught with a welcome roar. The hut was now a mass of fire, and Knight cast an anxious look into the lighted sky while Doyle climbed into his seat.

"Where'd he go?" demanded the stocky ex-Marine.

"I think I crippled him," Knight yelled back over his shoulder. He opened the throttle half-way, sent the Northrop trundling down-wind.

The ship had almost gone far enough for a turn into the wind when Slade's fighter came diving over the burning hut. The smoke and flames had concealed its approach until the last moment.

Doyle whirled his turret, and Knight braked the two-seater into a hasty turn. The 2KB's guns blazed briefly, then the false monk chandelled, wings screaming. As the fighter lifted skyward, Knight could clearly see Slade's head and shoulders by the glare from below. He was wearing a head-set, and with one hand he held a microphone close to his lips. Knight snapped on his receiver, twirled the dial. Strange words crackled into his ears, then he suddenly recognized them as Esperanto, the adopted language of the mysterious Four Faces.

He shoved the throttle open to the take-off limit, trying to catch a few words of the comparatively unfamiliar language. A startled cry from Doyle broke in.

"Dick! Look up to the north!"

**RICHARD KNIGHT** flicked a glance up through the snowy sky. Icy fingers seemed to pull at his scalp. For the second time that night, something was streaking earthward at terrific speed.

There was a blinding flash, a roar that cut through the radial's thunder as though it had been a whisper. Shattered trees and fragments of frozen earth went hurtling into the air a mile beyond the edge of the clearing. The blasted debris was instantly followed by a gigantic mushroom of dazzling white flame, and Knight felt the earth shake from the force of another explosion.

The Northrop was half-way down the field, wheels almost clear, when a second blurred streak showed nearer and to the south of the field. So fast his eyes could not follow, a bright spot in front of the blur plunged to earth and another explosion shook both earth and sky. Scorching heat swept out after the two-seater. He rammed the throttle wide-open, gasped for breath as the blazing white mushroom sent its huge tendrils snaking after the ship.

For a second he thought they were lost. The Northrop swayed, dropped almost to the ground in the buffeted air. Then the churning prop took hold again, and the ship slowly lifted into the cooler air beyond the clearing. He dragged the half-closed Plexiglas dome farther open, sucked in the cold air until his giddiness had gone. Doyle was wiping perspiration from his face, his eyes wildly dilated.

"That's twice that dirty louse has tried to burn us up!" he bawled into Knight's ear. "But what in hell are those things—and where do they come from?"

Knight made no answer. He was climbing steeply from the clearing, his eyes straining to see through the snow. Fear gripped at his heart as a third whitish blur became visible high up in the night. The blur became a streak—and again a weird flame spouted up into a giant geyser.

# CHAPTER IV
## Above the Border

**T**HE NORTHROP rocked in the fierce upblast, but Knight fought it safely away from the boiling currents of air. As the ship settled into level flight two miles beyond the clearing, he stared back. Four more of the strange white flame-masses had appeared, making a total of seven which roughly encircled the field. As he watched, an eighth struck almost in the center of the clearing, and the weird white fire spread out in all directions, hiding the already blazing hut and setting trees afire on both sides. The terrific heat had melted the falling snow while it was several hundred feet from the ground, and Knight could see distinctly into this oddly-cleared space.

Something flitted into view at one side, and in a moment he recognized the 2KB as Slade warily circled the stricken area at a height of six hundred feet. The Russian ship swayed and tossed in the unsteady air, but the Four Faces pilot held to his dangerous altitude while he continued to fly about.

"He must be looking for us," Doyle shouted from the rear cockpit. "Let's get him!"

"No, I want to see which way he heads," replied Knight. He closed the Plexiglas, switched on the ventilating unit. "Keep your eye on him while I climb a bit higher—I want to make sure he doesn't spot us."

The Northrop spiraled up to two thousand feet, then Doyle gave an exclamation.

"He's swinging north. And is he letting that crate out!"

Knight peered through the arc cleared by his windshield defroster and saw the 2KB settle on a course of 23 degrees. He followed, nosing down slightly so that he could not lose sight of the fighter as it raced away from the lighted zone. After a minute, the 2KB made a sharp turn, circled as though Slade were making sure he was not being trailed. Knight pulled up until he could barely see the other ship, and in a few moments the fighter resumed its former course.

Engine half-throttled, Knight sent the Northrop down in a power glide, holding back until the swiftly increasing gloom all but hid his quarry. He knew then that Slade was not likely to glimpse the Northrop, even if he were not already certain that they had perished. Carefully, he edged in, keeping a trifle under the other ship until he could dimly see the flash of its exhaust. The Northrop's stacks were shielded, and he had no fear that Slade would see the two-seater.

"How far we going to chase that rat?" demanded Doyle. "We haven't got any too much gas."

"We've more than enough to get over the border to Blagoveshchensk," returned Knight. "And that town's not so far off the course he's taking. If luck's with us, we may be able to locate the Four Faces base before we cross the border."

"Then you think it's in Manchukuo?" grunted Doyle.

"It would almost have to be," said Knight. "You could hardly build a gun big enough to fire those shells from the nearest point in Siberia."

"It's got me stumped," grumbled Doyle. "What are they up to, anyway? And why did we get dragged into it?"

"Your guess is as good as mine." Knight's eyes were fixed on the faint glow of the 2KB's exhaust stacks, as the fighter hurtled on through the darkness. "Here, take this map and turn your light on it—cover it so it won't shine up through the top. See if we're going toward that place covered by the question mark."

Doyle took the map, was silent for a minute.

"Hey!" he said suddenly. "We're heading straight for the dot under the question mark. It's about a hundred and fifty miles east of Blago—whatever-you-call-it, close to a river."

"So that's it," muttered Knight. "The dot's the location of the base, and Slade put the question mark there to keep anybody from guessing, if he happened to lose the map."

"You're doing a lot of guessing right now yourself," growled

Doyle. "If you ask me, we're in a bad enough spot without looking for more trouble. Maybe you think the Reds are going to give us the glad hand?"

"They won't start a row as long as we're not working against them. And I've an idea they'd like to hear about Slade's using a Soviet ship, and those other 2KB's."

"I wonder who he is," said Doyle. "He sure fooled me."

Knight answered without taking his eyes from the 2KB.

"There was a pilot named Brant Slade who did a lot of liquor smuggling by plane during prohibition. After repeal, he switched to running aliens and then suddenly disappeared. He'd made a lot of money—and a lot of enemies—so the Coast Guard supposed he'd been killed. I saw a picture of him some years ago. It didn't look like this man, except that he was about the same height. However, that doesn't prove anything, for glandular disorders could have distorted his features in that way in the meantime. One link between him and Asia is that he smuggled in a number of Chinese."

"He sounds like the kind of bird the Four Faces *would* get hold of," said Doyle. "But I can't figure how they've managed to build a hide-out in Manchukuo without the Japs finding it out."

"They'd have Japs on their roster, for one thing," said Knight. "But it does seem peculiar—" he stopped, eased the throttle back a fraction of an inch. The snow was getting lighter, and he could see the 2KB more plainly.

In a few minutes more the air was clear, and he was forced to drop still farther back; for now several breaks in the clouds began to appear, and occasionally shafts of moonlight shone through.

"He's climbing!" exclaimed Doyle. "We must not be near the base at all."

**KNIGHT FROWNED,** held the Northrop to a parallel ascent. After an interval, he switched on the radio, tried each special range. But there was no sound. He dared not use the transmitter for fear Slade would hear and discover a ship was close to him. The 2KB leveled out at about ten thousand feet, and for another twenty minutes held its course. A pin-point of light flickered from the darkness ahead, then a searchlight swung up the sky. Almost at once, two more beams came to life; then far below Knight saw A-A batteries blaze. A shell burst well off to his right. Another flamed ahead and to the left, and before he had time to swerve, the 2KB made a sharp turn to avoid the barrage.

Slade chandelled his fighter wildly when he saw the Northrop. Knight dived under him, then zoomed. Slade's guns blazed for a moment, then with engine wide open he climbed above the bursting shells, twisting and turning rapidly. Knight took a hasty glance downward.

"We're over the border! That strip between the batteries is the River Amur."

"Then both sides are popping at us!" howled Doyle. "This is a sweet mess."

A shell from a Soviet gun exploded two hundred feet underneath the Northrop, and bits of shrapnel thudded against the wings. Knight saw a small hole appear near the right wingtip. He shoved the throttle full open, and the two-seater thundered up into the gloom. A searchlight beam flashed past, pawed futilely at the heavens. The guns fired sporadically, then abruptly ceased. Knight shot a look at the altimeter, saw they were close to eighteen thousand feet. He stared around, but there was no sign of Slade's ship.

"Well, what now?" barked Doyle.

Knight glanced at the fuel gauges, made a brief estimate.

"We've enough gas to find out what that dot means and still get to Blagoveshchensk. What do you say?"

"I say we're nuts—but go ahead."

"Seal your end of the pit," said Knight. "We'll come in high, so there'll be no chance of Slade's dropping on us."

He likewise locked his own gear, turned the compressor valves so that supercharged air would be delivered to their cockpit as well as to the engine. He climbed the Northrop to 25,000 feet, and the plane droned on under the pallid moon, with only blackness beneath. The red dot, according to Doyle's measurement, was ninety-eight miles from the border. The strato-ship, cruising at only one-half its top speed in thin air, covered the distance in just sixteen minutes.

Knight's eyes were on the clock, and as he counted off the required time he idled the motor and started down in a slow spiral. Far below, a faintly grayish ribbon showed under the moonlight between two drifting clouds. He took out his field-glass, made a quick inspection.

"There's the river by the dot on the map, but I can't see anything else," he said as he replaced the glass.

"And I'll bet we don't find anything when we get down there," growled Doyle. "Of all the screwy—"

He stopped, and Knight sat up alertly—for the radio amplifier was blaring out a string of words.

"Esperanto again!" Doyle exclaimed. "Can you make it out?"

"No, but the station must be close to be that loud. See if you can get a bearing on the direction-finder."

Doyle turned to adjust the dial.

"Holy smoke!" he burst out. "It's movin' all over the place as though—Good Lord, Dick! *Look!*"

Knight whirled, went rigid. Something dark had flitted across the face of the moon so swiftly that it was gone before he could even guess at its shape. As he stared upward, a fiery streak appeared and vanished. Then the dark shape hurtled down at the Northrop!

*AT THE* speed of a meteor, the thing plunged down the moonlit sky. Knight had a blurred glimpse of short, thick wings. Streams of smoke eddied furiously from the rear ends of two strange-looking cones mounted on them. But there was no trace of propellers. The terrific speed of the mystery ship made a chill run up his spine.

Doyle was frantically trying to bring his .50s to bear on the diving craft, but before he could fire the other plane twisted aside. Knight tripped his wing-root guns, but the tracers went into empty air.

Wings screeching, the mystery plane skidded in toward the Northrop. Knight desperately kicked away. The other ship whirled in a vertical turn. There was a roar, and two blasts of white flame shot from the rear ends of the two huge cones. A scorching heat swept through the double Plexiglas enclosure into the Northrop's cockpit, and Knight sagged over the controls, gasping for breath. Dimly, he felt the ship whip into a spin, go twisting earthward with its motor still on. With an effort, he forced back the dark curtain which had almost descended over his senses. The ship had spun down three thousand feet. He closed the throttle, neutralized the controls, and brought the nose up. Doyle was dazedly clawing at the enclosure locking gear. It slipped open, and cold air howled into the cockpit.

Knight looked around hastily, felt his heart constrict as the sinister black raider again pitched down at them. His icy fingers slid over the stick-buttons, and then with a violent zoom he jerked the nose of the Northrop up at the other ship. The guns pounded viciously, but in the same instant two winking red spots appeared in the rounded nose of the raider. The spots grew at tremendous speed until it seemed the mystery ship would crash head-on into the Northrop with its guns still spouting. A trail of bullet-holes suddenly ran across the Plexiglas, sent tiny bits of dural spattering down into the cockpit. Then with a deafening shriek the black raider plunged by.

Knight kicked off as the Northrop started to stall. Five thousand feet below, two blinding white flames streaked the sky, and he saw the sky monster come racing upward again. Doyle was hanging in his gun-harness, gaping downward.

"Get back into your seat!" Knight flung at him. "Snap your belt! I'm going to try to out-dive them!"

"What the devil is it?" Doyle said hoarsely.

"Rocket-ship—jet-propulsion!" Knight rapped back. He

waited, crouching over the stick until the black raider was two thousand feet below and zooming at a mad speed. Then he jammed the stick to the firewall. The Northrop stood on its nose, went down with the radial bellowing. The rocket ship seemed to cartwheel in a split-second. With flames fifty feet long jetting from its nozzles, it came down after the diving two-seater. Doyle twisted around in his seat, pumped a wild burst from the .50s. The rocket-ship leaped sidewise two hundred feet, flung its tail toward the Northrop. Knight stood on the rudder, and the strato-ship lurched in the opposite direction. The streams of blazing gas flamed above them, and their force hurled the raider a mile across the sky before it could turn back.

Heart pounding, Knight watched the altimeter hand. The ship was already down to 16,000 feet and he knew the meter was lagging. Directly over the nose he saw lights flicker on the ground, making a rectangular pattern like tiny gems against black velvet. He threw a fearful glance over his shoulder. The rocket-ship was boring down at an angle from the point where it had reversed its course. But in another moment he knew that the pilot had momentarily lost sight of the Northrop, for the rocket-jets blazed and the black raider zoomed steeply.

He closed the throttle, started to pull out of the dive as the altimeter showed 10,000. The nose had barely begun to lift when an amber-colored beam probed up and caught the ship. Knight put one hand before his eyes, bent to watch the instruments as he pulled out. The Northrop was almost at its terminal velocity of 460. It would be only a matter of seconds to a crash unless he leveled out.

Above the frightful scream of the wings he faintly heard the clatter of Doyle's guns. Scant seconds from death, his chunky partner was trying to take the black raider with them. Brilliant flame lit up the sky and the rocket-ship for the third time skidded crazily past, its blazing jets pointed toward the Northrop. This time Knight thought they were finished, but as swiftly as the jets had whirled toward them they were twitched away. The amber searchlight was flashing wildly at the black raider, and from the corner of his eye Knight saw another ship racing in.

With both hands on the stick, he lifted the two-seater's nose. The ship was almost level, fifteen hundred feet above the ground, when a hail of lead crashed through the left side of the enclosure. He jerked to the other side, saw a stream of tracer cut diagonally forward into the cowl.

The twin-radial skipped a beat, broke into a ragged rhythm. Knight swore, glared back and saw a 2KB swooping in for another burst. It was Slade's ship.

"Get that louse, Dick!" he heard Doyle groan. "My guns are empty."

Knight grimly shook his head. The tachometer hand was steadily dropping, and they were practically helpless before the darting fighter. He kicked into a slip, straightened out as Slade sent a brief fusillade past his wingtip. The rocket-ship was swooping down toward the lighted rectangle, its jet-nozzles trailing plumes of white smoke.

**TWO FLOODLIGHTS** spread bright fans on the ground, and Knight saw that the rectangle was the only open space in a vast expanse of woods save for the frozen river which lay close by. For an instant, he thought the river might offer a chance at escape, then he saw that the ice was too rough for a landing.

With a heart like lead, he turned the Northrop and glided down toward the lighted ground. Slade followed, expertly shifting from right to left to ward off any attempt at escape, evidently not sure that the engine was really crippled. Knight stared gloomily over the cowl, saw hangars, barracks, and shops, dark bulks in the light from the flood-units. Men in fur parkas had swarmed out from the barracks, were rolling the rocket ship toward a platform at the base of a launching track. A car with cog-wheel drive stood on the platform waiting to receive the rocket-ship, and in front of it at the point where the rails began to tilt upward was a smaller car on which was secured a glistening rocket-shell some twenty feet long and three feet in diameter. The track extended upward at an angle of thirty degrees, being elevated from the ground by a huge trestle-work. Knight could vaguely make out a complicated braking apparatus near the end of the rails, three hundred feet from the platform. At least fifty of the sinister-looking rocket-shells lay in wheeled cradles on both sides of the platform. One was hooked to a derrick-boom, ready to be hoisted onto the launching-car.

Knight saw all this in a quick glance as he swung into the wind and leveled off. A dozen armed men ran toward the ship as it stopped, and in a few moments he and Doyle stood outside, hands lifted in the bitter cold air. The 2KB moaned down and landed nearby. Slade jumped out, his yellow robe flapping and strode over to the prisoners. The guards, Koreans except for one dour-faced Russian, apprehensively watched the approach of the false monk. An ugly smile twisted Slade's misshapen features as he came up to Knight, goggles pushed up on his forehead.

"You're a hard man to kill—but I think I can change that," he said sardonically.

Knight made no answer, whereupon Slade turned abruptly to a fur-clad man who had emerged from the cabin of the rocket-ship. The man was thickset as a gorilla, with a red, brutal face, and a drooping eyelid which lent him a look of sly cunning.

"Gunderson," rasped the robed pilot, "I told you not to use the jets on them except as a last resort."

"I suppose I should've let them shoot us down," said Gunderson sullenly. "Maybe you think it's simple to fly that damned ship—"

"I've told you a dozen times to cut off the jets while you're ten miles from your target," Slade retorted angrily. "You can get in line, fire, and—"

"—And crack into 'em head-on!" broke in Gunderson

sarcastically. "I tell you she's too fast for combat with an ordinary ship, even at one-third power. Anyway, you've got these two alive, if that's what you wanted."

"Not what *I* wanted," Slade said malevolently. "It was an order from *Them*. I think some special hell has been cooked up for these countrymen of ours."

# CHAPTER V

## Decree of the Four Faces

**G**UNDERSON SHIVERED as he heard Slade's words. "I'd bump myself off, if I ever thought *They* were after me."

"Well, I'll see that our 'friends' here don't have that chance," said Slade. Then he spoke briefly to the dour Russian, and the man turned to his squad of Koreans. Knight and Doyle were marched to the entrance of a thick-walled building between the main barracks and a hangar. Above the door, Knight saw a panel bearing Russian lettering. Translated it read: *Headquarters, U.S.S.R. Emergency Squadron 99.*

They entered a hall, turned, and stopped inside a large room at the opposite end of which was a groundglass television screen six feet high and eight feet wide. Powerful Kleig lights made the entire room blindingly bright. Two men sat at a complicated switchboard on the left side of the screen.

Slade and Gunderson followed the prisoners into the room, and the pseudo-monk dismissed all but the Russian and two of the guards. Knight and Doyle were quickly searched, and their guns taken. Slade nodded to one of the men at the switchboard, and stepped before the television screen.

"Number Thirteen reporting," he said, and his voice held a slightly uneasy note. "Knight and Doyle have been captured and are here at Base E. The stratosphere plane has also been captured, with only slight damage which is being repaired immediately."

There was a pause, then a faint humming sound. It died away, and an indistinct picture grew upon the screen. Knight stiffened as he saw four black-robed figures seated behind a high bar like a judges' bench. The picture grew clearer, and in a moment four grim faces looked out from the screen. All were identical, all had the same sunken eyes, rigid features, the same expressions of brooding menace. Though he knew the faces were masks to conceal the identity of the mysterious men who headed the criminal league, he felt the old, shuddering fear as he looked upon them. Doyle and he had stood in judgment in front of the Four Faces before, and only miracles had saved them. He knew they could expect no mercy now.

The first of the Four Faces leaned forward, and his voice sounded from the speaker behind the screen. It was so devoid of emotion as to be almost toneless, as though some mechanical man spoke:

*Report in full detail, covering all steps since the last report period.*

Knight stole a sidelong glance at Doyle. The ex-Marine was staring at the screen, perspiration running down his face. Gunderson and the guards were also watching with varying expressions of fear and uneasiness. Slade cleared his throat, spoke hurriedly.

"I took over the impersonation of Creele, as ordered. While I was in the air, spotting the hits of the first rockets, the Northrop appeared and was attacked by Japanese pilots."

**HE DESCRIBED** what had followed. The four masked figures looked at each other, conferred in whispers that the television speaker did not make intelligible. Then the First Face nodded.

*Number Thirteen, the attack on Harbin will be temporarily discontinued. Our reports indicate it has been successful, that the Manchukuan authorities believe the Soviet responsible. Tokyo has been informed. You will now carry out the second phase of our plan. Take down these orders.*

Slade jerked his head at one of the switchboard men, and the First Face went on impassively.

*Have the rocket-plane fueled for a flight to Tsingtao, China. There will be a ten minute interval for directing rocket fire, and then a return flight to Base E. On signal from the pilot of the rocket-ship that it is in position to direct your fire, you will launch three trial rockets to fall approximately ten miles north, south, and west of Tsingtao. As soon as corrections are received, you will then set the gyro controls to drop twenty rockets in rapid succession in the harbor and in the area including the Edgewater Mansions House, where three hundred Americans are now assembled. The United States cruisers "Marblehead" and "Sacramento," and the destroyer "Pope" are in the harbor, to protect or evacuate the Americans. All Japanese mills and property are being burned by Chinese communists, and Japanese naval vessels are en route for reprisal attacks. The rockets will undoubtedly be thought to be shells from Japanese battleships out in the Yellow Sea, and the destruction of the American colony and the three American warships will be certain to embrace the United States in a war with Japan, for America is already inflamed over the "Panay" incident.*

"I have the orders," Slade said tensely as the First Face ceased. "But what of the prisoners?"

The First Face spoke again:

*Their death has been decreed. But we intend to make use of them at the same time. A document is being prepared here which will be shown you by television in a few minutes. It will purport to be a code message from the American G-2 chief, General Brett, to Creele at his Manchukuo hiding-place, explaining certain secret plans for a sudden offensive by England and the United States against Japan. It will seem to instruct Creele to send the information to spies in Manchukuo, and across the border to the Soviet officials, who will also cooperate in the attack. It will name Knight as the senior secret agent of the United States, with authority from the White House. Have a photograph made of the document and then a handwritten copy made. This paper is to be found on Knight's body after he and Doyle are left in the Northrop.*

"I don't understand," Slade broke in. Thereupon the voice of the First Face became even more cold:

*Don't interrupt. I will explain everything. The Northrop is to be flown back to Manchukuo and landed at the field to the northeast of Harbin. One of the prisoners will be taken in the rear seat, drugged. The other also drugged will be taken across the border in one of your three-seater planes. Your pilots will return in the three-seater, leaving Knight and Doyle unconscious in the Northrop. As soon as your men are safely away, they will signal you, and you will relay the message to us. We shall arrange for one of our Japanese members to 'discover' the Northrop soon afterward. The prisoners will have frozen to death, and it will look as though they had lost their way and been forced down. The forged paper will give the Japanese evidence that they are about to be attacked by three powers—and the war we desire will be inevitable.*

Doyle gave a strangled curse, and Knight looked grimly at the Four Faces.

"It's a smart scheme—but it won't work," he said in a savage tone. "Neither Japan nor the United States wants that war."

A sound like a dry chuckle came from the television speaker.

*What they desire is not important, Mr. Knight. We have decided for them.*

The pictures faded from the screen, and Slade glowered at the two prisoners.

"Too easy a death," he said harshly. "If I had my way—" he broke off, his scarred face suddenly mocking. "Maybe I will, at that. Vornoff, lock them up with the Englishman—or did the fool die while I was away?"

**THE DOUR** Russian shook his head, grunted a command at the guards. Knight and Doyle were taken down the hall to a door which Vornoff unlocked. There was no light inside, but by the glow from the light in the hall Knight saw a man in a blood-stained yellow robe lying on the floor. There was a cut at one side of his shaven head, and his face was livid with bruises. The prisoner tried to raise his head as the two Americans were shoved into the cell. The door slammed shut, and Knight heard the man groan.

"Creele?" he said.

"Don't beat me again!" the other man cried hoarsely. "Let me die—I tell you I don't know anything else."

"We're not going to hurt you," Knight said gently. "We're prisoners."

"Prisoners?" Creele mumbled. His voice came out of the blackness, shakily. "Not—the two Americans?"

"Yes," said Knight. "Then you got the message from General Brett?"

"If you're lying, it won't do any good—I've told everything, I told you the message—"

"We're not Slade's men," Knight cut in. "We came up from Shanghai to get instructions from you, but Slade was impersonating you."

"I know—I heard them plan the whole thing," Creele muttered. "They intercepted your general's messages and then landed at my place. I thought they were Soviet pilots—I'd worked with Russia before. They almost killed me—I think they would have, but they thought I had some information I was holding back. One of Slade's pilots brought me over here in his ship—I've been in here at least six hours."

"What was Brett's message for us?" Doyle interrupted.

"It was about the rocket affair," Creele answered dully. "They had just discovered the secret plans were stolen at Guam."

"What plans?" said Knight.

"The design for the rocket-ship. I thought you knew about it—some American scientist named Chambers has apparently been working secretly at Guam for the last year."

"Chambers—the rocket designer!" exclaimed Knight. "But he was reported killed in an experiment in 1936."

"It must have been to cover up his work," Creele mumbled. "The messages didn't explain in full, but it seems that Chambers had built a rocket using hydrogen and ozone under high pressure. He was shooting test rockets out into the Pacific, with the Navy checking distances and speeds. And evidently he designed a full-sized rocket ship and was building it at his Guam station. The Four Faces learned about it and stole a copy of the plans and a rocket model, but Chambers didn't find out until two days ago when an assistant confessed he'd been blackmailed into doing it. I suppose you know about the Four Faces—your general mentioned them as though you'd understand."

"We've tangled with them—plenty," Doyle growled.

"I'd heard of the organization but never believed all the stories. They must have spies everywhere, even in the highest branches of a dozen governments. This base here," Creele went on wearily, "was built for emergency use by the Soviet in connection with the new defense plan for Siberia. Some one ordered it abandoned five months ago, and I know now that the Four Faces were back of that order. They've had men here since early Fall, building that launching-track and assembling the rockets from materials brought in by the river before it froze over. Vornoff bragged about it—I knew him at Vladivostok, the lying renegade."

"So that's how they got hold of the Soviet ships," Knight commented. "He's been playing a double role."

"That's right. He must have suspected me long ago, and had some one watch me at Harbin, or they'd never have known where to land today. Or maybe it was yesterday... I don't know what time it is... not that it matters..." his voice trailed off, hopelessly.

"We've still a chance," said Knight, though he knew there was practically none. "Tell me the rest of Brett's message— we may be able to work out something."

"I'll tell you—but it's no use. I was to help you reach the right Soviet officials at Khabarovsk, so you could have aid in finding where the Four Faces had built their rocket base. Chambers' assistant knew that they intended to work from somewhere east of Blagoveshchensk, with the idea of starting a world war. I don't know what side they're on—"

"The Four Faces are on nobody's side but their own," Knight said grimly. "They own munitions industries in several countries and probably stand to make a colossal fortune if another world war develops."

"And there'll be one if those rockets hit our ships and the American crowd at Tsingtao," Doyle said fiercely from the darkness. "But we won't know about it—we'll be feeding vultures down in Manchukuo."

"The rockets may not hit their mark," Creele said in a dull voice. "It's a long distance from here to Tsingtao."

"They've already arranged for that," said Knight moodily. "They're sending the rocket-ship ahead to spot the hits and radio back the corrections. If we could only have destroyed that ship!"

"I still don't see how the rockets carry so much explosive," said Doyle. "It must take a helluva lot of hydrogen and ozone to feed th' jets over a thousand miles—and it's all of that from here to Tsingtao."

"They don't carry explosive," Creele answered listlessly. "They simply arrange to detonate the remainder of their fuel on impact—hydrogen and oxygen is about as powerful a mixture as you can create, and ozone doubles the oxygen content. I heard the man called Gunderson tell some one the rockets would reach a trajectory peak of sixty-three miles on the way to Harbin, so they must go most of the way in empty space. That means they'd coast at least half the way, with the jets shut off after the rockets gained their momentum. They must reach a speed of 1500 miles an hour once they get above the stratosphere."

"Even more," said Knight. "The rockets began to strike near your hut within five minutes after Slade reached his ship. He couldn't have signaled for them any sooner."

"Well, it makes no difference now," Creele answered. Knight caught the labored note in his voice. "We're finished, and we might as well admit it. But I'd die happy if I had just one shot at that devil Slade."

"So would I!" Doyle grated.

# CHAPTER VI

## Hell's Holocaust

**"THERE MUST** be some way we could trick them," Knight muttered. "I wonder what Slade meant when he said he might have *his* way about killing us?"

Neither Doyle nor Creele had an answer. Then from out on the base the thunder of an engine suddenly was audible.

"That's our ship!" Doyle exclaimed. "They must've fixed it in a hurry."

"It was only a clipped distributor wire," said Knight. He listened while the engine ran for a minute. It stopped, and again silence fell in the darkened cell. Creele's heavy breathing was the only sound for almost ten minutes, then Knight snapped his fingers.

"What's the matter?" Doyle said hastily.

"It may not work, but I've an idea," Knight whispered. "At the worst, it's better than freezing to death, half-drugged. Creele, I'll take your robe and pretend to be you. They won't be expecting any attack from your direction when they come in here. If there aren't too many I might be able to seize a gun and cover them."

"It's probably your death-warrant," Creele said huskily, "but we might as well go out fighting. Here—help me get out of the robe."

Knight stooped over him in the dark, felt the Englishman's hand grope for his. Creele's flesh was feverishly hot and his hand shook.

"Don't try to get up," Knight said in an undertone. "I'll get out of this flying-coat and help you put it on. You'll have to wear the helmet and goggles, too, if we're to fool them even for a moment."

The exchange took a minute or two, and when Knight had donned the robe he felt along it until his fingers touched the bloody stain he had seen. He rubbed his fingers along the side of his head where Creele had been wounded. He was just starting to give Doyle whispered instructions when footsteps sounded outside and he heard Slade's voice.

"Have the crew ready for launching the ship. I'll be there as soon as I take care of the prisoners."

"You mean you're going to pilot it yourself?" came Gunderson's voice.

"I am," snapped Slade. "I've a special grudge against the Navy ever since they helped the Coast Guard put me out of business. I wouldn't miss this show for five grand."

Knight had bent over Creele at the first sound. He lifted the wounded man in his arms, carried him across the darkened cell. He started to put him down, but Creele gripped his arm with trembling fingers.

"No, no! Put me on my feet… Doyle can help me stand… best way to pretend I'm… you."

"He's right, Dick!" Doyle said in a hoarse whisper. "Here— lean on me—"

Knight sprang across the room, flung himself down where Creele had been as he heard the key grate in the lock.

"—and have the Northrop started, too," Slade's voice came, close to the door. "Our friends will be ready for their little joy-hop in five minutes."

The door swung open. Knight lay doubled up, one arm partly over his face, legs drawn up as far as possible under the yellow robe so that the difference in his height and Creele's would not be apparent. Light slanted in through the doorway, and staring under his arm he saw Slade come in, followed by Vornoff and two Koreans. A flashlight beam passed quickly over him, flipped toward the other prisoners.

Like a catapult, Knight's tense muscles shot him to his feet. The nearest Korean whirled with a startled yell. Knight's fist smacked viciously under his jaw, and the man went up on his toes. Knight wrenched a gun from the guard's resistless fingers just as Vornoff spun around. Fear shot into the Russian's eyes, and he frantically snatched at his pistol. Knight leaped in desperately, clubbed his gun into Vornoff's face. The Russian tottered back, blood pouring from a gash on his brow.

A half-muffled shot echoed through the cell. Creele gave a gasping cry, crumpled to the floor. Doyle crashed a left hook to Slade's jaw, knocked a smoking automatic from the killer's hand. The second Korean carried a bottle and a hypodermic syringe instead of a weapon. For a moment, as the fight raged about him, he cringed back against the wall, then suddenly he hurtled at Doyle, the syringe needle pointed at Doyle's neck.

**KNIGHT SPRANG** over the other guard, brought the butt of his gun down on the brown man's head. The Korean collapsed without a sound, and the bottle broke upon the floor. Vornoff was staggering around blindly, eyes half-filled with blood. He tripped over the second Korean, fell headlong. Knight wheeled to help Doyle, but his aid was not needed. His chunky comrade had the bigger man by the throat, and Slade was clawing wildly to break that deadly grip on his windpipe.

"Don't kill him!" Knight said swiftly. "We'll need him."

He scooped up Slade's gun, ran to the door and looked out. There was no one in sight. Evidently everyone else was out on the base preparing the two ships and the rockets. A horrible, choking sound made him whirl. For a second he thought Doyle had disregarded his orders, then he saw Vornoff writhing on the floor. Some of the liquid from the broken bottle had reached the Russian's gashed forehead. A terrible glare came into Vornoff's dilated eyes. His lips flew open as though for a scream of agony, but it never came. One last tortured gasp burst from the traitor's throat, and his face froze into a red-stained mask of horror.

Knight looked grimly from the dead Russian to Slade, who had sagged to his knees, breathing stertorously. He handed Doyle Slade's gun, stooped and picked up the hypodermic needle. Slade's eyes bulged as Knight came toward him.

"No! No!" he croaked. "Not that!" Doyle savagely hauled him to his feet.

"You dirty rat! I'd like to empty this gat right into your yellow belly!"

Slade cowered back, his misshapen face ashen. Knight looked down at Creele's body. Perhaps it was only imagination, but there seemed to be a faint, sad smile on the dead man's lips.

"He threw himself against Slade's gun," Doyle muttered. "I tried to stop him—poor devil."

"So that's what muffled the shot," Knight raised his eyes to Slade's face, and at the look in his eyes the Four Faces' pilot cringed. "We're going out of here, Slade—and if anything goes wrong, you're going to pay double for killing Creele!"

Slade's dark eyes stared down at the syringe. His lips moved, tremblingly.

"I'll do—anything. I'll get you clear—"

Knight's gaze flicked over Slade's fur parka.

"Take that off—and your helmet and goggles, too. Doyle, see that he gets into my flying-coat and helmet while I switch."

The exchange was quickly made, for Slade seemed to be completely cowed. Knight fastened Slade's winter helmet, drew down the combination goggles and breathing-mask which left only the tip of his nose and his lips exposed behind a fine wire mesh. Turning up the hood of the parka, he picked up the syringe, also the gun he had laid down.

"All right, let's go! Doyle, put Slade's pistol in one pocket and Vornoff's in the other. Keep your hands on them—but don't draw until you have to."

Doyle nodded, and Knight looked coldly at Slade.

"Turn up that coat collar, and when we get outside keep your head down in it. Stumble along as though you've been drugged. Make one move to attract attention and I'll jab this needle into your throat."

"But what are you going to do with me?" Slade said fearfully.

"That depends on you. Now go ahead."

They went into the hall, Knight keeping close to the Four Faces' pilot, gun poised and the syringe held significantly. As they passed the door to the radio and television room, one of the operators looked up, but Knight shoved Slade by and prodded Doyle with his pistol. The operator grinned, turned back to his instruments. Knight halted Slade when they came to the building entrance. Keeping the big pilot covered, he cautiously opened the door half an inch. Floodlights made the outside brilliant. The rocket-ship was on the launching-car, and he saw an engineer at the control board beside the platform. The crew was waiting, and beyond them a crowd of mechanics in parkas was waiting to place the rockets in position for shooting. He looked intently at the nearest gleaming projectile, saw a detonating pin in the nose. It had a safety-device to keep it from being pushed accidentally.

"Exactly what happens when one of those detonators is shoved into the nose?" he demanded of Slade.

"It releases a spring that opens the hydrogen and ozone tanks." Slade looked at him in sudden terror. "You fool! You'd kill yourself as well as the rest of us!"

Knight smiled behind the fur-lined flying mask. "And hydrogen explodes when it's mixed with more than fifteen percent of oxygen… I wonder how I could—"

**THE SPUTTER** of the Northrop's motor quickly ended his musing. It was the sound for which he had been waiting. He opened the door as the motor settled into a steady thunder.

"Head down!" he said in a harsh undertone, and Slade hastily obeyed, stumbling along the frozen ground toward the two-seater. Several of the mechanics stared at the trio, and Knight saw their frosty breath as they exchanged comments. He held the syringe in plain sight, knowing that the plan to drug the prisoners had probably become known to everyone on the base. The Northrop was only a short distance away, and his hopes soared as he saw there were only two men beside it. One of them had just climbed from the front pit after starting the motor.

"Be ready to grab the rear-pit guns," he whispered to Doyle. "I'll stand those two off while you jump in."

The man who had started the motor turned as Knight was speaking. It was Gunderson, red face half-covered by a parka hood. He took a step forward, went rigid as his eyes flicked to Slade's bent head. He leaped back, gloved hand clawing for the gun strapped at his hip. Doyle sprang to one side, jerked the two pistols from his leather coat. All three guns blasted. Gunderson spun around, pitched into a heap on the ground. The mechanic back of him dived for the gun he had dropped.

Knight fired, and the mechanic rolled over with a slug through his right side. It was only an instant—but in that split-second Slade whirled and raced under the Northrop's wing. Doyle triggered a shot after him, turned and vaulted into the ship. Across at the platform, the servicemen were breaking wildly for shelter. Knight saw one man sprint toward a machine-gun mounted near the main barracks. He fired, missed, was aiming again when Doyle's .50s broke loose with a deafening roar.

The running mechanic fell, riddled, and Knight sprang up onto the step of the two-seater. Machine-gun tracers shot above his head as he gripped the stick and throttle. He opened the radial and sent the Northrop plunging out into the center of the field. Doyle swerved his Brownings, raked the crew of the machine-gun which was blasting after them.

Knight bent over the controls, brought the Northrop around in a swift turn. His radial almost wide open, he hurled the ship toward the massed rockets. A furious cross-fire from three directions drove him into a zoom before he could trip his guns. He chandelled over the trees, nosed down to gain speed and to blanket the gunners' barrage. The Northrop, now a mile from the base, banked in a tight turn—and now the rocketship came racing up the inclined track. Half-way to the top, its jets belched out a blazing white streak, and the man-made meteorite leaped upward at terrific speed. The launching-cradle struck the braking device and rolled back, then the rocket plane screamed up into the night.

Doyle spun the rear-mount and fired, but his burst went two hundred yards behind the rocket-ship. Knight shoved the stick forward, dived back at the field. Another storm of machine-gun fire met the plummeting Northrop. He crouched, eyes fixed on the glistening rockets below. Bullets were pounding into the wings, but he held to the dive. A glare of white light reflected in the cracked cowl mirror. Slade was pitching the rocket-ship headlong after them!

With an unspoken prayer, Knight tripped the forward guns. Glowing pinkish lines stabbed down at the shining rockets. The Four Faces gunners broke and fled in panic. For an instant, Knight thought his desperate scheme would fail as his tracer lines hit the huge projectiles and ricocheted. Then suddenly a bolt of white flame shot from the rear of one rocket. He jerked the stick to his belt, and the Northrop zoomed madly.

**A TREMENDOUS** concussion shook the two-seater, and a dazzling glare lit up the sky. The Northrop whipped onto its side, was lifted vertically five hundred feet. Knight's senses reeled as once again a withering heat engulfed him. Dazedly he waited until stick and rudder had ceased their crazy flopping. The Northrop fell off, went into a wobbling glide from which he brought it into straight flight.

Out of the raging holocaust which a few moments before had been the base, another and still another explosion blasted, hurling masses of smoking earth and flaming wreckage high into the air. Knight stared back, and seeing Doyle slumped half-conscious in the rear cockpit, he raced away from the wrecked base.

But then something streaked across the sky at the Northrop, and the Q-agent's pulses leaped as he saw the black rocket-ship. Slade had escaped the inferno, was plunging in for a final vengeance!

Knight jammed the throttle wide open, trying frenziedly to reach the scattered clouds above. With jets roaring, the rocket-plane closed the gap. Knight kicked desperately at the rudder. The Northrop skidded wildly to the left and Slade overshot. Knight's fingers closed on his stick buttons, and with another furious kick at the rudder he raked the zooming ship.

The jet flames ceased. A jagged black strip tore from the top of the streamlined cabin, then the whole upper covering of the speeding monster ripped off in the wind. By the glare from below, Knight could see Slade pounding frantically at a lever.

A thin flame momentarily issued from the jet nozzles, then a blinding flash lit up the clouded heavens. An explosion followed that drowned the radial's thunder—and the rocket-ship was gone!

**KNIGHT SWIFTLY** banked to avoid the rain of blazing fragments. As he straightened out on the course back to Shanghai, Doyle sat up and gazed anxiously about the sky.

"Hey, Dick! Look out for Slade! He's around here somewhere."

Knight looked grimly down at the last falling bits of the rocket-ship.

"Yes, he's around here… somewhere. But," he added as Doyle stared bewilderedly, "the Dark Angel has fallen from Heaven."

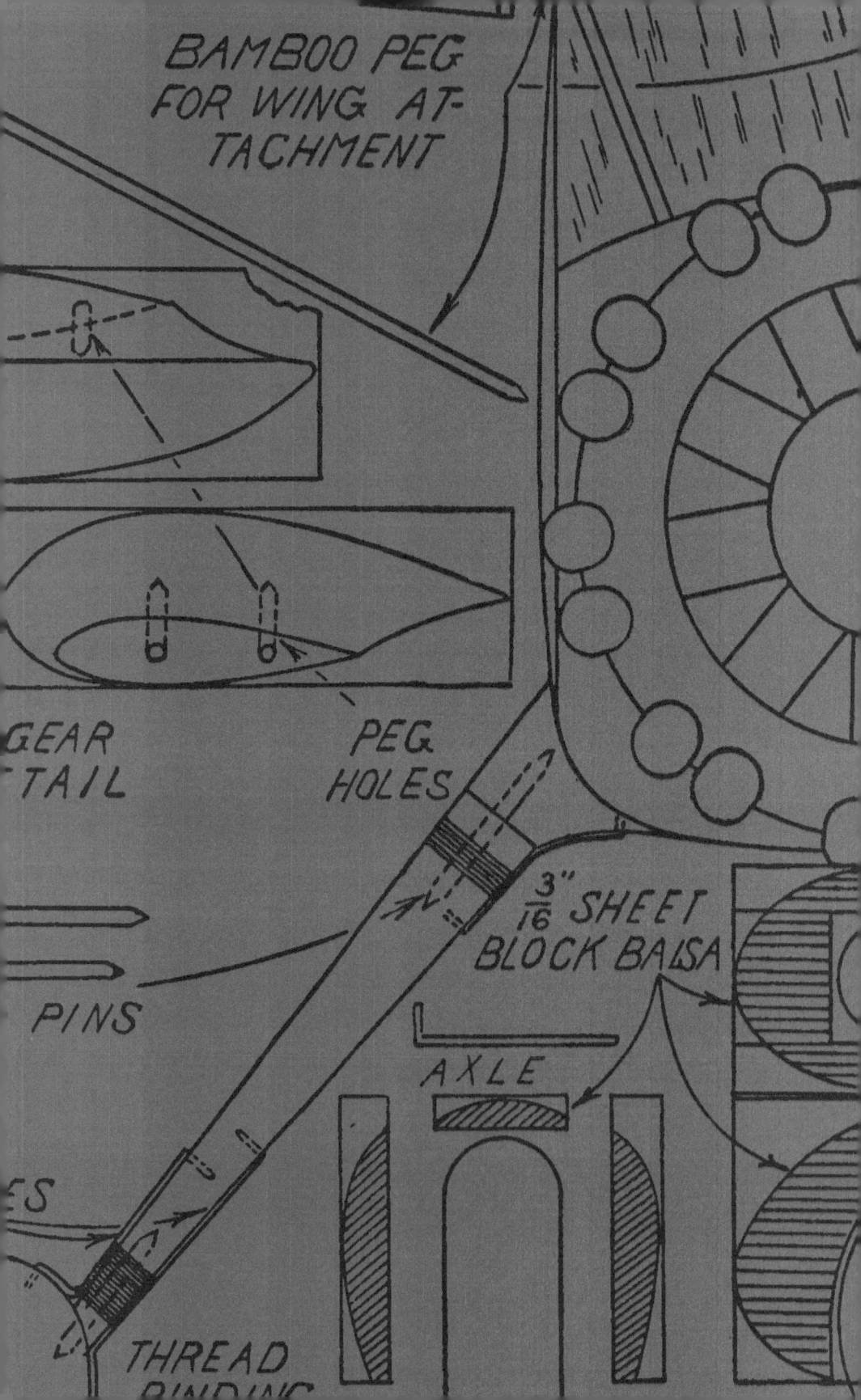

BAMBOO PEG
FOR WING AT-
TACHMENT

GEAR
TAIL

PEG.
HOLES

PINS

$\frac{3"}{16}$ SHEET
BLOCK BALSA

AXLE

ES

THREAD
BINDING

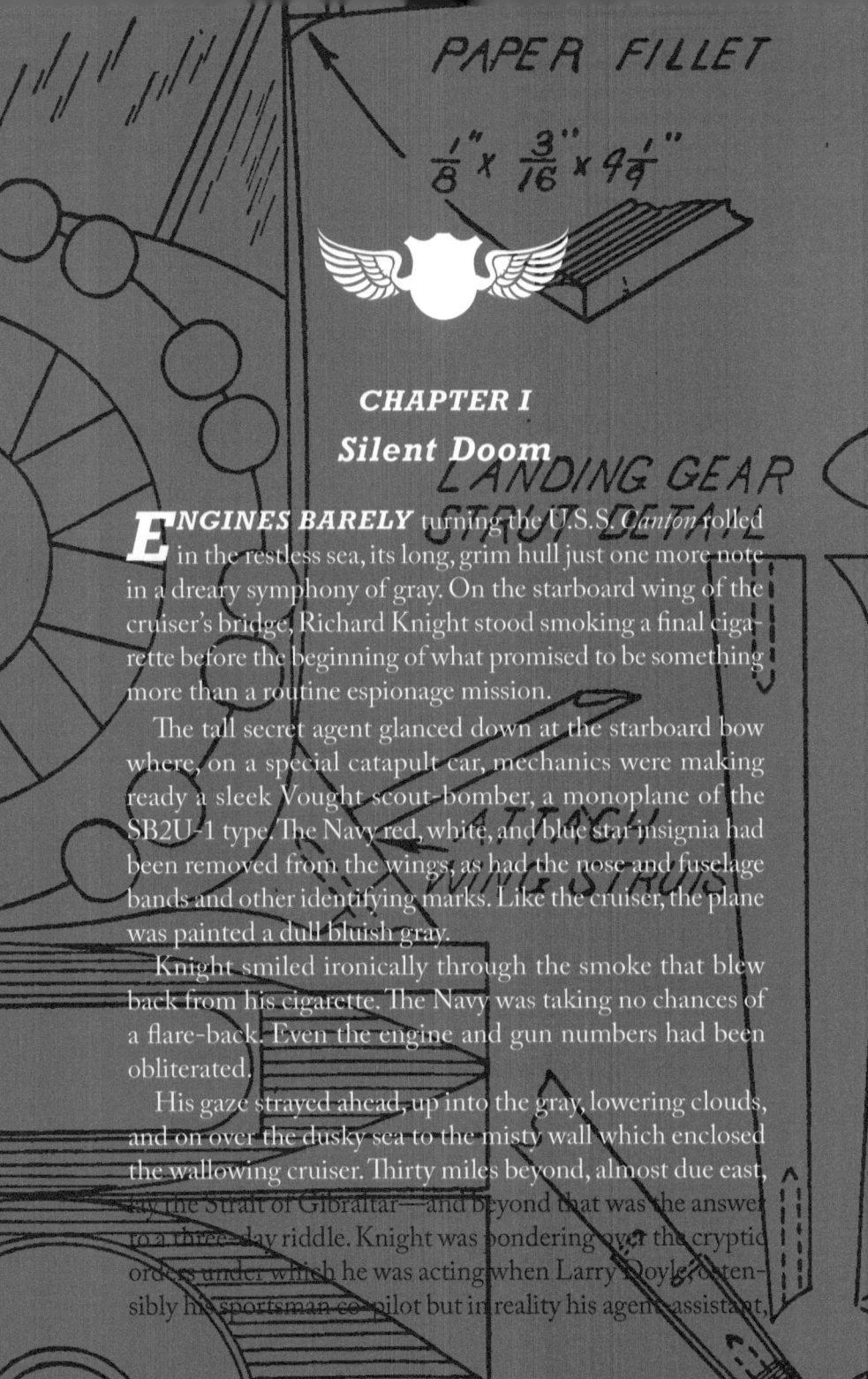

## CHAPTER I

### Silent Doom

**E**NGINES BARELY turning the U.S.S. *Canton* rolled in the restless sea, its long, grim hull just one more note in a dreary symphony of gray. On the starboard wing of the cruiser's bridge, Richard Knight stood smoking a final cigarette before the beginning of what promised to be something more than a routine espionage mission.

The tall secret agent glanced down at the starboard bow where, on a special catapult car, mechanics were making ready a sleek Vought scout-bomber, a monoplane of the SB2U-1 type. The Navy red, white, and blue star insignia had been removed from the wings, as had the nose and fuselage bands and other identifying marks. Like the cruiser, the plane was painted a dull bluish gray.

Knight smiled ironically through the smoke that blew back from his cigarette. The Navy was taking no chances of a flare-back. Even the engine and gun numbers had been obliterated.

His gaze strayed ahead, up into the gray, lowering clouds, and on over the dusky sea to the misty wall which enclosed the wallowing cruiser. Thirty miles beyond, almost due east, lay the Strait of Gibraltar—and beyond that was the answer to a three-day riddle. Knight was pondering over the cryptic orders under which he was acting when Larry Doyle, osten-sibly his sportsman co-pilot but in reality his agent assistant,

strode out on the wing of the bridge with Captain Becker, commander of the vessel.

Doyle, an ex-Marine pilot, was short, chunky, and possessed of a homely face the belligerence of which was heightened by a broken nose he had received in a long-forgotten brawl. He looked Irish—and was, with the Celt's quick temper and equally quick generosity. The *Canton's* skipper was taller, spare of form. His dignity, born of years of service, was somewhat relieved by kindly blue eyes.

Out of that weird black cloud of swirling doom there hurtled a million fragments of smoking metal. Then a silent concussion rocked the sky, pitched the Vought a hundred feet in the air before Knight could move the controls.

"No, I wouldn't care to be heading into that murk," he was saying to Doyle. "Even for an ordinary flight, that's mean weather—and when you don't know what lies ahead—" he paused, looked keenly at Knight. "Or do you? At any rate, now that you're about ready to start, perhaps you can tell me something else—just in case—" He stopped, a trifle confused.

Knight grinned.

"In case we don't come back? Thanks for the suggestion, Captain—but the truth is I'm as puzzled as you are. Doyle and I were loafing at Miami Beach, after a rather rough stretch in the Orient, when that code message came for us to board a specially-chartered Clipper at Dinner Key station. Before we made contact with the *Canton* south of Bermuda, the Clipper's first officer gave me those sealed instructions I've mentioned. He turned out to be a naval intelligence officer working undercover, and he'd flown the letter straight from Washington."

Captain Becker shook his head.

"I still can't understand. The Mediterranean is a caldron of intrigues and war-fever, and you shouldn't be sent into it without knowing exactly what you're up against."

"That's nothing new for us, Captain," Knight answered. "But we do have a hint. We know that secret agents from a dozen countries have all rushed into the Mediterranean for something. Washington heard of the rendezvous for which they were heading—but not the *reason*. It must be a vital secret—or a plot of some kind. Whatever it is, it's bound to affect the United States. So we're going to take a look-see, and I guess the Vought's ready—they're winding her up."

The howl of the inertia starter came up shrilly to the bridge, then the barking thunder of the Twin-Wasp-Junior filled the air. By the time Knight and Doyle had reached the catapult the engine was droning smoothly. The senior agent looked with dry humor at his partner.

"Sure you've thrown away all your love-letters, Lothario? Remember—no identifying marks."

"I've got a mole on my left shoulder," growled Doyle. "Want me to cut it off?"

Knight chuckled, fastened his chute-harness over his leather coat, and climbed into the front cockpit. Doyle settled himself in the rear, pulled the triangular-section Plexiglas enclosure shut. Knight revved up the engine, inspected his instruments, and tossed a salute to Captain Becker, who was leaning over the wing of the bridge with another officer. The captain answered, and Knight closed the front pit "greenhouse" after a signal to the catapult tender.

The *Canton* rolled to starboard, lifted slowly. There was a dull report as the tender ignited the gunpowder charge, and the Vought shot down the catapult track and into the air. Knight let the ship gain speed as it hurtled along above the waves. He was about to ease the stick back for a climb when a violent concussion of air hurled the Vought skyward. The ship whirled upward three hundred feet, dipped, then fell steeply on the left wing. He caught it, leveled out at sixty feet after battling the controls. A shout of amazement from Doyle made him twist around in his seat.

An enormous wave, twenty feet above the normal level of the sea, was racing along behind them. Throttle full on, Knight zoomed above it. Then, when he stared back, his heart stood still—*the cruiser had vanished!*

**A COLD** horror crept over him as he gazed down at the boiling sea. Where the *Canton* had been there was now only a vast, churning whirlpool into which a rain of smoking debris was falling from the sky.

Stupefied, he watched the smoking fragments plunge into the water. The thing was impossible! At the most, thirty seconds had passed between the moment of catapulting and the furious concussion of air. The cruiser *couldn't* be gone…

But it was!

He saw Doyle white-faced, lips moving, staring down at the steaming waters. Out of the chaos of his mind he tried to focus one thought: How could it have happened?

Only a colossal explosion could have so completely destroyed the Navy cruiser. Such an explosion would have come like a crack of doom, with a terrific detonation that would have cut through the drone of the Wasp like a thunderclap in the night. But there had been no sound above the engine's rumble.

Doyle had partly opened the rear pit enclosure in order to look downward, and Knight saw a jagged hole torn in the Plexiglas. Suddenly Doyle drew in his head, wiped his goggles. He had a sick expression as he glanced forward at Knight, and with a tinge of nausea the senior agent saw a faint reddish mist on the other man's hand and cheeks. It had come from a dark smear near the break in the enclosure, and the prop-blast had sent that gruesome vapor back onto Doyle's face.

"It's blood!" Doyle said hoarsely through the interphone system. "And we were almost a mile away. Think how close we—" he did not finish, but Knight dully nodded. Only a miracle had kept them from being a part of that fragmented mass upon the heaving Atlantic. A moment's wait for the cruiser to roll into position for catapulting… another drag or two at his cigarette—the slightest pause, and they would have been doomed by the ghastly, silent fate which had overtaken the *Canton* and its crew.

Into the agent's mind came a vision of Captain Becker, with his kindly look of concern. He seemed to hear Becker saying:

*"You shouldn't be sent into it without knowing exactly what you're up against."*

And now Becker and his crew were gone, wiped out by some horrible thing which must have brought instant annihilation. Only Doyle and he and the Vought remained—without a base to which they could return, facing he knew not what. He banked slowly, gazing into the fast-deepening gloom to the East. The clouds, the wall of mist, all seemed suddenly ominous as though conspiring to hide something dreadful, some fate that awaited them in the fog. Doyle's voice, harsh with emotion, came through the interphone and brought him up with a jerk.

"Dick, what in Heaven's name did it?"

Knight's stiff lips touched his mouthpiece. "I don't know, old man. I haven't the slightest idea."

"Maybe a spy was on board—might have blown up her powder magazines," Doyle mumbled.

"No, we'd have heard such a blast—and there wasn't a sound above the engine. Besides, that wouldn't have torn her completely apart. She'd have been blown up... been on fire... sinking. But not—this."

"What are we going to do?" Doyle said huskily.

"We can go ahead," Knight said, his face grim, "or we can make for Gibraltar. The British carrier Furious is stationed there, so we could land. I'll leave it up to you."

He waited, sure of what the answer would be, though after the awful thing which had happened he would not have forced Doyle to carry out their original mission. In a moment, Doyle's decision came with a hard and savage note.

"Whatever's ahead must be the thing that 'got' poor old Becker and his men. Let's go!"

Knight pulled his cockpit enclosure shut again, circled above the spot where the *Canton* had been destroyed. He had asked Captain Becker to stop the cruiser at a dead-reckoning position of 6 West by 36 North, a spot in the Atlantic just outside of Gibraltar. The rendezvous of the international spies had been reported as 5 West by 36 N, just inside the Mediterranean, and about twenty-three miles southeast of Gibraltar. By flying straight East along the 36th parallel, it would be fairly simple to pass over the spot in question— unless the mist thickened and blotted out everything.

**THEY CLIMBED** to three thousand feet, and the Vought roared ahead, cruising with the air-speed needle exactly on 200. In just seven minutes the lights of Tarifa, at Point Marroqui on the southernmost tip of Spain, passed under their left wing. They twinkled up dimly through the murk, and he felt a tinge of relief at seeing them. It meant that the clouds were thinner here than out in the Atlantic, and they would have a fair chance of sighting their goal.

The nearness of that goal helped him forget the tragedy of the *Canton,* for at this speed it would be only about eleven more minutes till they crossed the fifth meridian. He spoke again into the mouthpiece:

"Turn on the radio, Doyle, and see if you can pick up the Gibraltar station or catch some vessel in the Mediterranean reporting its position. We may hit a wind-drift inside the Strait."

His phones clicked as Doyle switched on the receiver. In a moment the voice of an Italian operator was audible, apparently in conversation from a Mediterranean patrol vessel with the radioman of a freighter. Doyle tuned to the Gibraltar wavelength, but only a steady hum sounded. Knight glanced at the bearing-indicator on his instrument board.

"Hold that," he said to Doyle. "It'll give us a partial check."

Nine minutes passed, and the bearing-indicator steadily shifted until it pointed almost southeast. Knight was peering down into the gloom, expecting to glimpse the lights of a vessel at the rendezvous point—then a blurred shape abruptly plunged out of the night. He whipped to one side so hastily that his tense fingers touched the gun-clamp on the stick. The single highspeed Browning on his cowl spat out a brief stream of tracers. The oncoming ship, a huge flying-boat, pulled up swiftly, and an answering blast of fire shot from its nose-turret.

Bullets spanged from the dural framework of the forward enclosure, ripped through the upper section of Plexiglas. Knight stood on the rudder, and the Vought jumped sidewise, so that the other ship's tracers curled off into empty air. In his hasty skid, he saw that the plane was a French Loire 70, one of the three-engined monoplane flying-boats France had designed for coastal defense. But though it was French-built the big flying-boat carried the cocardes of the Loyalist Spanish Government, and with dismay he realized that the crew thought they had encountered one of Franco's planes.

The Loire was twisting around, and now another gun was blazing from a port in the rear of the control cabin high up under the wing. Doyle bellowed angrily through the phones.

"Cut in under 'em, Dick! I'll show those—"

"No!" rapped Knight. "We're not here for that. Hold your fire."

The last word had hardly left his lips when like a winged bullet a biplane single-seater hurtled out of the mist. It whirled into a vertical bank as the pilot saw the Vought, and Knight dimly perceived the circle insignia of Great Britain on its wings. The fighter was a Gloster Gladiator, a type which he knew carried four guns at more than four miles a minute. The pilot's goggled face stared across—a pale blur in the semi-darkness—as he chandelled tightly above the pivoting Loire.

The British fighter had barely passed above the Loyalist ship when a gun pounded up at it from the flying-boat's rear turret. With a steep zoom, the Gladiator pilot fled up into the night, twisting sharply at the top of his climb. The abrupt appearance of the British plane had caused Knight to sheer away to the other side, bringing the Vought again in range of the Loire's nose-turret. Machine-gun fire drilled in a fuzzy red line toward the American ship, curved swiftly to follow as Knight renversed. Doyle was cursing like a madman in the rear cockpit. He pleaded wildly through the phones:

"Let me blast that guy, Dick! I'll blow him right out of that turret!"

"We're getting clear," Knight insisted. "I want to find out what's going on."

**HE BANKED** a few seconds later and looked back. The Loire was almost invisible, a dark hulk circling in the gloom, its crew apparently searching for the supposed attackers. On the sea below it a spot of light suddenly appeared, widened, became a broad neon beam ploughing up through the mist. Knight ruddered away, but the light did not follow. Instead, with a quick swerve, it caught and held the huge flying-boat. The Loire ponderously twisted aside, started to climb. The neon beam, a bright orange-red, followed easily, widening until a large pinkish circle showed on the clouds above. Far out in the edge of the circle, parallel with the Loire, the Gloster Gladiator appeared, cruising at reduced speed. Knight had now climbed above both of the planes.

Suddenly the steady hum from the Gibraltar radio station was drowned by a different, sharper sound, as though a more powerful transmitter had been switched on. For a moment only this carrier wave was audible, then there came a strange, metallic voice.

*"Garde à vous,"* it said with an icy calmness. *"Watch—and see that the Master of Death does not lie."*

There was something about that icy voice that made Knight's scalp creep. Every nerve screamed a warning for him to flee, but something stronger than fear kept him there, staring down at the Loire as it clumsily tried to escape the mysterious beam.

The deadly voice spoke again—

*"Now!"*

A swirling jet-black cloud instantly hid the huge ship. A silent concussion shook the sky—*and the Loire was gone!*

Out of that weird black whirlpool, a million fragments of smoking metal came hurtling. The Vought pitched onto its back, was lifted a hundred feet before Knight could move the controls. A sliver of dural pierced the enclosure beside him, and another piece cut through his helmet. He felt warm blood run down his temple, trickle across his lips.

Half-dazed, he moved stick and rudder until the prop again took hold and brought the Vought out of its stall. He held the stick back until the inverted ship nosed down, then pulled it out of its dive and looked back anxiously. Doyle, too, had been hit. He was holding his right shoulder, and Knight saw blood oozing out on his hand.

The Vought had been struck in a dozen places, but fortunately both motor and prop had escaped. Beyond, a gigantic space had been blasted in the misty night, and a veritable cloud of fragments, all that remained of the ill-fated Loire, could be seen falling toward the sea. The wide neon beam still glowed, but in a moment it narrowed and swung toward the Gloster Gladiator. In a swift turn, the British fighter evaded the light. Knight hastily throttled the Wasp, but he was too late. Like a great, crimson finger, the beam whirled across at the Vought!

## CHAPTER II
## The Man Without a Face

**K**NIGHT TRIED to plunge aside, but the beam passed across the left wing. He shoved open the throttle, swiftly changed direction. The light probed after the two-seater, began a mad dance in the effort to catch the twisting ship. Knight was about to release a flare, hoping to blind the men below and then zoom above it, when the strange, icy voice again sounded in his phones.

*"Find the British plane. I will take care of the Americans after the Englishman is finished."*

The beam swerved quickly, but as it moved Knight saw its reddish light reflect from the wings of a diving ship. He shouted a warning to Doyle, pulled up as the other plane came out of its headlong descent. It was an Italian Breda fighter equipped with small pontoons instead of the standard landing gear. It carried the colors of Italy.

A burst flamed from the Breda's cowl guns, and Knight barely missed charging into the fusillade. There was a berserk roar from behind him, and Doyle's twin-mount crashed into action. The Breda shot into an Immelmann. Knight followed through, grimly holding his fire, but just as he reached the top of his zoom another Breda pitched down at the Vought. His hand clenched the Browning trip, and over the scarred cowl he saw his tracers eat into the second ship's flippers. The other pilot kicked off and dived, came back in a terrific chandelle. Knight flung into a sharp bank, cut inside the first Breda's turn just as a barrage from all four of the fighter's guns blasted at the Vought. Doyle whirled his twin Brownings, howling exultantly as the Italian pilot frantically renversed.

"That's enough!" Knight shouted into the phones. "I'm going to shake them off if I can."

He swept the stick back, and the Vought screamed up into the darkness. He had purposely turned the ship north so that it would be headed away from the neon beam, and in a few seconds the two-seater was shrouded in comparative gloom. He climbed a little higher, circled tightly, and looked back. The beam was slowly moving back and forth, piercing the mists to the south and west. Knight thought he saw the two Bredas diving near the edge of the light, but before he could make sure Doyle gave a wild yell.

"For the love of Heaven—*look!*"

Knight cast a startled glance upward. Two reddish eyes were glaring down at them from a human skull, and the skull was dropping straight at the Vought!

He slammed the two-seater into a vertical turn and twisted around in his seat. To his dismay, the skull pitched after them, two tiny lines of crimson light focussing on the ship from the weirdly glowing eyes. With a jerk, he stood the Vought on its tail. The skull whirled by and to one side, and as it did he saw the outlines of another Breda, silhouetted against the distant beam.

The skull was mounted on the cowl of the Italian fighter, and now he could see that the light also showed, though more dimly, through its nose and leering mouth. Before he could see any more, the skull turned swiftly, as though on a pivot, and the tiny streaks of light crossed the Vought's tail. The Breda pilot, crouching low in his cockpit, shot his plane up in a tight turn. Knight snapped a flare release, and the dazzling brilliance of a magnesium torch lit the heavens. The flare dropped almost in the path of the climbing fighter, and the pilot skidded hurriedly out of the way.

Bathed in the glow, the Breda was for a second completely exposed. Knight gave a crisp order for Doyle to hold his fire, while he peered down at the other ship. This one did not carry the Italian insignia. Instead, it was coal-black and devoid of markings except for the skull on the cowl. Knight started as he saw the pilot. The man wore a skull-mask, and his eyes had a weird reddish glow!

In his amazement at this discovery, Knight for an instant was off guard. The masked pilot whipped into a furious turn, and a hail of lead tore into the Vought's right wing. Knight threw the ship into a half-roll, changed direction so swiftly that the masked man overshot.

"Judas Priest!" Doyle said hoarsely. "Did you see that? It's a damned skeleton!"

"That's only a mask," Knight clipped back, but his face was tense as he saw the skull-ship charge again. He kept in a fast climbing turn, waiting for the other man to unleash his guns and waste precious ammunition. If he could only force that masked devil down instead of killing him....

T-t-t-t-t-t-t! The ominous thud of bullets drilling the left wingtip sent him zooming in consternation. There had been no flash of guns, no tracers, no faint, staccato pound of guns to warn him. But bullets were hitting the Vought!

His zoom gave Doyle an almost straight aim at the mystery ship. The ex-Marine poured out a fierce blast, started a yell of triumph. But it changed, and Knight heard him swearing fluently.

"The yellow devil!" howled Doyle. "The second he even gets a wing scratched he runs."

**KNIGHT LEVELED** out, gazed downward. His flare was still burning, though by now it was almost two thousand feet below. The neon beam had disappeared, and the only thing he could see in the water was a small freighter. The skull-ship was now diving at terrific speed toward the Gloster Gladiator, which the other Bredas were trying to bring down.

"Three to one!" the American agent muttered. The Vought was nosed down and the Wasp drumming even before his words were finished. Whoever the fellow in the Gladiator was, he was fighting against that masked fiend in the Breda, and so were they.

Stung by the interruption, the four battling ships seemed to leap upward at the Vought. Knight ringed the first Breda in his gun-sights, but the pilot frenziedly kicked aside as he opened fire. Doyle crashed out a burst at the other Italian fighter, then Knight back-sticked and they stormed through a venomous crossfire. The British pilot had snatched his radio-mike from its prongs, was trying to fight off the skull-ship while he switched on his transmitter. Knight flung a stream of tracer in at the masked pilot, and the black Breda dived under the Gladiator. The Britisher, white-faced, threw a startled look at the Vought, then lifted the mike to his lips.

"*Stanley—to the Furious!*" The words crackled into Knight's ears on the Gibraltar wave-length. "*I may be downed—take my report! Saw French Loire destroyed in mid-air by silent explosion—*"

The two Italian-marked Bredas charged in with redoubled fury, but before they had time to open fire on the Gladiator, the masked pilot plunged in and forced them aside. In the same moment Knight heard the icy voice which had spoken before, and he knew there must be a special transmitter in the black ship. The masked man was speaking tensely.

"*Signores!*" he said in hasty Italian. "*The Englishman— Stanley—must be taken alive!*"

There was a sudden passion in that heretofore icily-calm voice, and Knight saw one of the Breda pilots stare at the masked pilot. That brief stare spelled his finish. With a lightning turn, Knight centered his Browning and snapped the trigger grip to the stick. The high-speed gun hammered a straight bright line into the terrified pilot. He jumped as though an electric wire had shorted through his body, then the life went out of him and the Breda shrieked down to crash in the waiting sea.

The sight of his comrade's death seemed to drive the other Italian pilot into a frenzy. Disregarding the masked man's order, he hurled his ship in at the Gladiator, guns blazing. With a wild skid, the man in the skull-ship ranged his sights on the charging Breda. The Italian threw one hand before his face, tried to get clear. His head flopped backward, goggles shattered, his sheltering hand and his face a mass of blood. Knight felt a chill go up his spine. The man was dying—was being riddled before his eyes. Yet he was ready to swear that the masked man had not even fired!

A high-pitched, bubbling laugh dinned into Knight's phones. Still gripped with horror, he heard the masked killer's voice:

*"Fool—I am still the Master of Death!"*

The Englishman, like Knight, had stopped his attack as the black Breda charged at the other. The pilotless fighter went up in a crooked climb, veered sharply toward the Gladiator. Forced to turn swiftly, the Britisher came racing between the two Bredas. The masked pilot banked with a savage skill, apparently intent on forcing the other man down. Doyle's twin-guns roared thunderously, and the top of the black Breda's cockpit enclosure vanished under his bullets.

The masked man instantly dived. Knight pitched after him, and the two ships drilled down into the glow of the slowly-settling flare. The skull-ship pulled out sharply at a thousand feet, made as though to renverse away from the light. The wind ripped away the rest of the transparent enclosure, and with it went the skull-mask.

One hand before his eyes, the pilot banked away. As his ship turned from the glare, the man dropped his hand. Knight half-rose in his pit as he saw what was revealed.

*The pilot had no face!*

**A MASS** of scarred and twisted tissue, evidence of some horrible disaster, hid the man's eyes except for two hideous dark holes. His mouth was a crooked slit without lips, and Knight could not see any nostrils in the bloated-looking maze of scars. For the fraction of a second, that frightful ruin twitched toward him, then the black Breda raced into the darkness.

Belatedly, Knight turned the Vought for pursuit, but the faster ship quickly outdistanced him and was lost in the night. He pulled up, saw the Gloster Gladiator swinging in parallel with the two-seater. The Englishman beckoned hastily and pointed toward the northwest. Knight nodded, and the two ships roared away toward Gibraltar. The parachute flare had dropped into the sea, and when Knight looked back he could see no lights on the freighter. For a minute he kept close enough to the Gladiator to see its exhaust-flames, then the Englishman blinked his lights and left them turned on. Taking the hint, Knight dropped back to safer distance, hand on the throttle in case of a sudden maneuver. Without glancing around, he spoke into the interphone mouthpiece.

"Are you all right, Lothario?"

"I guess so," Doyle mumbled. "That is unless I've gone clear nuts."

"No, that ghoul was real enough," Knight said grimly. "But how did he destroy that Loire?"

"I've never believed in a real death-ray," Doyle said in a shaken voice, "but after that—"

"It looked like ordinary neon light to me. Whatever it is, I see now why all those foreign agents were rushing into the Mediterranean. The country that monopolizes that secret could master the world."

"And that fiend calls himself the 'Master of Death!'" Doyle grated. "Maybe he's got that notion—thinks he'll control the world."

"There are too many angles that I don't—" Knight broke off, hurriedly closed the throttle. The British fighter was in a glide, its lights blinking out a code signal. Well ahead, but not more than two-thirds the distance to Gibraltar, the signal was quickly answered. Five minutes later, lights marked the landing-deck of a carrier, and the Gladiator dipped down, obeying the commands signaled by the officer at the stern.

"It's the *Furious*, all right," Knight said. "At least we'll have a dry landing—instead of stalling in alongside the *Canton* as we originally planned."

"Yeah," Doyle said dully. He was silent a moment. "I'd forgotten about Becker and the others—with all this other happening."

A blinker-light from the bridge focused on the circling Vought almost as soon as the Gladiator landed.

"*B-l-i-p m-o-t-o-r i-f f-a-m-i-l-i-a-r w-i-t-h c-a-r-r-i-e-r l-a-n-d-i-n-g,*" came the terse message.

Knight blipped the Wasp several times, then glided toward the vessel. Watching the lighted wands in the landing-officer's hands, he made a careful approach after lowering the wheels which he had retracted immediately after being catapulted. The Vought came in smoothly, hooked the retarding-gear, and came to a quick stop. The landing-crew had barely secured the ship after Knight switched off the engine, when the pilot of the Gladiator came running up to the Vought.

"Before anything else," he said quickly, "thanks for helping me back there. I'd have been down, I'm afraid, if you hadn't jumped in."

"I think the honors are even," Knight answered as he stepped down. He shook the hand the Englishman held out, saw the questioning look in his eyes.

"Perhaps we'd better talk in private," he said in an undertone.

The other man looked at the curious crowd of sailors and marines. He nodded.

"Right—and I've a report to make, too. If you'll both come along—"

The lights went out as he spoke, and Knight and Doyle followed across the darkened deck to a hatch. A minute later they entered the captain's cabin, where a ruddy-faced, slightly younger edition of the typical British sea-dog was waiting.

"One moment, sir," the pilot said. He glanced uncertainly at Knight and Doyle. "I'm fairly certain, of course, that you're special agents for the United States. If you could help me on that point, we could save time—"

Knight thoughtfully wiped away a trickle of blood on his cheek.

"If you'll radio the Commanding Officer at Gibraltar, mentioning a certain 'Q'—"

"Q?" the English pilot exclaimed. He took a closer look at Knight and Doyle. "A hundred pardons, Mr. Knight! I saw you that other time at Gibraltar—I know how you and the others wrecked that Four Faces' scheme to involve us in the Spanish war. But with that blood and oil on your face—"

"That's all right," Knight said pleasantly. "I take it, then, you're in British Intelligence?"

"Commander John Stanley, Royal Naval Intelligence," said the other man. "This is Captain Farrington, in command of the *Furious*. Captain, Richard Knight, the American agent I told you about—and this is Mr. Doyle, the other half of the team."

Farrington shook hands, looked with concern at the blood spot on Doyle's shoulder.

"You've been shot! I'll call the ship's surgeon."

"No, it's only a flesh-cut from a dural splinter," said Doyle. "It's just about stopped bleeding. How about you, Dick?"

"We'll need a little bandaging up later," said Knight. "But right now I'd like to get straight on this hellish 'Master of Death' business."

**CAPTAIN FARRINGTON** looked at Stanley. "We caught your message about a silent explosion. I can't believe it. Your engine must have drowned the blast."

"No, sir," Stanley replied, his face suddenly grave. "There was not a sound. I had idled my engine and was spiraling down to see where the light came from."

"Light?" said Farrington. "What light?"

"I'd better start at the first," Stanley answered. He turned to Knight and Doyle. "You probably were there on an observing mission, as I was; I imagine you know as much as I." He faced the captain again. "I reached the assigned location ten minutes ahead of the time specified, so I had plenty of time to circle down from ten thousand feet. Then I saw gun-fire, and discovered one of the Loyalists' Loire flying-boats—the type France lent them—attacking an American Vought."

Briefly, he summarized what had followed. Farrington

looked stupefied when he described the destruction of the Loire, and he listened intently as Stanley told of the encounter with the Master of Death. There was a hush as Stanley concluded, and Farrington dazedly shook his head.

"Incredible! The latter part is uncanny enough. But for one of those huge planes to disintegrate utterly—and without a sound! It's impossible!"

Knight and Doyle looked at each other, then the senior agent spoke up.

"If you find that hard to believe, Captain, then you had better brace yourself. Less than one hour ago, the U.S.S. *Canton* was destroyed in exactly the same manner!"

All the color went out of Farrington's ruddy cheeks. He plopped down in his chair. "This is not a jest?" he said in a whisper.

"Where the lives of hundreds of men are concerned," Knight said, a trifle coldly, "I don't jest."

"Forgive me," muttered Farrington. "I didn't mean it that way. Surely, this is a terrible blow. If they can destroy a cruiser that easily, they could do the same with this carrier—even the *Hood*, our greatest dreadnaught. Why, the whole Fleet would be in peril."

"It *is* in peril," Knight said solemnly. "But before we try to find some defense against this thing, tell me—who is this ogre who calls himself the Master of Death? Can you tell me?"

The two Englishmen looked at each other, then Stanley slowly shook his head.

"We haven't the slightest idea."

# CHAPTER III
## Clue From the Sky

**THERE WAS** a silence, while Knight stared at the intelligence officer. "But why," he said finally, "did he countermand his first order and direct that you be taken alive?"

"I don't know." There was a puzzled sincerity in Stanley's eyes. "It does seem peculiar. I suppose the man is half mad—and madmen change their minds without reason."

"No, there was more to it than that." Knight hesitated. "Suppose we lay all our cards on the table. I'll give you all the information I have—and you do the same."

"Agreed," said Stanley, "with one exception. I am under orders to seize the secret for Britain—if that's possible. If anything leads to it later, I shall have to carry out those orders."

Knight smiled wryly.

"I'll make the same reservation—for the United States."

Then swiftly, he sketched what he knew about the situation. Stanley listened intently.

"That's about what we heard, in regard to the foreign agents," he said as Knight finished. "I learned they were chartering several boats—that freighter was probably one of them. But I've something to add to your story. About three weeks ago we first heard of this 'Master of Death.' One of my agents said there was something going on at Rome—an intense effort to learn who the man was that called himself by that fantastic title. My man couldn't learn any more. Shortly after that, three of our planes failed to return to the *Furious* after an observation flight. They had been sent over to get pictures of certain spots in Spanish Morocco, so we thought they had been shot down by Franco's planes. But that night, we caught a peculiar radio message from the 'Master of Death' thanking us sarcastically for the use of our planes in a certain test. He said they would not be back."

"Could you take a bearing on the sending station?" Knight interrupted.

"No, it was over too quickly for the operator to check it. However, we did get ranges on other messages, though that did not aid us. The transmitter was moving—probably in a plane, as tonight."

"How many other times has the Master of Death struck?" asked Knight.

"Twice that we know of. One of our destroyers disappeared, and also a submarine. Each time, we received one of those gloating messages. A search failed to reveal any traces of the missing vessels."

"Whoever he is," growled Doyle, "he must be on the Fascist side of the fence. Maybe—"

The phone rang sharply. Captain Farrington answered, then his face went tense.

"Why didn't you fire on him—get planes up after the devil?" he said in a harsh voice.

The receiver diaphragm squeaked and crackled. Farrington swore under his breath.

"Very well, then. Send down the parcel at once."

He dropped the phone, turned to the others.

"Your planes were followed here—by that black skull-ship! The officer-of-the-deck reports it came in against the wind, without a sound, spotted the deck with a beam of red light and flew past before anyone could fire. The pilot dropped a parcel. It's marked for you, Commander Stanley."

Stanley looked startled. And when an orderly appeared a minute later he hastily took the package and opened it. A wad of cotton batting was disclosed. He spread it apart, then jumped back, his face ashen.

A plastic mask of a woman's face lay there. Its contours had a marked beauty, and instead of empty slits, eyes as blue as sapphires looked up at the four men. Captain Farrington stared from the mask to Stanley's stricken face.

"What is it, man? I don't understand."

"My wife," the younger man said hoarsely. "This mask is an almost perfect duplicate of her face."

He picked it up, looked on the back to see if there was any message.

"Wait!" said Knight. "Hold it up toward that light again."

Stanley did so, recoiled with a strangled cry. For when viewed against the light, the mask appeared as a leering skull!

**HE DROPPED** the thing from his trembling fingers. Then, Knight retrieved it, examined it carefully.

"Clever construction," he muttered. "It's been made to fit some kind of a frame. I've an idea there was a light behind it that could be switched on or off."

"But why?" Stanley whispered.

"Where is your wife now?" Knight countered.

"In London—I had a message from her only this morning, at Gibraltar."

"Then she's safe, at least. This must have been made from a photograph, or several of them, rather." Knight looked shrewdly at the Englishman. "Does this give you any better idea of the identity of the Master of Death?"

Stanley helplessly shook his head.

"For some reason," said Knight, "the man hates you—and evidently your wife. Think back. You must have known some one who—"

"There was such a man," Stanley broke in. "But he's dead—thank Heaven!"

"Who was he?" Knight said quickly.

"An Austrian—Stephen Brauer."

"How was he killed?"

"In an explosion. He was a research chemist. That was seven years ago—in London. He had come there from Austria to work. But why discuss Brauer? I tell you he's dead."

"A chemical explosion," Knight said, half to himself. "That would explain those horrible scars—"

"What do you mean?" Stanley said, white-lipped.

"When the black Breda pulled out of that dive," Knight

replied slowly, "it tore off the cockpit enclosure, and also the skull-mask the pilot wore. I saw then why he wore a mask." And with grim detail, he described the ruin he had seen.

"Brauer—alive!" Stanley clenched his hands convulsively, made an effort to hide his emotion.

Farrington took his arm. "Suppose," he said not ungently, "you give us the whole story?"

Stanley sat down, eyes fixed on the beautiful mask.

"I met Brauer in 1931. He'd come over from Vienna, and approached the Royal Navy with an idea for a faster-burning explosive than T.N.T. His ideas sounded good, but we were suspicious of him. He explained that Vienna was now only a mockery—that he hated the present government and wished to become a British citizen. He was more than a chemist—he also had some ideas for silencing airplane engines. For some reason, you see, he hated noise, and he was interested in aviation as well as chemistry. Finally, the Admiralty arranged an experimental laboratory for him—but I was assigned to keep watch on him, though I pretended to be cooperating on his scheme for cutting down the exhaust noise on our planes.

"I was engaged to be married, and one day Brauer met my fiancée. He was a moody, neurotic fellow—but he changed completely after he met her, and in a week I could see he had fallen madly in love with her. The upshot of it was that he tried to make her break off our engagement and marry him. When she refused, he flew into a rage and swore he'd be revenged on both of us. The night before the wedding date I received a call, supposed to be from my senior officer, telling me to meet him at Brauer's laboratory at once, that they'd found the man was a spy. As I approached the building, I saw a man—I thought it was Brauer—hurrying inside. A second later there was a violent explosion and the building burst into flames. A body was found later—unrecognizable, of course—but on the basis of my evidence it was believed to be Brauer. A search was made of his lodgings, and information was found indicating that his helper was implicated in some scheme. We supposed the man had fled, but now I suppose the body we found must have been his."

**"IT PROBABLY** was," agreed Knight. "Brauer must have been somewhere near, waiting to set off the blast. It looks as though he intended to kill you and place the blame on his helper. Perhaps the helper discovered that and rushed to the laboratory to confront Brauer—and Brauer had to set off his bomb prematurely, to kill the other man."

"It may have been like that," Stanley admitted. "But I wouldn't have thought it humanly possible for anyone to escape from that explosion alive."

"Hate gives a man uncanny strength sometimes," said Knight. "He must have been frightfully mutilated. The strange part is that he wasn't seen later, or that some hospital didn't report his case."

"It was foggy—that's how I mistook the helper for Brauer, I suppose. And it's fairly certain that he must have had connections with a clique of secret agents. They no doubt took care of him."

"And he's evidently been planning all these years to revenge himself," Knight added. "His allying himself with Italy, as seems obvious, would be motivated by his desire to even the score. He evidently hates all Englishmen."

Stanley nodded dully. Doyle fingered the mask.

"I guess he dropped this to get you to worrying—maybe he figured you'd dope out who he was. But how did he come to be carrying the thing, anyway?" Knight pointed to the edges of the mask. "You can see where it's been torn from a support. His hatred must be such an obsession that he kept one of the objects of his hate before him all the time. It must have been mounted in his cockpit, where he could flash a light behind it and turn it into a skull whenever he wished."

Stanley shivered. "I'm afraid for my wife—what if he had some idea—"

"I'll radio London and arrange for her to be guarded," interposed Captain Farrington. "But right now the main thing is to find that madman and get his secret. I'm going to order two squadrons up at dawn to make a careful search of this area—and if they can do it, the Insurgent-held islands, too. But now I'd suggest that these gentlemen get their wounds bandaged. And perhaps a little brandy wouldn't hurt any of you. Take care of them, Commander, and then we'll discuss our plans."

Doyle's homely face lit up at mention of the brandy. He and Knight followed Stanley from the cabin. Half an hour later, their cuts cleansed and bandaged, they were sitting down to a snack of sandwiches and brandy-and-soda, when a junior officer hurried up to Stanley and saluted.

"The Captain wishes to see you, sir—and the Americans. We've just had an S.O.S.—from Lieutenant Clarke."

Stanley jumped.

"Clarke! Are you sure?" He whirled to Knight and Doyle. "That's one of our missing pilots. Come along!"

Doyle gulped down the rest of his drink, snatched a sandwich, and trailed after the others. They found Captain Farrington and the navigator poring feverishly over a map of the western Mediterranean. From up on the flying deck came the rumble of engines being started.

"No island along that line, sir," exclaimed the navigator. "It must have come from a vessel of some sort."

Farrington turned haggard eyes on Stanley.

"An S.O.S. came in ten minutes ago—the radio officer recognized Clarke's voice and Clarke identified himself. He tried to add something but was cut off. The radio officer heard sounds of a fight, then the transmitter was switched off. However, he had time to take this bearing."

Knight saw the line they had drawn. It ran almost due south.

"Somewhere between here and Spanish Morocco," said Stanley. "How many planes are to make the search?"

"Too many might defeat the purpose," replied Farrington. "I thought if you three men—" he glanced at Knight and

Doyle. The two Americans quickly assented, and in another minute they were shifting back into flying-gear and following Stanley up to the flight-deck.

"I'll take off first," said the Englishman. "We'd better fly at different altitudes—and I'll blink my lights if I change. If you see anything, signal me with your lights—give me an 'ST' and I'll follow you."

"Okay," said Knight. "I'll cruise at 200, so you'll have to hold the Gladiator down a bit. And we'd better keep low, or we won't be able to spot anything."

"I'll hold three hundred feet—you take five hundred," Stanley said fastening his goggles over his eyes. "The *Furious* will be following that bearing-line, and the skipper will have a squadron of fighters ready if we call for them."

**STANLEY VAULTED** into his ship, and the deck officer gave him the takeoff signal. The Gladiator roared down the deck and up into the darkness, and a few seconds later the Vought raced after it. Knight climbed to five hundred, leaving the bullet-torn Plexiglas shoved back so that he could lean out and peer down at the sea.

The course was 173, leading about twenty miles to the east of Point Almina, on the rocky little isle of Ceuta. Knight's eyes narrowed thoughtfully. It was possible the radio operator had made a mistake, and that the message had come from an Insurgent station on Ceuta, a stronghold of Franco's forces. But to fly over that area would probably mean quick attack by a flight of Insurgent ships and A-A batteries on the coast.

He opened the Wasp a trifle until he caught the flash of the Gladiator's exhaust stacks almost directly below. Ten minutes passed, and the dim flare of the other ship's exhaust began to fade out. Knight frowned. They were running into light fog again, and not only that, Spanish Morocco lay just about ten miles ahead. At their speed, three minutes would bring them to the rugged coastline southeast of Tetuan. He nosed down, trying to keep the Gladiator in sight, then started to blink the lights in a fear that Stanley had forgotten the nearness of the African continent. The mist had thickened, and he could barely make out the British fighter.

Then, without the slightest warning, a neon-red light streamed out from the fog ahead. Knight shot the two-seater up swiftly, shading his eyes from the glow. As he twisted around at the top of his zoom, he heard the rear-guns clatter.

"Bredas!" bawled Doyle. "They're after Stanley!"

Knight pitched back toward the red light, which as before had partly penetrated the murk, but without revealing the source from which it came. Three or four Bredas were milling madly around the Gladiator, obviously trying to force it down.

Stanley had pulled up to four hundred feet, was battling desperately to break through. Knight saw his wing-guns blast at the nearest Breda. The Italian fighter slipped off, but the pilot caught it before it hit the water. Stanley then hurled the Gladiator between two Bredas, whipped around in a tight bank as a third one charged into his way. Knight ringed the last Breda in the Browning sight, tripped his gun. In the weird glow, he saw the pilot pitch sidewise in his cockpit. The Breda nosed down, went onto his back, and crashed into the sea with a roar that came dully through the din of motors. Another Breda spun furiously on its wingtips, darted in at the Vought.

Until this moment, none of the Italian pilots had opened fire, but as this one saw the Vought he loosed a murderous torrent from all four guns. Doyle swerved the rear-mount, raked the Breda broadside. Flames burst from the Italian fighter's cowl, streaked back onto the pilot. The unfortunate man sprang up, clawed his way over the side. His chute billowed out as he dived, but the silk was already on fire. Flame ate swiftly through the top, and the doomed Italian vanished in the misty sea.

Knight's plunge had carried him beyond the fight. He renversed, came back with the Wasp wide-open. From somewhere behind the neon-light, machine-guns pounded fiercely. He was forced into a hasty turn to the left. The Vought roared away from the light. Gloom was about to swallow it up when a rugged cliff suddenly appeared dead ahead. Knight slammed the stick back, heart pounding as the Vought screamed up past the face of the cliff. The ship started over into a loop. He rolled into level flight, sent the Vought thundering away from the rocks. It had lost speed, and it settled dangerously close to the sea. Against the murky redness beyond, he saw the battered hulk of an old wrecked freighter. It lay on his right, apparently on a submerged reef. On the left, briefly seen as the red glow abruptly shifted, was a large bell-buoy with a light at the top. It was rolling sluggishly with the waves.

The Vought was now picking up speed. Knight climbed, saw the two remaining Bredas frantically darting in at Stanley's ship. The Englishman was charging in the direction of the cliff, and Knight kicked in front of him, crashing out a burst to warn him off. Thinking the fire had come from a Breda, Stanley whirled his Gladiator into a lightning turn with his cowl guns blazing. The Vought's Wasp skipped a beat, broke its steady thunder. Knight flung the ship aside, pitching a burst at the closest Breda as he turned. He heard Doyle cry out hoarsely. He whirled, thinking Doyle was hurt, but the other man was staring down at the British fighter.

Knight froze. Stanley was racing straight for the precipice!

## CHAPTER IV
## The Secret of the Cliff

*T*HOUGH HE knew it was too late, Knight seized his hand-mike and snapped the transmitter switch. Even as he did, he saw the Gladiator zoom to escape the rocks. Through the reddened fog he dimly saw the fighter twist sidewise and strike the cliff. There was a flash, then darkness, and the Gladiator was gone!

Knight stared toward the spot, but the neon light below stabbed up and caught the two-seater, blinding him. He banked as swiftly as he could, with the motor missing badly. Then the Vought shook under a sudden hail of lead, and in consternation he felt the rudder go slack.

Using the ailerons and stick, he managed to hold the bank. He was turning away from the cliff when with a final dismal bark the engine went dead. Almost in the same instant, the neon light vanished, and the Vought was lost in darkness. Knight shoved up his goggles, glided the craft carefully. He was not sure, but he thought they were headed toward the derelict. If he could stall in near the wrecked vessel, they would have a place where they could hide while they decided on the next move.

"Be ready to unfasten your belt," he flung over his shoulder at Doyle.

Doyle's answer was lost in the boom of the buoy's mournful bell. It came from close by, and Knight swept the stick back as he saw the buoy flash under the right wing. Bracing himself, he stalled the Vought above the waves, then threw one arm before his face.

The ship struck flatly, dug its nose into a wave, and stopped. Knight was tossed against the instrument board, but his arm took most of the shock. He snapped open his belt, turned, and saw Doyle jerking at the flotation-gear control.

"Let that go," he said hastily. "They'll be over here looking for us in a minute or two. If she goes down by then, so much the better—maybe they'll think we went with her."

Doyle clambered out onto the wing. "And where the devil are we going?" he demanded, peeling off his coat.

"To that wrecked freighter," Knight said in an undertone. "I think it's over this way."

He had discarded both his coats, was about to kick off his shoes when a muffled throb sounded from not far away. Voices sounded indistinctly. With a whisper to Doyle, he lowered himself into the water, struck out for the derelict. He heard Doyle splash into the waves, but he was unable to see him in the dark. The throbbing sound grew louder. He redoubled his efforts to reach the wrecked vessel, then realized that he had lost his way. Treading water, he tried to orient himself. There was no sign of Doyle. Holding his breath, he dropped his feet down; but the water was over his head.

The throbbing now became a loud rumble, and as he came up, he was electrified to see a dark hull slowly moving toward him.

It was a big submarine!

The next moment a voice spoke sharply in Italian. "There on the starboard beam—turn on the light."

The neon light swung from a skyward tilt down to the water, spotted the sinking Vought. Knight heard a volley of explanations and with dismay saw Doyle between the submarine and the plane. Doyle started to swim away, but a pistol instantly barked.

"Over here, *Signor* American!" ordered a man near the neon light. "Unless you want a bullet through your head."

Doyle cursed him but sullenly swam to the side of the submarine.

Meanwhile, Knight had hurriedly maneuvered to pass around the stern of the vessel, but the sub was too long. He grasped at a brace on the fantail, hauled himself up, panting. Silhouetted against the light was a long narrow catapult projecting up from the after hatch. Forward he could see Doyle being dragged aboard and hustled toward the conning-tower.

"Where is the other man?" an officer demanded.

"He went down, damn you!" Doyle snarled.

"Perhaps he did—perhaps not," retorted the Italian. "Ah, here comes one of the boats. We can leave the search to them."

Knight flattened himself on the fantail as a motor-boat with a spotlight in the bow came alongside the submarine.

"We caught one of them," said the officer who seemed to be in command. "The other may have drowned, but make sure."

"*Si, signor,*" replied an ensign in the boat. "But be careful going inside—the big door will not fold all the way."

**THE NEON** beam shifted, and with a start Knight saw an opening in what had seemed to be a solid cliff. A high, folding door, made like an accordion and well camouflaged to look like rock, was drawn back so that only a third of it was extended flatly. In this flat part, there was a large hole, near the top.

"*Per amor di Dios!*" exclaimed the submarine commander. "That fool dived clear through!"

"No, he tried to turn at the last moment—and saved his life. The plane crashed through sidewise and toppled into the water. He was only bruised—luckily for all of us, *Signor.*"

"What do you mean by that?" said the officer.

"The pilot was no one but Brauer's hated Englishman—Stanley. That is why that Austrian devil ordered the Bredas to fend him away from the cliff."

"Excellent news, Ensign!" exclaimed the sub commander. "Now that our mad friend has achieved his purpose, the rest should be easy. We also destroyed the freighter and the two motor boats those spies had chartered—so *Signor* Brauer's scheme to get other nations interested if we failed him will not bother us any longer."

He gave an order, and the sub slowly forged ahead, the

neon beam shifting from side to side. Knight glimpsed the derelict to starboard, the bell-buoy to port, and he knew there was a channel leading to a cavern inside the cliff, a channel not shown on regular charts. The wrecked vessel had evidently been left on the reef to help mark the passage instead of buoys which would excite suspicion.

There were dim lights moving around far inside the cavern. He crawled to the opposite side of the fan-tail as he saw that it would be away from the huge door on which men were already beginning to work. The submarine slowly glided into the hidden base, and by the shifting neon-beam and the hooded lights inside he could get a fair picture of the cavern. Its dome was so high that it was lost in darkness; he estimated it must be at least two hundred feet above the water. There was a wide ledge on the right toward which the submarine was carefully making its way. He could not be sure, but he thought the cavern was almost half a mile long. The neon light, swerving across the base, seemed to reflect from water at that distance.

The ledge was a wide shelf of rock obviously well supported, for it was covered with boxes, fuel drums, portable military huts, and a variety of supplies. Men were stringing lights on the rocky walls at the back of the shelf, and still other workmen were connecting a large communication cable which came up out of the water like a long snake. Two hundred yards from an improvised dock, where a crowd of uniformed Italians waited, there were rows of small tents, seemingly quarters for the enlisted men. Between this point and the dock, a number of Bredas were secured, and farther on Knight saw some larger ships, flying-boats and an amphibian. His heart sank still farther as he realized there were nearly five hundred men in the base, not including the crew of the submarine.

He kept on the side away from the ledge, praying that no bright lights would be turned on. Huge rope buffers had been adjusted, and in a moment he saw a line whiz through the air. Another line followed, and soon after he felt the vessel grate to a stop against the heavy buffers. The crowd shoved along the ledge toward a gangway which was being pushed to the side of the sub. Knight lowered himself into the shadowy waters, knowing all eyes would be momentarily focused on Doyle and the group by the conning tower. He took a deep breath, dived, and swam as hard as he could to a point where the rock shelf curved. Here, where it narrowed near the entrance, there were a few boxes but no tents or huts. The only men near that spot were the ones working on the big door sixty yards away, and he could barely see them in the gloom. He cast a hurried glance toward the crowd, drew himself up, and crawled across the dark ledge until he was hidden by a turn in the jagged wall.

"What of the second man?" he heard a voice demand in Italian. He tensed as he recognized the unmistakable tones of the Master of Death.

"My men are searching the inlet and the reef, *Herr* Brauer," the Italian commander answered quickly. "He probably drowned—"

"It is not important," the Master of Death said curtly. "This English swine is the one—that one I have waited all these years for!"

**HIS VOICE** lost its chill calm, rose to a note of frenzied triumph. Knight pulled up cautiously beside a jutting rock in the cavern wall, and looked around the edge. Stanley was back against one of the larger portable huts, held there by two armed guards. Standing before him, hands curling like talons, was the Master of Death.

In place of the skull-mask he had lost, he wore a molded wax face that might have been taken from a tailor's dummy, and under the dim light, he appeared to be woodenly handsome. But Knight shuddered as he thought of the horror which lay underneath. The man's eyes flashed oddly when he turned his head, and now it was plain that there were glass lenses in the eye-slits of the waxen face. Evidently Stephen

Brauer's eyes had been injured in the explosion, and instead of wearing ordinary glasses he had put the correcting lenses in the masks which hid his ruined features. It was these, Knight now knew, which had caused his eyes to shine so weirdly during the first battle, when the neon light inside the skull on the cowl had reflected back on the lenses.

For several moments, the Master of Death stood before his prisoner, his hands quivering as though in a mad rage to grip Stanley's throat. Then he slowly forced them to his sides.

"No," he muttered, in his own tongue. "Seven years have I waited—I will do as I planned."

He made a peremptory motion, and the guards hustled Stanley into the hut. The submarine commander, a tall man for an Italian, came up to the masked Austrian, fumbling nervously with his mustache.

"Now that you have your prisoner, *Herr* Brauer, I should like to have the rest of the formula."

The Master of Death whirled on him angrily.

"*Nein!* It is only one-half the bargain! *She* is still in London."

There was a madman's fury in his mention of Stanley's wife, and the Italian officer hastily stepped back.

"But I told you—our agents will soon be able to spirit her out of England. They must work carefully—"

"And until then, I keep the formula where it is safe—in my brain." A crazy laugh came through the parted lips of the mask, then abruptly Brauer's voice regained its icy composure. "Have no fear, *Signor* Latti, I shall keep my word. After my revenge on those two, I will have nothing to live for. Your Italy can have every secret I possess."

He turned, glared through the mask lenses at Doyle, who stood dripping, surrounded by a half a dozen armed Blackshirts.

"Take this meddling American inside, also. I have an idea he will be of use."

"But, *Herr* Brauer," objected Latti uneasily, "I must question him and Stanley to learn how much they know of your work—and also what has happened on the *Furious*."

"Very well," the Master of Death said coldly. "Question him now—then let me have him."

He stalked into the hut, and Latti ordered Doyle taken inside. Knight waited until he saw Latti go into the building and close the door. The awe-stricken crowd began to disperse and resume their work.

The American agent had lost his Navy issue automatic, but he still had a .38 short positive in a clip-holster under his left arm. If he could steal to the rear of that hut unseen, there might be a way of surprising Brauer and Latti. It all depended....

**HE SPUN** around, jerking the .38 from its holster. Thirty feet away, one of the men who had been working on the big door was striding toward a supply shed near the dock. Knight held his breath. The workman, a Blackshirt with dungarees over his uniform, was almost abreast when he halted abruptly, staring down at the ledge.

Too late, Knight saw he had left a watery trail behind him. The man lifted startled eyes and saw him. Knight leaped, frantically hurled the pistol as the other man started to yell. The gun caught the workman in the jaw, and he staggered back with a groan. Knight brought him down with a flying tackle, then raised his fist for a silencing blow. But it was not needed, for the Italian's head had hit with enough force to knock him senseless.

Knight pulled him back into the darker shadow, quickly stripped him of dungarees, shoes, and his black shirt. There was no time to take his uniform. Knight peeled off his own wet shoes, shirt, and trousers, changed with fast-moving fingers. Up on a scaffolding, floated into position behind the folding door, men were completing their makeshift repairs, and he knew they would be coming along the ledge in a minute or two. He took the unconscious man's cap, put it on so that it hid the bandage on his head. Jerking the visor over his eyes, he thrust his pistol under the dungaree coat and stole toward the first group of huts.

There were men on the dock, mostly the crew of the sub, which he had noticed bore no markings. But they were not paying any attention, and the only hazard he feared at the moment was being stopped by some officer. He was fairly certain that the first huts were quarters for the officers of the secret base.

He took a quick glance toward the planes at the edge of the rock shelf. With one exception, the seaplanes were Bredas equipped with folding wings for submarine use. Forward of the conning-tower of the sub, he saw what looked like a large round tank. It was open, and mechanics were taking out a small Macchi two-seater seaplane, its wings folded. Men in hipboots pushed the little plane to the shelf, where other mechanics unfolded the wings, locked them into position, and began a routine examination.

"At least, the hangar did not leak this time," Knight heard one of them say with relief. He slid in between two large boxes, hurried toward the hut where the prisoners had been taken. It was more solidly built than he thought, for he could hear only an angry mumble through the walls. He was stealing past, toward the side in deepest shadow when suddenly the door opened. A man started out. It was the masked Austrian.

## CHAPTER V
## The Master of Death

**K**NIGHT STEPPED back, and the other man stared at him through the glass lenses of his waxen mask.

"What do you want?" he said coldly.

Some of the ice left Knight's heart. The semi-darkness had saved him from recognition.

"I was told to inspect the light-wiring, *Signor,*" he mumbled in Italian. Beyond Brauer he saw Doyle and Stanley, carefully guarded, and Latti at one side. The two prisoners were not facing his direction.

The Master of Death made an impatient gesture.

"Very well, go ahead with your work; we are leaving. Now Captain Latti, if you will have those two taken to my laboratory, I shall show you how to make them talk.

Knight stood aside. There were too many men nearby to attempt a rescue in the open. Already, the Master of Death had walked by him, and the guards were bringing out Stanley and Doyle.

Suddenly there came a stentorian shout from the direction of the great door: "Entrance closed! Turn on the lights."

Knight tried to avert his face so that the prisoners would not recognize him and give him away. But before he could retreat, a 500-watt lamp blazed up from a pole nearby. The masked Austrian went rigid as Knight's face was brightly illuminated.

"Seize that man!" he shouted. "It is the other American!"

A dozen Blackshirts came racing up from the dock. Knight's hand had flown under his coat, but he saw it was useless to resist. Helplessly, he raised his hands. Stanley and Doyle were looking at him in utter dejection, and he knew they had been hoping he might save them. Captain Latti gazed at him incredulously.

"But how—he is wearing one of our uniforms," he sputtered. "Are you sure—"

"I would know him anywhere!" the Master of Death said icily. "It was he who almost shot me down tonight. I saw his face clearly under that flare."

An Italian petty officer took Knight's revolver, then searched him while two others covered him.

"Nothing else, sir," he reported to Latti.

Latti confronted Knight angrily. "How did you get in here?"

Knight did not speak. The other man struck him a vicious blow.

"Answer me!" he cried, rocking Knight's head with another blow, but the Master of Death stopped him.

"Not that clumsy way, *Signor*. I will show you a *much* more efficient method."

Latti grudgingly nodded, turned to one of his officers. "Have the base searched. He must have overcome one of our men to get that uniform."

The officer saluted. Knight's arms were twisted behind his back, and with a gun prodding his ribs on each side he was marched along behind Doyle and Stanley. They came to a windowless structure made of stone from the wall of the cave. There was a smoke-vent at one side. The masked Austrian unlocked a heavy door, closed it when the others had entered. Knight shot a quick glance about the place. It was fitted up as a chemical laboratory and workshop. At the other end was what at first appeared to be a large model plane, but as Knight's eyes raced over its burnished dural fuselage he realized the sinister truth. It was an aerial torpedo, with some unknown means for guiding it to a target.

The explosive container, which formed most of the fuselage, was about four feet long and ten inches wide, with small gyro-actuated controls. The wings were very short, but powerfully made. A curved panel just aft of a one-bladed propeller had been left open, permitting a view of several knobs, dials, and switches.

A compact, cylindrical battery stood on the floor near the

aerial torpedo, and Knight surmised that the winged projectile was driven by an electric motor. This accounted partly for the silence with which the Master of Death had struck. There were holes of varying size in the counter-weight stub on the propeller, with some sort of adjusting screw, apparently a means for silencing the sound of the blade. But there was still no indication of how Brauer had contrived a silent, flashless explosion.

**AS KNIGHT** was shoved toward a door at the rear of the laboratory, he glimpsed an opening in the prop-boss of the aerial torpedo. Something like a round, staring eye was visible, and he could see wires running through the hub, evidently leading to some connection with the control panel.

The Master of Death unlocked the rear door, revealing a space hollowed out of the cavern wall. Rusty iron rings set into the rock showed that this place had been occupied many years ago. There were initials and cryptic marks chiseled crudely in the walls, and Knight guessed that the cavern had once been a hiding-place for Mediterranean pirates, probably only recently discovered by Brauer or the Italians. Its entrance had been enlarged and fitted with the massive folding door.

Knight's hurried inspection of the place was cut short by a cry from Stanley.

"Clarke!" the Englishman groaned. "What has this fiend done to you?"

A half-naked figure lay on a narrow table, his arms and legs secured by ropes which ran underneath. His face was ghastly, and his eyes held a fixed, unearthly stare.

"Stanley!" he whispered, as he heard the commander's voice. "Good Heavens—has he finally caught you?"

His staring eyes shifted, but they did not focus on the other man. Stanley looked at him in horror.

"Blind!" he said hoarsely. He jerked around toward the masked Austrian, oblivious to the gun jabbed into his ribs. "You've done this, you butcher!"

"He will not find it so easy to reach the radio and call for help next time," the Master of Death said with a grim amusement. He turned, looked coldly through his mask at Latti. "I warned you he should have been chained—or killed. He nearly gave away the whole secret."

"He will be tried and executed," Latti muttered. "There was no need for this."

"Stanley!" the blinded pilot said huskily. "Does England know? Have they found out about this place?"

Stanley glanced sidewise at the masked Austrian.

"Don't worry," he answered soothingly. "You'll soon be out of here, old fellow."

"You're lying," cried Clarke dejectedly. "They trapped you... they'll get everyone... the whole Fleet. They've got some frightful new explosive that's ten times worse than T.N.T.—and it doesn't make a sound. They fire it in regular torpedoes with infra-red eyes that guide by the heat of the ship's funnels—and aerial ones they catapult—"

One of the guards moved menacingly toward the blind Englishman, but the Master of Death stopped him.

"Let the fool rave. He can do no harm now."

He faced Stanley, who was watching him savagely. "You see, I was not the numbskull some of your British experts thought when I said the most deadly weapons of the future would all be the silent ones." His voice held a mixture of hatred and gloating as he went on. "A silent plane! That was the simplest of all. A vacuum box for the exhaust to pass through—and the engine is completely muffled. I did it five years ago—and the Americans are just waking up to the idea. Their one-bladed propeller could be just as silent. It's merely a trick of neutralizing the propeller roar by sounds of varying pitch made when the slipstream passes through that device in the counter-weight. I had the idea when you were spying on me in 1931, just as I had the idea of a silent explosive, one with such a terrifically fast rate of burning that the soundwave of the blast would be inaudible to the human ear. I found the key to it in the laboratory your government so kindly furnished me. But it was not until last year, here in this hell-hole, that I discovered how to create with it a completely flameless powder."

"*Herr* Brauer," Latti interrupted, "we are wasting valuable time. I must know how much the Americans and British have learned."

The Master of Death turned on the Italian fiercely, then controlled himself with an obvious effort.

"Untie that fool," he ordered one of the guards, pointing to Clarke. "Then put this smart American in his place."

Knight's blood ran cold as Brauer's eyes sardonically rested on him. The Master of Death laughed.

"So you do not feel so brave now, *nein?*" He stalked over to one corner of the hollowed-out space where a number of gleaming torpedo war-heads reposed behind a heavy wire grating. He returned in a moment wearing a heavy chemist's apron and gloves. In one hand was a small bottle, in the other a tiny glass funnel.

"Fasten the others to those two rings," he ordered the men guarding Doyle and Stanley.

Doyle fought back, knocked one man over. But he was finally subdued by a blow in the stomach. He hung, gasping, hands tied above his head and to the iron ring, while Stanley was likewise overpowered and secured. Knight had watched tensely for a chance to break into action, but Latti had his pistol out and the two remaining Blackshirts did not relax their vigilance. Clarke's bonds were untied, and one of the Italian soldiers started to guide him across the chamber.

"Take him outside," directed the Master of Death.

**AT THAT** instant, the blinded English-man whirled and made a frantic leap at him. Brauer sprang back, hurled the bottle. It struck Clarke on the forehead, shattered. Acid ran down his face, smoking as it ate into his flesh. A scream of agony burst from Clarke's lips, and he tottered back, clawing at his face: There was a sharp report, and his cries ended. He slumped to the floor a few feet from where Latti stood with smoke curling from his gun.

"*Schwein!*" raged the masked Austrian. "Why did you shoot him?"

"You devil!" Latti said hoarsely. "You could stand there and see him eaten alive by that acid?" It was obvious that the Italian did not relish alliance with Brauer and that only the desire for the formula sustained it.

"I could see him cut up inch by inch!" snarled the Master of Death. "If you are so squeamish, get out!"

Fury darkened the Italian officer's face, and for a second Knight thought he would shoot down the other man. Then Latti slowly lowered his pistol.

"No, *Signor*," mocked the Master of Death, "don't forget there is still the formula for Brauerite. Il Duce would be very much annoyed if you deprived him of the secret when it was about to give him power over all his enemies."

Latti turned and without a word left the laboratory. The Austrian sent a sarcastic laugh after him, turned to the gaping Blackshirts.

"Take off the American's dungarees and tie him on the table. Then get out of here, and take the corpse with you!"

Knight cast a desperate look around him, then hopelessly submitted as he was stripped to the waist. He was quickly stretched on the table, and his legs tied as Clarke's had been. He took a deep breath, held it as a rope was passed across his middle and looped around both wrists. One of the guards knelt, avoiding the broken glass on the floor, and fastened the rope under the table. The Master of Death waited until they were finished and had left, then he leered down through the mask-lenses at Knight.

"Now, if you will just be patient, while I go for another supply of vitriol...."

Stanley groaned. "May Heaven forgive me! Knight, I brought this on you—I fired on you by mistake when you tried to drive me away from the cliff."

The Master of Death chuckled.

"I am indebted to you, Stanley. I have needed a human guinea pig or two for my experiments—so that I'll not make any mistake on you, later."

"You murderer!" rasped the Englishman.

"Murderer?" said the Austrian. "Ah, you think I am going to *kill* you? No, that would be too easy—a few hours, perhaps a few days of torture—and it would be over. Do you think I have waited seven years just for that?"

Stanley looked at him with a new dread. The Master of Death slowly lifted the waxen mask, and the Englishman cringed at sight of his ruined features.

"You find it hard to look?" the Austrian said harshly. "It makes your stomach sick—you feel as though you might faint.... You trembling English pig! That is what *your* face will be when I am through with you!"

All the color fled Stanley's cheeks. Brauer dropped the mask back over his face, stood glaring at the man he hated.

"Like mine—or worse! I'll learn when I'm finished with these two meddling Yankees just what I need to know. Your face will be a masterpiece, I promise you—and I shall have an audience to watch me work! A very lovely audience!"

Stanley's jaw fell. "You fiend, you wouldn't—"

"She will be here, tied to one of those rings and when I am through it will be her turn. A woman with a death's-head for a face! I'll give you back to each other—you can return to your damned England after this brief war is over and Italy has ruined her. But you'll live in a hell that will never end—as I have lived. Behind masks, afraid to see a mirror, wishing for death and afraid to kill yourselves...."

**BRAUER'S VOICE** had risen to an hysterical screech. He broke off, shaking, then turned and went into the laboratory. Knight began a desperate attempt to loosen his right arm, and the veins stood out on his forehead. But in a moment he had shifted what slack there was to the right side. He twisted his head, looked feverishly for the spot of acid which had spilled onto the edge of the table when the bottle broke. He had seen it just before they had tied him to the table, a dark splotch slowly eating into the wood.

In another second, the strand of rope which encircled his wrist was pressed hard against the spot. He heard Doyle mumble something to Stanley, heard the two men struggling against their bonds. The Master of Death came back with another bottle of sulphuric acid. He set it down on the floor, picked up the tiny glass funnel he had put on a chair.

Knight lay motionless, fighting back the wild impulse to act instantly. There was a faint warmth on his wrist, and he knew that a speck of acid had touched it. That meant the rope must be partly severed....

"Dick!" came Doyle's frantic voice. "Try to kick loose. Don't lie there and—"

"*Stille!*" grated Brauer. He threw a ferocious look at the ex-Marine. "Unless you want what I gave Clarke."

In the second or two that his head was turned, Knight pulled with all his might at the loop on his wrist. For one heart-breaking instant he thought it was going to hold, then it parted with a jerk.

The Master of Death whirled just as Knight's freed hand shot toward his throat. He jumped back, but the agent's fingers closed on his apron and jerked him over the table. His mask fell off, and a wild yell came from the scarred slit that was his mouth.

Knight swiftly raised his left hand, bringing with it the severed rope which had gone underneath. He whipped the rope about the Austrian's neck, gave it a terrific pull. Half-strangled, the Master of Death tumbled across Knight's legs, pawed madly at the loop about his throat. Grimly Knight held on, and in a few moments Brauer slumped to his knees. His fall pulled the rope away, but he lay motionless, breathing stertorously.

"Thank Heaven!" he heard Doyle whisper.

Knight sat up, hastily untied the rope at his feet, and swung his feet to the floor. He bent over the Austrian, took his gun, and ran toward the two prisoners. He had Doyle almost freed when from outside there sounded a sudden commotion, as of men running toward the laboratory.

"Stay there—pretend you're still tied up," he warned Doyle. Then he leaped back and stripped off Brauer's long apron and gloves. Lifting the Austrian to the table, he looped the ropes about his arms and legs, tucking them under so that they appeared to be tied. Pulling Brauer's black shirt up over his face, he snatched up the fallen mask and ran for the other room. The gun was under his belt, but he had barely slipped the mask over his face when the outer door burst open.

# CHAPTER VI
## *Masked Fate*

*L*ATTI AND another officer came in, panting, with at least twenty Blackshirts behind them. Knight stepped a trifle to one side, to avoid being caught in the bright glare from out on the base.

"The *Furious*—we must have warheads for the torpedoes!" Latti said breathlessly.

"What has happened?" Knight demanded, imitating the slightly accented Italian Brauer the Master of Death used.

"The British carrier—steaming straight this way!" Latti's eyes were filled with alarm. "They are using their searchlights. They must know part of the secret. If they turn their guns on this place—"

"Nonsense!" Knight said coldly. "They are only cruising aimlessly. I just forced the truth out of that American."

"I'll take no chances!" Latti flung back. "The *Furious* must be sunk before her planes can get into the air—even if it starts another world war!"

He rattled off an order, and the Blackshirts hurried into the rear with padded bomb-conveyors devised to fit the charges of Brauerite. Knight stalked in on the heels of the first group, stood beside the partly covered figure of the Austrian. Only two of the Blackshirts glanced at the table, and they quickly shied away from that ominous-looking form. Latti stood at the connecting-door giving crisp directions as the war-heads were taken out.

"The first one to the Macchi... the second and third to the amphibian... the rest to the submarine, Lieutenant!" he snapped his fingers at the officer supervising the work. "See that two of the under-water torpedoes are loaded in case there is any more difficulty with the projector for the aerial ones."

"*Si*, my Captain!" The lieutenant said, then disappeared. Knight stole a side glance at Doyle and Stanley, saw them watching tensely. He was thanking his stars that the last warhead was being taken out and that nothing had betrayed him.

But then, without warning, Brauer flung the shirt from his face.

"Latti!" he shouted. "Kill that devil with the mask!"

Knight jumped back, snatched the gun from under the apron. Latti stood paralyzed with amazement, made a belated attempt to draw his pistol. As though shot from a cannon, Doyle hurtled across the room. Latti went down, and his pistol clattered on the floor. Doyle grabbed the gun, jumped up and covered Brauer and the Italian officer.

The four men who were carrying out the last war-head backed up, eyes bulging, as Knight whirled toward them. Helpless, and afraid to drop their burden for fear of setting it off, they stood there open-mouthed.

"Put it down—carefully!" he snapped in Italian. "Now, back up—behind that grating."

Brauer, Latti, and the four Blackshirts were quickly crowded into the enclosure. The Master of Death was cursing insanely. Knight covered them while Doyle released Stanley. The Englishman ran toward the outer room.

"Wait!" Knight clipped out. "You can't do anything alone."

"But the *Furious*. You heard what Latti said! They'll be killed—blown to bits!"

"Not if we use our heads. Take Latti's gun and cover the prisoners. Don't shoot if you can help it."

"How are we going to work it, Dick?" Doyle cut in hastily.

"Take Latti's uniform coat and hat," said Knight. "Your trousers are dark enough—by the time we get near enough for them to see they're wet you'd be recognized anyway. I'll take a look outside."

He hurried to the outer door, made a guarded inspection. The huge folding door was still closed, but the submarine was almost ready to cast off its lines. Men were racing up the gangway, sprinting toward the hatches. The projector for the aerial torpedoes was pointing up at an angle of sixty degrees, and he saw that one of the winged missiles was already in place at the bottom of the catapult track.

He tore his eyes from the sub, looked toward the planes. The Macchi's engine was being warmed up, as were those of two or three Bredas. Mechanics were working on the motor of the amphibian, which seemed to have balked. He turned and ran back to the rear space.

"Go ahead—you and Stanley—to the outer door!" he told Doyle. "I'll be there in a few seconds. We'll pretend we're guarding Stanley when we go to the ships."

As they obeyed, he lifted the mask, looked grimly at the six prisoners.

"I'm going to walk backward to the laboratory entrance, and I'll be aiming every second at that war-head. If any one makes a break before the lights go out, I'll blow you all to smithereens!"

**HE STARTED** backward, pistol trained on the nose of the gleaming shell of Brauerite. As he reached the connecting door Brauer crouched, but three of the Blackshirts wildly dragged him back.

"*Dumkopf* swine!" he screamed. "He's tricking you—he'll never blow himself up!"

Knight stepped back out of sight, whirled, and ran at top speed. At his signal, Doyle and Stanley started outside.

"There comes one of Latti's officers!" Stanley said in a tense voice.

"Motion to him!" Knight said swiftly to Doyle. "Signal him to go ahead."

Doyle flung up his hand, pointed toward the submarine. The officer, apparently coming to see what had detained his commander, turned and hastened back to the dock. The bright lights dimmed, went out.

"Run!" Knight muttered. "Head toward the dock until we're opposite those ships. Doyle, you and Stanley try to get the Macchi. I'll cover you and grab one of the Bredas."

A wild yell from the direction of the laboratory split the air just as they came abreast of the planes. The mechanics around the Bredas turned and stared. Knight dashed toward the largest group.

"The prisoners have escaped! Head them off!"

All but two of the men ran for their rifles. Doyle raced toward a Breda which was just being swung around for taxiing out. A blow from his fist sent one mechanic headfirst into the water. Before the other man could recover from his amazement, Doyle had leaped onto the wing and was slugging the pilot. The frightened Italian tumbled out of his pit, splashed in beside the mechanic.

Doyle hit the throttle, and the Breda lurched away from the ledge amid a bedlam of yells from the Blackshirts. A petty officer came dashing back from the direction of the laboratory, and Knight saw Brauer and Latti charging toward the ledge followed by the rest of the men who had been captured.

"The Macchi!" Knight shouted at Stanley. He dropped a mechanic who had snatched up a rifle. The Macchi pilot had been waiting beside his ship, evidently for final orders from Latti. He darted under the wing and jumped at Stanley, clawing a gun from under his flying-coat. Knight fired point-blank, and the pilot tumbled back, shot through the head.

By now a terrific hubbub had arisen, echoing through the huge cavern. Stanley made the rear cockpit of the Macchi in a wild spring, and Knight vaulted into the pilot's seat a split-second later. Over near the dock, a Blackshirt swung a pivoted machine-gun, but an officer knocked it aside before he could fire.

"Imbecile!" he shrieked. "You'll hit the Brauerite bomb! We'll all be blown to pieces!"

Knight seized the throttle, shoved it open. The Macchi forged out under the drive of its silenced motor. A spot of reddish light flickered across the right wingtip. Knight jerked a look back and saw the Master of Death hurtle over a fallen

Blackshirt and scramble onto the wing of the black skull-ship. The neon-light in the skull had already been turned on, and a mechanic was scurrying out of the cockpit. Brauer tore a pair of goggles from the man's head, fastened them over his slits of eyes.

The clatter of a machine-gun broke through the din of voices. Doyle's ship was in the air, twisting around toward the ledge, and a terrified Italian gunner was blasting at the Breda. At the same time, another Breda which had already taxied out came racing across the gloomy water. It zoomed the instant its pontoons broke free, then whipped into a turn, plunging after Doyle.

Knight held the Macchi onto the step until it was streaking at well above flying speed. He pulled the stick back, then tripped the muffled guns before him. No tracers showed, there was nothing but the vibration of the guns to indicate they were firing. But the Italian pilot gave a sudden leap, stiffened, and fell over his controls. His ship pitched head-long into the water below.

**THE SUBMARINE** was now half-way through the opening, and Knight could dimly see the crew at the folding door making ready to close it as soon as the undersea vessel was past. He pulled up to Doyle's level, hurriedly waggled his wings. Doyle shot after him as he nosed down to pass through the opening. The fan-tail of the sub was passing the door, as the vessel put on more speed. Knight flung a burst above the heads of the door-crew, and the men scattered madly.

A vicious thudding into the wings told him that muffled guns were firing from somewhere behind, but he dared not look back. He crouched over the stick as the Macchi raced into clear air, then zoomed up into the darkness. The sub was a black shadow about to be swallowed up in the night—and not ten miles ahead searchlights were methodically sweeping the water from what he knew must be the *Furious*.

Two tiny red spots showed in the darkness, and Brauer's

grim skull-ship plunged through the entrance to the secret base. Knight saw Doyle's Breda skid aside, vanish in a tight chandelle. The skull-spotlight twitched to the left, passed over the Macchi's wing. Knight zoomed, banked above the submarine.

"Drop a flare!" he shouted back at Stanley.

"Can't find the releases!" the Englishman yelled. "Dive lower—we've got to finish that sub!"

Knight made a desperate search of the cockpit, trying to locate the flares. He had already found the bomb-pull, with a safety-catch to make certain the lethal charge of Brau-erite was not dropped by error. But unless he could see the target....

T-t-t-t-t-t-t! Another burst from silent, masked guns cut through the Macchi's wings. He felt the rudder pedals quiver as the bullets raked back across the tail. With a swift renversement, he was out of the fusillade. But he had hardly banked when a dazzling light blossomed directly overhead. Doyle had dropped a flare!

The black skull-ship was two hundred feet on the right, circling swiftly, and the submarine was almost out of the channel. Knight hurled the Macchi after the vessel, climbing at full-throttle. Like a shot, the Master of Death plunged in at them. Doyle pitched down under the flare, but before he could get into range another Breda streaked out of the cavern base and drove him to hasty defense.

Machine-guns were tilting up from the submarine, and aft of the conning-tower Knight saw a crew frantically preparing to launch one of the aerial torpedoes. The sub was also swinging to launch a full-sized underwater torpedo.

Knight pointed straight toward the *Furious,* pawed at the bomb-pull. Once the bigger torpedo was launched, he knew that the infra-red eye would guide it straight to the British vessel, and all on board would be doomed.

His fingers closed on the safety-catch, snapped it open. The Macchi was almost in line with the sub when like some apparition from Hell the black skull-ship plunged straight into its path. Knight's heart turned to ice as he saw the scarred horror of Brauer's face glaring over the cowl.

The vengeance-mad Austrian meant to crash them head-on and explode the bomb in mid-air!

**WITH A** frenzied jerk, Knight stood the Macchi on its tail and pulled the release. The Austrian skidded wildly, fell into a spin. For one instant, Knight thought Brauer's ship would hit the falling bomb. One instant of freezing dread—waiting the blast that would hurl the three of them into eternity. Then he saw the bomb plunge on down toward the unmarked sub.

Under the glare of the drifting flare, the doomed vessel lay starkly revealed. Knight had one last glimpse of terrified men diving into the sea, of Brauer pulling out of the spin. Then the deadly bomb struck!

A jet-black cloud whirled out over the sea, and skull-ship and submarine vanished! From the center of that black cloud a terrific geyser spouted up. Prepared though he was, Knight was slammed half-way out of the seat. He clung to the stick, staring dazedly down into the inferno of hurtling wreckage. The thought of Doyle wrenched his gaze from that scene of horror. He turned, felt a great thankfulness as he saw his partner's ship twisting in toward them through the turbulent air currents. The other Breda was wobbling down to a landing in the sea.

He started as Stanley violently thumped his shoulders. The Englishman was pointing back toward the base, a look of awe on his face. Knight looked back. The whole face of the cliff was sliding down, as the tremendous concussion loosened some hidden fissure. The rumble of the avalanche swelled to a roar—then finally slowly faded away.

From the approaching *Furious*, searchlights swept over the sea, rested upon the pall of dust which hid the wrecked base. The shroud of dust lifted, disclosing a vast slide of rock where the opening had been. There was no sign of life.

"Wiped out—to the last man," Knight muttered. He saw

Doyle signal toward the *Furious*. He gestured back, and side by side the two planes began long power glides to land beside the carrier.

Once Knight looked over his shoulder. Stanley was staring back at the heaving sea, and he knew what the Englishman was thinking. Stanley shivered, turned and saw Knight watching him.

"Think what it would have been," he said huskily, "if the secret of that vulture of silence had lived! It would have meant the end of civilization. He'd really have been the Master of Death!"

Knight slowly nodded.

"You're right—but Death finally proved the real master!"

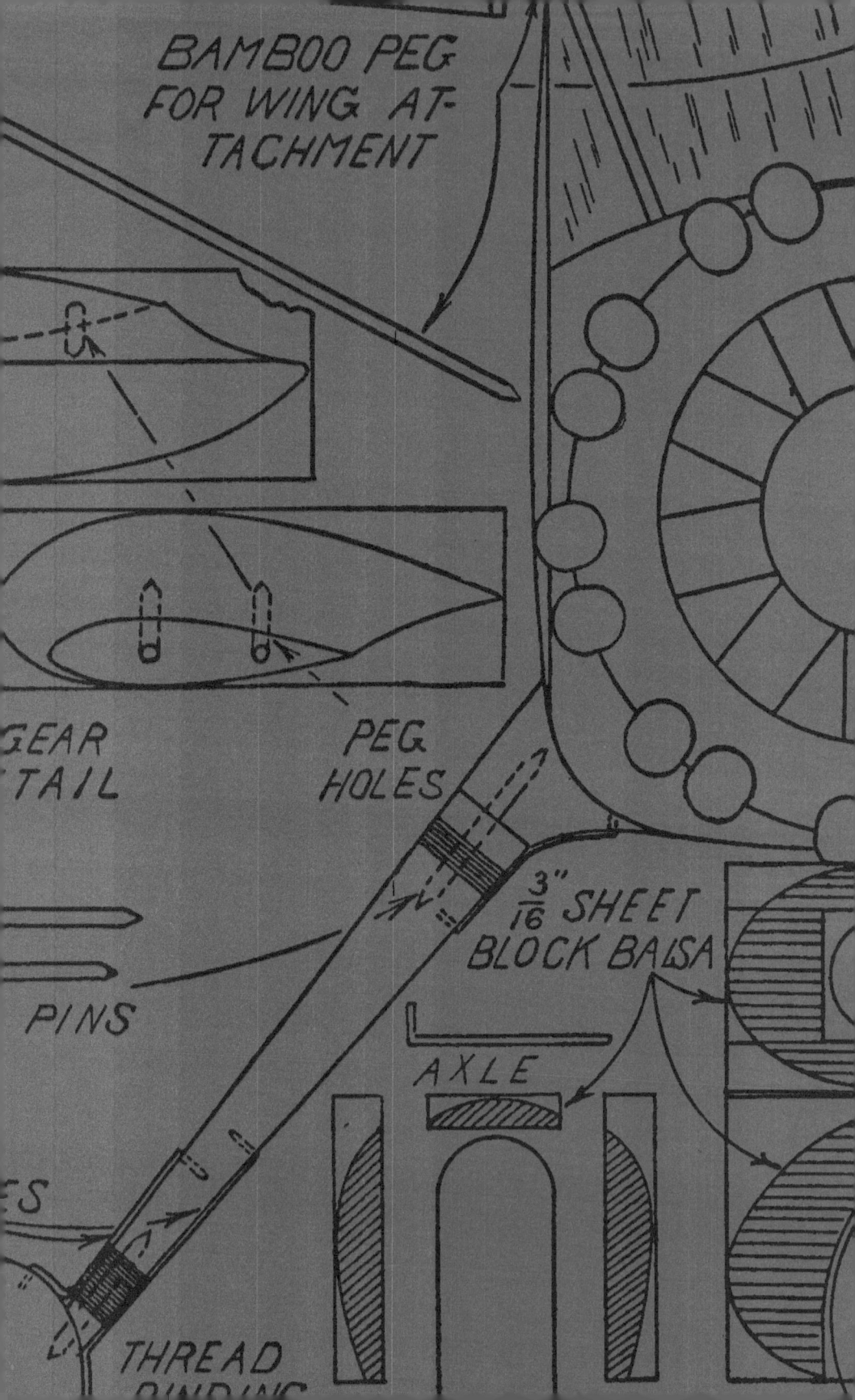

BAMBOO PEG
FOR WING AT-
TACHMENT

GEAR
TAIL

PEG.
HOLES

PINS

3"/16 SHEET
BLOCK BALSA

AXLE

ES

THREAD

# Hell's Hangar

## CHAPTER I
### Death Rides the Dewoitine

**I**T COULD have been a tomb—that strange, paneled room buried deep in the ground "somewhere east of Luxembourg." A deathlike hush pervaded it, save for the jerky breathing of the square-headed colonel in one corner.

The other man in that room hardly moved, hardly drew a breath. His pale, gaunt figure might have been a corpse propped stiffly behind the great desk, glassy eyes fixed on the huge wall-clock.

Like a long, bloody dagger, the red second-hand once more traversed the clock's dial. As it reached the sixtieth second point, the eyes of the gaunt German lit with a fanatical glow.

"Five minutes!" he whispered. "Think, Moltke! Only five more minutes, after all these years!"

The color went still farther out of Moltke's fat face, and he stared in fascination at the dagger-like hand.

"*Ja*, General Hiede. I am thinking! But what if it should go wrong?"

"You white-livered *Dumkopf!*" the general said with contempt. "No one else knows of it—only you and I. Even after I give the signal, word cannot reach der *Fuehrer* or that lummox of a Goering within anything less than four hours.

Doyle swung his twin-mount for a death blow. But the Messerschmitt pilot did not hesitate. He plunged in recklessly, his guns hurling blazing tracers that tangled with the fire of the ex-Leatherneck.

I have seen to that. And by that time, they can do nothing but—"

He broke off as a muted buzzing came from a spot on an enormous wall map of Europe which hung directly opposite the big desk. A tiny green light flashed out a swift code signal, then burned with a steady emerald glow. Hiede inhaled sharply, stabbed a look at a photostat chart which lay before him. His bony finger traced down to the word "Paris," and across to one of several numbers bracketed with it.

"Von Lehr's signal! We are ready!"

Drops of perspiration stood out on Moltke's square, fat face. He reached toward a phone, took it up in shaking fingers.

"*Herr Kommandant,*" he said hoarsely. He gulped, had to force himself to go on. "It is—it is the time."

"*Sehr gut!*" an answer crackled from the receiver end of the instrument. There was a brief pause, then something like a muffled explosion sounded over the wire. A roar followed, quickly lessened in volume and died out. Moltke put down the phone.

"*Gott* help us!" he mumbled.

"Stop blubbering, you fool," Hiede bit out harshly. He stood up, an amazingly tall and skinny figure, his major-general's uniform flapping like the clothes on a scarecrow as he strode across the room. He pressed at the side of a panel, and it moved sidewise, revealing a steel door two feet square fitted with a dial-lock similar to that of a bank vault. His long fingers spun the knob, and the door opened to reveal a compact switchboard with numbered and lettered buttons. He threw in a master switch at the top, then methodically began to press the buttons. As he finished with the last, his feverish eyes briefly rested on a small single-bladed switch at the bottom. It was secured with two separate locks which kept it from being closed.

"Give me the other key," he snapped at Moltke.

The colonel's jaw sagged.

"But—but you have barely given the stand-by signal!"

"They will have enough time," grated Hiede. "I will not follow through until the hour we planned. But I'll take no chances on your suddenly changing your mind."

**MOLTKE TOOK** a key from his wallet, dropped it on the desk. The general pocketed it, closed the steel door. By now, colored lights were beginning to flash at several points on the huge map. Hiede checked each one with the photostat, occasionally referring to a red leather book in which names and numbers were entered with a paragraph after each entry. In ten minutes, all but five of the bulbs on the map were burning steadily.

"The others will come in soon enough," Hiede said, half to himself. He looked at the clock. "Switch on the amplifier and make sure that von Lehr is on the right bearing."

Moltke bent over a box with wires plugged into the wall, and in a moment a series of high-pitched signals became audible. There was something oddly harmonious about them as they blended in a chord, then sounded separately and blended again like the bells of a carillon or the high notes of an organ.

"Beautiful, *nein?*" Hiede said with his hatchet face grimmer than ever. "A pretty little song, eh, Moltke?"

The square-headed colonel managed a ghastly smirk. "Very pretty, *Herr General.* But what if some one heard and suspected—"

"For the hundredth time, I tell you it's impossible!" rasped Hiede. "My agents checked every country in the world, and there has been only one other such set built."

"But you told me there was *none!*" Moltke said in dismay.

"That one was destroyed," retorted the scarecrow German. "It was built by the radio engineers of the United States Army for that spy-devil who caused so much trouble in Spain and in the Mediterranean two months ago."

"You mean the one they call 'Q'?" exclaimed Moltke. *"Mein Gott,* if he should find out—"

"What could he—or any other man—do in three hours? And as I told you, his set was ruined. I have a complete report. It was installed in a special Northrop which was built for stratosphere flight. Also, my agents finally discovered the identity of this *verdammt* Q-agent. His name is Richard Knight, and he poses as a wealthy sportsman pilot. But his money comes from the secret counter-espionage fund of the United States, and his companion on his travels is a former Marine Corps pilot named Lawrence Doyle—a fellow who was discharged from that service after being entangled in a battle with Jap flyers in China. They work with various civil departments of their Government, as well as with the Army and Navy, so you can judge the power they have."

"But this ultra high-frequency set?" insisted Moltke.

"It was destroyed when they made a forced landing at Guam after that rocket affair we heard of in Manchukuo. Knight and Doyle left there by Clipper, and my men lost them at Singapore. They are probably back in the United States now."

Moltke exhaled a sigh of relief, sat down, and again watched the lights on the map. Two more had flashed up, one of them at a point marking Le Bourget Airport, just north of Paris. A third, near London, was flashing a brilliant purple when suddenly the sweet harmony from the amplifier was broken by a staccato, rasping signal. Both Germans leaped to their feet.

"Von Lehr!" cried Moltke. "Something must have gone wrong."

"It can't be von Lehr!" snarled the general. "He'd have to switch off his automatic transmitter, and you can still hear the chimes."

For almost a minute, the discord continued. Then there was an interval, following which the mysterious new signal came through again. Hiede clutched the direction-finder knob of the high-frequency receiver, frantically adjusted it until the signal all but drowned out the bell-like tones.

"*Du Lieber Gott!*" he said furiously. "It has twice the volume! Do you realize what will happen?"

Before Moltke could answer, the rasping signal ended and a voice spoke, deep in tone, and with a guarded inflection—

*Q to W-A-R… Q to W-A-R… If new code, have not received key. Please shift to Code F. Shift to Code F. Go ahead W-A-R.*

Hiede sprang for the phone, his gaunt face livid.

"*Kommandant!*" he rasped. "Order three of the 109s started for emergency flight. I'll be there to give the full instructions in a minute."

"*Herr General!*" Moltke said wildly. "I don't understand! Who is W-A-R and what—"

"W-A-R is the United States Army station at Washington," Hiede flung back as he started for the door. His sunken eyes held a maniacal glare. "Those damned agents of mine have been tricked! If that Q-agent isn't found—and that set destroyed in thirty minutes or less—we're lost!"

The door boomed shut behind him.

Moltke, his fat face ashen, continued to stare at the amplifier. But the voice remained silent, and only the sweet harmony of the chimes came to his ears. He shivered as he thought of what that music meant.

**THE FOG** now seemed to be slightly less thick, for the wingtip lights of the speeding Northrop again showed plainly. Dick Knight looked thoughtfully into the murky gloom ahead, then cut in his gyro-pilot and lifted his long legs from the rudder pedals.

"Try it again," he said over his shoulder.

Larry Doyle bent his chunky figure and switched on the special spy-set which had been built for their use in counter-espionage. After a few seconds a clear, sweet harmony came from the tiny speaker-box in the front cockpit.

"There she is," grunted Doyle. He rubbed his crooked nose with the back of his hand. "Hanged if I can make it out. Brett never said it with music before."

"It's not coming from Washington," said Knight. His eyes, so darkly blue they appeared almost black, rested for a second on the bearing indicator. "Whatever it is, it's coming from the heart of Paris—if my dead reckoning is anywhere near right."

"Where are we?" demanded the ex-Leatherneck.

"Just about over Versailles, I think. The wind may have

changed since we swung in from St. Nazaire, but the last bearing I took on the Le Bourget beacon shows we're just about on course."

"I still think we should've pushed through to London," grumbled Doyle. "Here we go to all the trouble of hopping across Spain, with both sides ready to smack us in the klink if we get forced down there, and then a water-jump over the Bay of Biscay. And now you go chasing bells!"

Knight chuckled. "Don't worry, Lothario, that girl up at Croydon will wait another day. And then there's always Paris."

"You know I can't talk Frog worth a nickel," retorted Doyle.

"I thought," Knight said with a grin, "that you lovers had a universal language."

"Go sit on a prop," snorted Doyle. "Say, those bells are getting louder."

The taller secret agent leaned over the bearing indicator, then switched off the gyro and took the controls. Without lowering the special retractable landing-gear, which with a souped-up twin Wasp enabled the Northrop to show a top speed of 365, he nosed the spy-ship downward.

"What's the idea?" said Doyle.

"I'm going to see if we can break through this stuff and find where that chimes signal is coming from."

**BLURRED LIGHTS** began to show beneath, and the fog masses took on a whitish glow, indicating a city of considerable size below. Knight leveled out at 1500 feet. The mysterious chimes grew steadily louder, and in a moment he switched on his transmitter and held the hand-mike to his lips.

"Q calling in—Q calling in," he said crisply.

"I thought you said it couldn't be for us," cut in Doyle.

"Might be some one from G-2 with a special mission— some fellow using one of those portable sets," Knight said, his thumb on the mike circuit-button. Then, when he had barely switched back to the receiver, a voice spoke with a note of frantic haste—

*W-A-R to Q. Don't send any more. Land at Le Bourget and wait for contact!*

Knight's eyes narrowed, for the voice had a foreign inflection, although the words were English. He threw the sending switch.

"Who's calling? Give your identification number. And who am I to contact at—"

"Dick, look out!" shouted Doyle.

Knight sprang up in his seat. A giant Dewoitine airliner was plunging head-on out of the fog!

He gave a desperate jerk at the stick and stood on the left rudder pedal. Thereupon, the Northrop screamed up into a skidding split-turn, wingtip almost scraping the French airliner.

"The crazy fools!" howled Doyle. "Not a single light showing! Let's get out of here!"

Knight stared down into the mists. Against the glow of the city lights below, the Dewoitine was darkly silhouetted. It was turning back toward them, starting into an upward spiral. From its size, Knight knew it must be one of the thirty-passenger jobs used by the Air France Company.

"What the devil do they want now?" yelped Doyle.

"Look! They're chasing after us!"

Knight turned on his landing lights, swung the controlling grip so that the beams focused slantingly on the big ship. Faces showed at the windows of the climbing airliner. And a cold chill went over the American when he saw them. There was something horrible about those faces—a queer rigidity, a total lack of expression as though—

"Good Lord!" Doyle burst out. "They're dead! Even the pilots!"

Knight froze. Yes, the pilots, too, were sitting rigidly in their seats, unmoved by the glare of his lights. But the Dewoitine continued to zoom straight for the Northrop!

## CHAPTER II
## *Enter Capitaine Robard*

**WITH A** jerk at the stick, Knight pulled up over the Dewoitine, then pivoted into a vertical bank. The big airliner settled into level flight, and he cautiously edged in alongside. The glow from the Northrop's wing-lights reflected from the fog back into the cabin. He stared across, through the Plexiglass enclosure of his cockpit. The passengers were still sitting there, motionless, their faces oddly waxen.

And then the truth burst upon him. "They're wax dummies!" he exclaimed.

The Dewoitine swerved abruptly, and he had to kick into a hasty skid to avert collision.

"Maybe they're dummies," howled Doyle. "But there's somebody on board workin' those controls."

"I'm going to slide in close again," clipped Knight. "Watch the cockpit—there might be some one crouched down between those dummy pilots."

Braced for a quick zoom, he inched the Northrop in beside the big airliner. In tense silence, Doyle and he peered across toward the pilot's compartment as the two planes swung together. The Dewoitine again was flying level. Knight twisted the light-control grip and pointed the starboard light into the cockpit. There was no sign of a living person— only the two staring wax dummies, in pilots' uniforms, tied upright in the seats.

Meanwhile the amplifier of the ultra high-frequency set had been silent. But suddenly the music of the chimes again sounded, this time with greatly increased volume.

"I've got it!" yelled Doyle. "The transmitter's on board th' Dewoitine! Turn your light back in the cabin and— Holy smoke, look at the ship!"

The airliner was yawing violently from right to left. Knight zoomed a hundred feet above it, then for the first time he realized that searchlights were probing the fog. Bright spots showed in half a dozen places where the mists blocked the powerful beams from the ground. The Dewoitine nosed down sharply, leveled out again, and in the same moment something plunged past one of the shifting circles of light.

Knight banked swiftly, and his recessed wing-lights flooded a sleek black ship. The plane whipped out of the glare, but as it did it turned broadside and in amazement Knight saw the swastika emblem of Germany on the tail. It was a Messerschmitt fighter—the famous Bf-109, cream of the Nazi air service, with a reported speed between 335 and 370 miles per hour. But what in Heaven's name was a German fighter doing over the heart of Paris?

The answer to that came with the speed of lightning. With a furious turn, the Messerschmitt plunged back at the Northrop, and from hidden guns in the cowl two streaks flamed at the circling spy-ship. Knight flung the two-seater into a tight split, almost crashing the Dewoitine. The German pilot dived under the airliner, renversed hastily.

"Kick her around, Dick!" Doyle bellowed. "I'll blast that devil!"

"Hold it!" Knight said tautly. "We're likely to start a war!"

He hurled the Northrop into a chandelle, bent on escaping from the German. But almost instantly two more Messerschmitts charged out of the murk, guns blazing. Knight's jaw hardened, and his fingers shot up to the buttons on the stick.

"You asked for it!" he muttered, and clamped the second button. Sliding flaps whirled open in the cowl, and with a roar two high-speed Browning 30s went into action. Tracers flung two yellow tracks across the gap and into the metal side of the leading Nazi fighter. The pilot kicked aside, then his gun fire ripped dural from the left wingtip of the Northrop. Doyle's twin-fifties now clanged up into position from their secret niche in the turtleback, and the two-seater vibrated with their thunderous chant.

The searchlights had gone mad, were dancing wildly

in all directions in a vain effort to break through and find the battling ships. Knight saw a swastika-marked wing flit through a blurred glow at one side. He whipped around, crashed out a burst. The radio stub-mast aft of the German's cockpit crumpled under his bullets, and the antenna flipped back over the tail.

For a second, Knight thought the ship would go out of control, but with a frantic jerk the pilot shook off the broken mast and came back. Crimson eyes winked from his wing-roots, as two more guns joined in with the ones on the cowl. The sudden blast ripped half the Plexiglass from above Knight's head and spattered bits of dural into his pit.

He snapped the Northrop down and around in a screeching renversement. Behind him, Doyle pounded out a barrage that drove the nearest pursuer into a frenzied climb. Knight slid his hand up to the master-button at the top of the stick. He had been saving the 50-caliber guns hidden in his wings, but the time for waiting was past. Whatever the reason, those Germans were out to annihilate them at any cost.

Above the thunder of the Wasp came the sharp clatter of Doyle's guns, fired broadside. Knight jerked his head. One of the Messerschmitts had zoomed high above, was diving headlong from the right. Knight whirled the two-seater, thumb hard on the master-button. All four guns burst forth with a grinding roar, and a gaping hole appeared just aft of the fighter's cockpit. As the pilot whirled, horrified, the shattered fuselage broke in two and the forward section went hurtling down into the mists.

**KNIGHT ZOOMED** over the tail section as it started to fall. The Dewoitine airliner had vanished in the fog, but it reappeared on his left, just as the two remaining Nazis came in furiously for vengeance. A fusillade from the first Messerschmitt raked the Northrop's cowl. Knight ducked with a shout of warning to Doyle, and splintered bits of metal swirled rearward, banging over the riddled enclosure.

The second Nazi fighter charged around the Dewoitine

to catch the Northrop in the clear. Doyle spun his twin-fifties and crashed out a long burst. Then just as he fired, Knight ruddered away to avoid collision with the first Messerschmitt, thus causing the last tracers from Doyle's guns to rake the Dewoitine's cabin.

A blinding flame shot from the windows of the airliner, and it disintegrated with a terrific roar that shook the sky. Hurled back against his head-rest, Knight dazedly clawed at the stick. And the Northrop was on its back, starting to spin, before he recovered control.

He quickly rolled rightside up, stared around in stupefaction. Greenish smoke was spreading in every direction, and below was a hole literally blasted in the fog. He could see the Seine and two of its bridges, and almost directly below was the Quai d'Orsay and a row of Government buildings. A searchlight spotted the Northrop before he could see anything else, so he hurriedly kicked away.

He was climbing blindly when Doyle gave a frantic shout. A gigantic structure loomed straight before him, and just in time he whirled the Northrop aside. By the glare of the searchlight he saw a platform with a railing, and suddenly recognized that colossal framework.

It was the Eiffel Tower!

A small but powerful light flicked out from the top platform, and he could dimly see two or three men. Tracers smoked past the right wing as he turned. He thought for a second they came from the tower, then he saw another black Messerschmitt darting in, with the two other fighters behind it. The new leader's ship overshot, and as it whipped into a vertical bank Knight glimpsed a gaunt face, with glaring eyes covered by huge goggles. The enclosure of the Messerschmitt was open, and he saw the pilot make a savage gesture toward the other Germans.

Knight jerked his throttle, and the leader overshot. With a swift touch at the rudder, he swung the Northrop toward the Nazi fighter. The wing-root fifties crashed out a lethal blast, but before he could center his tracers on the now zooming ship the other Messerschmitt darted in frantically. He hurled the Northrop into a tight chandelle, booting the tail around so that Doyle was in line with the nearest Messerschmitt.

In the same moment, his sights caught the leader's left wing. He thumbed the third stick-button, and the 30s hammered a burst into the aileron of the Nazi ship. Doyle's guns roared simultaneously, and a spout of flame lit up the misty sky and the fading greenish smoke. As Knight followed the leader into a dive, he flicked a look sidewise and saw one of the fighters tumbling down in flames. The other Messerschmitt was plunging in recklessly, guns blazing, tracers tangling with Doyle's as the husky ex-Leatherneck spun his twin-mount for a death-blow.

Suddenly a bright red rocket streaked between the Northrop and the ship before it. A single-seater with French cocardes shot out of the fog and squarely into the glow from light on the Eiffel Tower. The light went out, but not before Knight recognized a Loire-Nieuport 46.

As the French ship whipped around, flame belched from both its 20 m.m. guns. Both Knight and the Nazi leader pulled up hastily, for the cannons were blasting in between them. The other Messerschmitt flung a wild burst at the Loire, then whirled at a signal from the leader.

In another second both Messerschmitts were lost in the fog.

**THE PILOT** of the Loire now warily eased in parallel with the Northrop and turned on his landing-lights. The glare reflected from the mists partly illuminated both ships, and Knight saw the pilot nod vigorously and point downward. He signaled back in the affirmative and nosed the bullet-scarred Northrop into a parallel glide.

"See if you can pick up the Le Bourget radio-beacon," he said to Doyle through the interphone. "This chap may know what he's doing. But I'm not following anybody in a blind landing."

Doyle switched to the Le Bourget beacon wavelength, and as the signals came in Knight glanced at the compass. As he had surmised, the Frenchman was heading for the great air terminal.

The Yank agent made a quick check of air-speed and altitude, was about to pull up and work out his own descent problem when the fog thinned enough to give a vague picture of the ground.

Blurred lights sharpened, revealing main arteries leading into Paris, and ahead he glimpsed the boundary markers and beacons of Le Bourget. He was lowering the wheels when without the slightest warning the Loire pilot jerked his throttle and dropped behind them. Instinctively, Knight kicked away—and saved Doyle and himself from instant annihilation.

A shell from the Loire's right-wing cannon smoked within a foot of the cockpit, and as he opened the Wasp full-out a second shell barely missed the cowl. Doyle's bellow of rage was drowned in the roar of his fifties.

Knight gripped the retracting-gear valve and pulled the Northrop into a thundering Immelmann as the wheels folded into their niches.

The Loire flung to one side as he pitched around after it, and he lifted his fingers from the gun-buttons. Doyle's burst had gone into the Frenchman's engine, and the single-seater was twisting down with a dead stick.

"The louse!" howled Doyle. "I hope he cracks up and breaks his neck."

"If he does we'll be in a fine jam," retorted Knight. "There'll be no way to get at the truth, and the French will be taking care of our necks with a guillotine."

"Holy cow!" cried Doyle. "Then we'd better dig out of here and make for England."

"No, that would only make matters worse. And we'd probably be intercepted, anyway. The best thing to do is tell the

French officials the truth before our friend there has a chance to talk."

Lowering the wheels again, Knight dived for the terminal, with a hasty survey preparatory to landing. The Loire was a mile behind, stretching its glide. But when the American swung in at three hundred feet, he swore to himself. A transport was taxiing out to take off, and a red light from the tower peremptorily signaled him to sheer away. He made a tight circle, intent on plunging down the moment the airliner was off the ground. But suddenly the transport stopped. The men in the tower had seen the crippled Loire and were giving it the right-of-way.

Knight kicked into a forward slip, landed cross-wind on the runway which angled across the one with the airliner. But the Loire was already gliding in against the wind, and as he raced in toward the row of buildings he saw the fighter come to a quick stop and the pilot jump out, waving his arms excitedly.

A spotlight from the tower swung toward the Northrop, and a motor car darted out as Knight braked to a halt. He cut off the motor, slid back the enclosure, and jumped down. But before he could say a word he was seized by three airport police, and two others covered Doyle with their pistols.

A second auto now drew up, and the Loire pilot sprang from its running-board. His goggles had been pushed up, revealing protuberant blue eyes close-set beside a large aquiline nose. He threw a swift glance at Knight and Doyle, wheeled to the senior *agents de police.*

"Take them into one of the private offices before a crowd collects!"

"*Oui,* Major Foix," said the policeman. He scowled at the prisoners. "Get into the car, *espion* pig!"

The machine swiftly conveyed them past a staring crowd of air-travelers and airport attendants, to a side door from which Knight and Doyle were hustled into a deserted office. One of the police switched on a light, pulled down the shades.

Knight's attempts at speech were brusquely silenced, and he motioned his infuriated partner to keep still.

In a minute, Major Foix entered, and Knight saw a furtive glance pass between him and the senior *agente de police,* a swarthy, heavy-set officer.

"Have you searched the prisoner, Monsieur Mireau?" demanded the major.

*"Oui, commandant, "* said Mireau. "They were both armed. But we found no papers aside from their passports."

"None are needed," said Foix, with a malevolent grin at the two Americans. "I know all about them—they are spies for Germany."

One of the policemen looked uncertainly at Mireau. "Shouldn't we be reporting this to the Prefect, sergeant?"

*"Non, "* Foix snapped before Mireau could reply. "It is a matter for Intelligence; and we can afford no publicity just now. Sergeant Mireau, arrange to have that special Dewoitine started—the one with the experimental radio in it. The prisoners will be transferred in it to a more private spot. Also, have their plane refueled at once; I intend to turn it over to our engineers to examine those secret gun-mounts and bomb-racks."

**MIREAU SALUTED** and went out. Doyle looked desperately at Knight. "What'd he say?" he asked. "What're they going to do?"

Before Knight could answer, the door to an adjoining room quietly opened.

*"Bon soir, messieurs, "* said a voice. "What seems to be the trouble here?"

Foix started perceptibly, then covered his alarm with an oily smile.

"Ah, *Capitaine* Robard! You are just in time. I have caught two spies!"

Knight looked quickly toward the man in the door way. He was blond and quite tall for a Frenchman. His uniform fitted him smartly, and there was a languid grace about him as he stepped into the room.

"Spies, eh?" He gave Knight and Doyle a cold glance. "Well, we of Intelligence will make short work of them if you can prove your charges."

"I can explain this matter—and tell you something else of interest," Knight said quickly.

But Foix broke in with an oath. "*Nom de Dieu!* I suppose you can explain shooting me down—and dropping a bomb on Paris!"

"So it was *these* men who caused the explosion?" exclaimed Robard. "We heard a plane had exploded in mid-air."

"No, these swine tried to bomb the city," Foix said hurriedly. "The fuse must have been set wrong. The bomb exploded prematurely in the air. Then they attacked me—"

"Ask the observers on the Eiffel Tower," Knight interrupted as Foix paused for breath. "They saw the entire affair. There were four German Messerschmitt fighters and a Dewoitine 620—"

"He lies!" snarled Foix. "I insist on their removal to safe detention for questioning."

Robard slowly nodded, reached over and picked up the Colt .38 which had been taken from Knight. With a tight little smile he turned and pointed it at Foix.

"I am indebted to you, *Herr* von Lehr. This saves me much trouble."

The color went out of the major's face, and the policemen looked dumbfounded.

"But, *Capitaine* Robard," gasped one of the men. "I don't understand."

But Robard was still smiling.

"It is very simple," he said. "In the name of the Republic, I am arresting the man known as Major Foix for espionage and treason."

# CHAPTER III
## A Single Chance!

**"THE MAN'S** insane!" Foix cried hoarsely. "I command you to arrest him." But without moving his pistol, Robard reached his other hand inside his uniform coat and withdrew a folded paper.

"I have a signed warrant, *Herr* von Lehr—made out three days ago when we finally traced the mysterious F-9 radio calls to the experimental radio you put in that Dewoitine."

"This is an outrage!" von Lehr said, white-lipped. "I am the victim of a conspiracy."

Robard smiled. "If the workings of French Intelligence are a conspiracy, you are undoubtedly right." He turned to a staring police corporal. "Manacle the prisoner and take him into the next room. The rest of you go with him and see that this wily *Allemander* does not use any tricks and escape."

Still protesting, von Lehr was led into the adjoining office, his wrists secured with the twisted chains which serve as the French version of handcuffs.

Robard turned back to Knight, who was standing at one side looking at his features keenly. "I see you recognize me, *monsieur*," he said to the American.

Knight matched the Frenchman's smile with one a trifle ironic. "I seem to recall your taking a couple of shots at me in Madrid not long ago."

Robard looked somewhat embarrassed.

"*Oui*, I mistook you and your comrade here for anti-French spies when you were trying to break up the Four Faces group. I hope you do not hold it against me?"

"Not as long as you didn't hit me," said Knight. "And I take it, then, you know who we are?"

"In a vague way," nodded Robard. "I was working with the Loyalists then, and my investigations indicated that you had been sent over by the American Government. Also I heard later of your affair with the Italians in the secret Mediterranean station—so it seems, at the least, that you are engaged in my profession, *n'est ce pas?*"

"*Oui,*" said Knight. They had been talking in French, but now he switched to English and introduced Doyle. Without revealing more than was necessary, he explained their presence in Europe, then briefly described the strange events of the evening, beginning with the chimes-signal and ending with von Lehr's treacherous attack.

Robard's whimsical expression slowly faded into one of intense seriousness. "I do not like all this. We have not heard such a signal, so they must have built special sets which this *diable* von Lehr knew, from his radio work with us, that we could not hear. But the explosion of the Dewoitine—and the wax dummies—are you sure of that?"

"We're plenty sure," interjected Doyle. "That crate came close enough to shave me with a wingtip if I hadn't ducked."

Robard looked amazed, then he smiled lamely.

"I see you have the sense of humor, *Monsieur* Doyle. I wish I could retain mine—but too many grave things are happening. France is surrounded by enemies—German and Italian spies are everywhere—"

"This von Lehr," said Knight. "Can't you drag something out of him? He must be a key agent."

"He is *the* key agent," Robard said sternly. "I have suspected him for months, and finally I learned how he had been planted in the French Army, nine years ago. We watched him to see how many other spies we could trap before actually arresting him. But he is clever. When he wishes to communicate, he takes to the air, usually at night, or in bad weather. Where he lands, what he does, no one can tell. Perhaps he goes into Germany, or lands at an isolated spot in France. Or he may communicate with another plane in mid-air by signals or his secret radio. But *oui*, we shall make him talk, even if we have to—"

Robard broke off, as there came a timid rap at the door which led to the hall. He opened it, still holding the gun which had covered von Lehr. A white-haired old man in a wheel chair was a few feet away, and a skinny little man in rusty black clothing stood at the door. Both the skinny man and the invalid looked dismayed at sight of the gun. Robard lowered it with an apologetic smile.

"Pardon, *mon pere,*" he said to the man in the chair, "I had forgotten this little toy. What did you wish?"

The skinny man answered, in a high-pitched voice. "Colonel Reposte here, has a letter asking him to come here. It is from—who is it from, *mon colonel?*"

"I have it here," said the man in the chair, feebly. He fumbled in one pocket, then another, finally nodded his white head, as he reached inside his coat.

"Here it is," he quavered. Then with a lightning movement his hand came out with a Luger and he leaped to his feet before Robard could raise the gun he held.

"Don't move!" he rasped, and with a start Knight saw where his white hair had slipped, exposing a close-cropped head. "Raise your hands, the three of you. A shout for help will bring you a bullet!"

**THE WORDS** were in guttural, staccato French. As Knight backed into the office with Robard and Doyle, the pseudo-invalid swiftly followed, and the skinny man pulled the wheel-chair inside, then also produced an automatic.

The bright lights revealed the false invalid's gaunt, fierce countenance, and with new amazement Knight recognized the man who had piloted the fourth Messerschmitt. Robard was staring at the be-wigged intruder as though he saw a ghost.

"General Hiede!" he whispered. "*Sacre Dieu,* you must be mad!"

The German's lips curled scornfully. "What danger is there—with such fools as you in French Intelligence? Hitler himself could come over here in masquerade, and you would never doubt him."

Some one came hastily down the hall, and General Hiede stiffened.

"Be ready, Hans!" he muttered.

The skinny man opened the door a little farther, then looked relieved. Sergeant Mireau and another man in police uniform entered hurriedly, came to rigid attention at sight of Hiede. The gaunt German made an impatient gesture.

"This is no time for formality! The two of you go with Hans and straighten out that affair in the next room. Hans, you had better take the outer door, to attract attention for a moment."

Hans disappeared, and in a moment a confused murmur of voices sounded from the next room. Hans burst in, gun poised, and Knight saw one of von Lehr's guards jerk frantically at his gun. Hans fired, and the policeman dropped. A brief bedlam followed, then von Lehr appeared, carrying his chain manacles. And Knight noted that there was blood on one end of the set of links.

"Imbecile!" Hiede snarled at Hans, as the skinny spy came in. "Why did you have to shoot?"

"He would have killed me," whined the little man. He spread his hands in a gesture, and inadvertently brought his pistol within a yard of Knight. The tall agent leaped instantly, but Hans' gun went spinning before he could get a firm hold. At the same moment Robard lunged at Hiede. The gaunt general jumped aside with amazing swiftness, cracked the butt of his gun against Robard's head. As the Frenchman toppled, shouts of alarm sounded in the hall. Hiede whirled to von Lehr, who was now covering Knight.

"Take charge! Blame it on the Americans! Get rid of everyone you can!"

He was now back in his wheel-chair, wig straightened, and Hans was behind the chair, pale, shaking, when the door burst open and an airport official came in, two attendants behind him.

"*Pardieu!*" exclaimed the official, as his eyes fell on the unconscious Robard, and a dead policeman near the doorway in the next room. "What in the name of Heaven has happened?"

Von Lehr had a gun rammed against Knight's ribs, and Mireau was likewise covering Doyle.

"These two spies tried to break loose—they killed the officer and assaulted *Capitaine* Robard,"von Lehr said savagely.

The official and his attendants broke into a babel of Gallic oaths and exclamations, but von Lehr cut them short.

"Go back and tell everyone it was nothing—only an electric light bulb dropped on the floor. This spy-matter must be kept secret until we can learn all its ramifications."

The official seemed to notice Hiede and the skinny Hans for the first time. His brows drew together as though he were trying to recall something, but von Lehr gave him no time.

"This is Colonel Reposte, a retired officer of Artillery, who gave Captain Robard a tip leading to the identity of these spies."

The other man turned to go, looked down at Robard.

"Hadn't I better send for the doctor, *m'sieu le commandant?*"

"No, it is only a scalp wound—we will take care of him," von Lehr answered quickly.

**THE AIRPORT** official and his men went out. Von Lehr waited until their footsteps had died away, then closed the door and wheeled to General Hiede.

*"Lieber Gott, mein General!* You are taking a great risk to—"

"Forget that!" snapped Hiede, springing up from the chair. "We have work to do, if we are to save our plans. We must make off with the Northrop to eliminate the American's set—also, I have a scheme for using it later. But we still need another plane. I flew one of the Messerschmitts and was forced to abandon it and take to my parachute, in order to get here in time."

Von Lehr looked dismayed.

"But what if the ship is found? The crash must have attracted attention?"

"I flooded the engine, and made sure it would burn when it struck," Hiede retorted irritably. "And before I jumped, I radioed Hans to be ready with a car at the old field east of Aubervilliers. I had the plan for my invalid act all ready, so I managed to get here in time to offset your stupid blundering."

Von Lehr flushed. "It was not my fault, *Herr General*—"

"We will settle that later! Our main problem is to get away at once—and take these prisoners with us."

"I had already planned that—at least to take the Americans. My special Dewoitine has been started—" von Lehr turned inquiringly to Mireau, and the spy-policeman hastily nodded.

"*Gut,*" said Hiede curtly. "The rest should be easy. I shall want all three prisoners taken; we can undoubtedly force them to give us details of American and French Intelligence which we can use. And the *Plan* must be carried on immediately."

Von Lehr lost some of the color he had regained.

"Then it has really been ordered?" he whispered.

"Certainly!" snapped Hiede. "And every lost minute makes the victory less sure. Hans, wheel me out into the hall. Von Lehr, you and one of Mireau's men come along with the *Amerikaners*. Mireau, you and the other one carry Captain Robard. When we get outside, von Lehr, you will order the Northrop started at once. The engine will still be warm, so it should take only a moment. Meantime, tell the airport superintendent you need a pilot to fly the Dewoitine for an Intelligence matter at Versailles, and that the prisoners and myself and Hans are going in that ship. If they insist on an extra guard or two, very well—Hans and I can take care of them once we are in the air, and then also 'relieve' the pilot."

"And I am to fly the Northrop?" asked von Lehr.

"Did you expect a ghost to fly it?" grated Hiede. He glowered at the false major, jerked his head at Hans. The skinny man pushed the chair into the hall, and Knight and Doyle were marched along behind at gun-point, Mireau's two traitorous policemen brought up the rear, grumbling at Robard's weight.

**ON THE** field, the Dewoitine was ready, motors idling, when the group arrived. At von Lehr's order, a mechanic quickly started up the Northrop's motor. Hiede was lifted from his chair and between Hans and an airport attendant was carried into the Dewoitine.

Knight watched desperately for a chance to break, but von Lehr and the man guarding Doyle never relaxed for a second, and the increasing crowd of spectators was growing more audibly hostile every instant.

"I'm going to take a chance, Dick," Doyle muttered through set teeth. "Get set!"

"Idiot!" von Lehr cut in before Knight could answer. "You'll be dead before you lift a hand! Move on!"

"I forgot th' dirty louse could speak English," Doyle moaned to Knight. "What I'd give for just one crack—"

*"Espion!"* came a sudden strangled cry. Robard had recovered his senses, shouted the alarm before his captors could stifle him. "Help! Major Foix is a German spy!"

One of the spy-policemen struck him a furious blow, but the damage was already done. Half a dozen mechanics and airport attendants dashed through the milling crowd of air-travelers, and customs guards and officials came darting on their heels. The two men carrying Robard lifted him and threw him headfirst into the Dewoitine. And now Hiede reappeared in the doorway with his automatic leveled.

*"Espion! Allemander!"* Knight shouted at the top of his lungs.

Von Lehr had spun half around to face the charging officials. He now whirled back, but Knight caught him with a furious left hook and shoved his gun-hand upward. The gun blasted skyward, and the next instant Knight jerked it from the spy's hand.

Hans was almost at the door to the cabin. He crashed two

shots into the crowd, was triggering a third when Knight fired. The skinny little spy fell on his face, a black hole between his eyes.

Von Lehr dived madly for the door of the Dewoitine, Mireau and the false police behind him. Doyle brought down one man with a flying tackle, and Hiede's hasty shot at him drilled the shoulder of a mechanic close behind. Knight pumped a bullet at the German general, but Hiede sprang back as he leveled the gun and the slug harmlessly pierced the door. Then von Lehr scrambled inside, and before Knight could reach the airliner, it lurched ahead under hurriedly opened throttles. The sudden blast blew him from his feet. He rolled over, came up to find Doyle struggling in the hands of three or four infuriated Frenchmen.

Doyle thudded an uppercut to one man's jaw, sent another somersaulting backward as Knight jumped into the fight. In a split second, the other two men were in full flight, yelling for help. Knight dashed for the idling Northrop with Doyle at his elbow. A pistol spurted flame as he sprang into the cockpit, and two more guns opened fire before Doyle could get aboard. One of the slugs drilled the already bullet-torn cowl, and as he ducked he recognized the gunman as one of the false police. The man had missed the Dewoitine, and was now desperately trying to cover up the truth by attacking the supposed spies. Doyle recognized him in the same moment, snatched a flare-pistol from its socket and pulled the trigger.

A rocket-flare streaked across the intervening space, struck the spy in the chest. Above the drone of the engine, Knight heard the man scream, then the rocket-charge burst with a blinding light. Pawing madly at the flames, the man rolled over on the ground. Knight opened the throttle, sent the Northrop racing away from the mob which was surging toward them.

"We're in a swell fix!" he shouted back at Doyle. "Robard's the only one who knows that man was a spy!"

"They can't get any madder than they were," Doyle howled

back. "What could I do—let him stand there and blast us down?"

"I'm not blaming you," Knight answered over his shoulder. "But we've only got a single chance of getting a clear ticket. We must force that Dewoitine down and save Robard so he can explain it all. Be ready with your guns!"

# CHAPTER IV
## Trapped

**D**OYLE LEVERED the twin-fifties up from their niche, and Knight reached toward the retracting-gear valve, lifted the wheels the moment they were off the ground. The Dewoitine was climbing swiftly into the northeast. A searchlight speared out, crossed the airliner, then swung to the Northrop. Knight ruddered to the left, zoomed at full gun. Hardly a second later, tracers made pinkish white lines through the space where the two-seater had been. Another searchlight angled up the sky, and he had to whip into a vertical bank to avoid it. The Dewoitine again was spotted by the first light, but no gunfire followed. Knight grimly whirled the Northrop and aligned it with the big ship.

"They won't fire on it, as long as they know Robard is in there," he said into the interphone. "Watch out for any ships following us—I saw a fast interceptor back there in a military reserve hangar."

"They probably haven't got a pilot," Doyle yelped back. "It hasn't been wheeled out yet."

Tracer lines suddenly probed down the sky from a point near the Dewoitine's tail. Doyle swore like a pirate as Knight rolled out of the burst.

"Guns in the tail! How do they get that way with a passenger ship?"

"Half the airliners in Europe are made for conversion into bombers," said Knight. "Hold your fire—I'm going to see if I can find a blind spot."

He raced above the Dewoitine in a tight climbing turn. But before he had more than started to close in a gunsnout poked through a round opening in the top and another blast barely missed the Northrop.

"I'm going to take a crack at their props!" raged Doyle.

"No—you might set the ship on fire!" Knight stopped him. "We've got to think of Robard."

"In twenty minutes more they'll be over the border into Germany," lamented the ex-Leatherneck. "You know what we'll be then—the men without a country! When Paris kicks about this to London, they'll cover up about how they let us use these British registration letters on this job—and Washington won't save our necks."

"I know that," Knight said, half to himself. He knew that was the lot of spies who get caught or who get into a jam. They could expect no direct help from their government, and they were expected to take what came without a word, even if it meant a firing squad.

"Then what are we going to do?" demanded Doyle. "Are we going to let those bums get away with it?"

"No," Knight said flatly. He changed the propeller pitch, climbed at a steep angle until they were well out of range. By now the searchlights at Le Bourget were far behind, but others between Paris and the German border were flicking their way up the sky, trying to pierce the clouds. Both the Dewoitine and the Northrop were soon above the first layer, and as the lights lost their brilliance Knight warily descended, watching the blurred shape of the airliner as the shifting light-beams illuminated the clouds below it.

"Listen!" Doyle said abruptly. He had switched on the radio, turning to the high-frequency wave they had used before.

Sweet and clear, the mysterious chimes were sounding again. For half a minute they continued, then the harmony was shattered by the grating, unmistakable voice of General Hiede:

*Hold the second unit! Wait for my orders. M–13, switch off your transmitter and wait for further directions.*

"Now what the devil does that mean?" exclaimed Doyle.

Knight had been staring at the bearing-indicator.

"The chimes signal came from somewhere in Paris, or on a line with it. I'm beginning to get a hunch on this business."

"What is it?" grunted Doyle.

"That first Dewoitine must have been guiding on—" Knight broke off, for the high-frequency receiver was again speaking:

*Orders received. Will signal as directed.*

**THERE FOLLOWED** a low-pitched buzz, lasting about three seconds, then two short ones. After an interval of half a minute, this was repeated.

"That's not from Paris!" Doyle said excitedly.

"No, it's from somewhere on a line north of Longwy, near Luxembourg. That's the nearest German border."

"It must be a radio-beacon to guide that ship in to a field," Doyle said through the interphone. "The fog's probably thicker near the Meuse, and Hiede figures he can't get in without a beacon."

"There's something queer about it," Knight answered. "Why did he switch to another wavelength to give the order for the beacon? If I've figured that old fox anywhere near right, it's a trap for us."

"Well, we don't have to land," Doyle pointed out. "And with this low ceiling, we can duck into the clouds if the going gets too tough."

"We'll have to risk it, anyway," said Knight. "Keep your eyes open."

"I wasn't counting on going to sleep," Doyle retorted. "Hey, look at the Dewoitine! They're trying to lose us!"

The airliner was now nosing down, turning in a northerly direction. The searchlight spots on the clouds were now few and far apart, and it was with difficulty that Knight managed to keep the big ship in sight.

After a minute or two it turned east again, resuming its first course. Knight dropped the Northrop to within a thousand feet, gradually lessening the distance as the darkness increased. Five minutes, and a dozen lightzones showed ahead, as unseen searchlight crews vainly probed at the drifting mists.

"Must be the border, somewhere near Montmedy," Knight

said after looking at his map. "I think they're heading just north of Longwy and into the southern part of Luxembourg."

The light spots now fell behind, and he had to close the gap again as the stolen airliner plunged down through the clouds. They had passed, he estimated, the tip of the French area just north of Longwy, and were a few miles into Luxembourg when the beacon-signal faded into silence. At the same moment the Dewoitine dived steeply into the gloom.

"Must be the cone of silence on the beacon!" Doyle yelled.

Knight made no answer, but sent the Northrop into a swift plunge after the stolen ship. His hand went to the landing-light switch, then he shook his head. Better to risk overrunning the Dewoitine's tail than to expose the Northrop to concerted fire from the airliner and the ground. And if his guess were right, there would be massed guns below.

Re-setting the altimeter after checking the map, he eased the Northrop from its fast glide and banked into a spiral, straining his eyes for the first sight of ground. The radio-beacon was still silent, though he switched to alternate wavelengths to see if he could pick it up. The mists darkened, and he knew that ground was near. Suddenly, their ship broke through into clear air, and he cast a hasty look on both sides.

He could see nothing of the Dewoitine!

Several kilometers distant, the headlights of a car made two tiny spots in the gloom. Another car passed, going in the opposite direction. With this as an altitude check, Knight came down to a hundred feet of the ground, circling carefully. As his eyes became accustomed to the gloom, he could vaguely see that they had come down in a broad valley, with rolling hills on both sides. He was about to start climbing, to be sure of not hitting a hill in the darkness, when Doyle gave a shout.

"Turn back, Dick! I just saw a light flash, a mile south—I think I saw the Dewoitine taxiing."

Knight whipped the two-seater into a turn, and in a few

seconds was circling the Northrop over the area Doyle indicated. His pulses leaped as he made out the shape of the stolen Dewoitine, gray against the darker ground. It had stopped moving, but his anxious survey failed to reveal any buildings or hangars nearby. Bracing himself for a quick maneuver if guns should blast, he flicked the landing-light switch. The tilted beams swept over the Dewoitine, caught a solitary figure running toward the cabin. A swift circle, with the lights sweeping over the flat bosom of the valley, failed to reveal any other sign of life.

"Stand by your guns," he said to Doyle. "I'm going to land."

"Look out for that ridge!" Doyle warned him. Knight swung away, made a wide turn into the wind, lowering the wheels as he prepared for the approach. The Northrop moaned down, engine droning just above idling speed. He tilted the light-beams more steeply to flood the landing area, and in a moment the wheels touched. He pulled the throttle full back, stared ahead with fingers on the gun-buttons. Then a wave of astonishment swept over him.

The Dewoitine had vanished!

"Hell's bells!" howled Doyle. "They beat it while we were landing."

Knight braked the ship to a halt, peered up through the Northrop's riddled Plexiglass enclosure. There was no sign of the airliner above.

"They couldn't have got clear that fast," he muttered. "They'd have had to turn around and taxi for enough room to take off."

**ABRUPTLY THE** implication of his words hit him. He sprang up in the cockpit, bumping his head against the enclosure. A crawling sensation went up his spine. Something was moving in the darkness, off to the right. He dropped back in the seat, jazzed the motor to turn and spot the area. In the same moment, a dazzling light shot out and blinded him. He kicked away, stood on the brake pedals.

A gun hurled tracers out of that dazzling light. Doyle

answered with a crashing barrage from the 50s, and above the din Knight thought he heard a scream. He shielded his eyes, sent the Northrop rolling around until his back was to the light. Guns were clattering from two angles, and Doyle was furiously swinging his twin-mount to blast at both. Above the choked thunder of the Northrop, the roar of another engine came with a booming force. Knight shoved the throttle open, praying his half-blinded eyes would not fail.

The Northrop's controls stiffened, and the two-seater bellowed away and broke into the air with the manifold pressure dangerously over the red mark. Off to the left, a sleek black shape raced into view, as a Messerschmitt fighter strove to head them off. Doyle flung a burst at the German, and the pilot pitched over the stick. The Messerschmitt slued around, went onto its back and burst into flames.

The night was instantly turned into daylight brilliance, as the blazing gasoline leaped skyward. Another Nazi fighter was charging across the smooth carpet of the valley, and with consternation Knight saw five more fighters taxiing swiftly into the wind. Back of them yawned a black maw, where the huge door of an underground hangar had opened in the side of a hill. Lit by the flamer, the Dewoitine was revealed just inside the entrance, with dozens of men running about.

An anti-aircraft battery mounted on a truck came whirling out of the secret hangar, behind it two machine-gun trucks. The truck which held the searchlight was pulling to one side, the crew feverishly trying to keep the Northrop spotted.

One of the Messerschmitts pulled up in a perilous zooming take-off, shot back at the Northrop. Slugs gouged for a second at the side of the two-seater. Knight snapped a quick burst at the Nazi pilot, but the other man was out of range in a flash. He gripped the retracting-gear valve, groaned as it came away in his hand. One of the German's bullets had scored a lucky hit. With its wheels down, the speed of the Northrop would be cut considerably.

Desperately, he hurled the ship around and down at the searchlight. If he could blind the Messerschmitt pilots, there still might be a chance. But a terrific fire from the ground drove him into a hasty chandelle. Doyle's guns roared for a second—then went dead!

"Run for it, Dick!" he shouted. "I'm out of ammo!"

Knight grimly booted the nose around toward the nearest fighter. Its smooth dark sides were almost in line with his wing-root 50s as he pressed the master button. Battered dural and steel and bits of wiring shot from the Messerschmitt's cowl as the burst raked over the top. Knight rammed the stick forward, and the blasting force of his guns hit squarely into the German ship's nose. Literally knocked out of the bearers, the engine went smoking and flaming down the sky, and the fighter whipped into a crazy spin.

With a sudden hope, Knight drove through the space he had opened—then snapped the ship around in a violent turn. A hill had loomed straight before him, too high to zoom across. Tracers from three directions flamed past the wings as he came back. For an instant his taut hand hesitated on the throttle. There was still a chance in a thousand—of plunging straight through, he might by a miracle miss connecting with German bullets. But he slowly pulled the throttle back. It would be practically suicide—and he had no right to doom the man behind him.

With the Messerschmitts swarming around and above, he leveled off and landed—for that was his only alternative. As the ship stopped, he turned and looked at Doyle. A crooked grin was frozen on Doyle's homely face.

"You should have gone ahead, Dick," he said huskily. "It'd be better—that way."

**THERE WAS** no chance for answer. At least a score of armed Nazi brown-shirts closed in around the ship, with von Lehr in the lead. The spy's jaw was swollen and discolored where Knight had hit him, and the Q-Agent read murder in the man's protruding eyes.

"Get those *schweine* out here!" von Lehr snarled, and a dozen storm-troopers leaped to do his bidding.

As Knight was dragged to the ground, von Lehr stepped up and struck him furiously across the mouth. Knight lunged at him, but a horde of brown-shirts threw themselves on him and he went down. Kicked and beaten, he was lifted to his feet and carried half-senseless toward the secret hangar. He could dimly hear Doyle cursing the Germans, and the sounds of a scuffle.

But as he was taken into the entrance of the hidden hangar, the shock of his beating began to wear off, and though the pain increased he could think more clearly. In spite of the agony which the jolting of his captors caused him, he tried to take in the details of the secret base.

It was obvious that the cavern was artificial, an excavation made for the purpose of hiding a large air unit. Walls, floor and roof were of concrete, with iron pillars to support the roof trusswork. The hangar was divided into three sections, with several huge Junkers 86 bombers on one side, and two rows of Messerschmitts on the other. In the rear were shops and partitioned space for war-time quarters, only part of which seemed to be occupied now. The entire space was lighted by electricity, and he saw that the big balanced door, camouflaged expertly to look like the rest of the hillside, was operated by electric motors.

He kept his eyes slitted, so that his captors would not realize he was conscious, though now and then a jerk brought pain that almost made him groan. Ahead, he saw Robard, guarded by two Nazis, and General Hiede in the midst of a group of officers. Hiede glared toward the approaching brownshirts.

"I told you not to kill the American!" he said savagely.

"He is not dead, *Herr General*," one of the men spoke up in haste. "He was only knocked senseless when he tried to kill Major von Lehr."

"And the other?" demanded Hiede. "*Ach*, I see they have

him—and alive. Put this one down and douse him with a bucket of water."

Knight was dumped on the floor. He opened his eyes, knowing further shamming was useless.

"So, you were trying to fool us—hoping for a chance to escape!" fumed Hiede. "Stand up, *Amerikaner* dog!"

Three Nazis gripped Knight and yanked him to a standing position. But for their support he would have fallen. One of the officers, a square-headed colonel with a face as fat as a pig, looked at him in fascination.

"Then this is the Q-Agent—Knight?"

"*Ja*, Moltke," said Hiede, "this is the great American spy. He does not look so very clever now, *nein?*"

Moltke shook his head, twitched a glance at Doyle, whose crooked nose was bleeding copiously from a blow it had received.

"*Gott*, what an ugly-looking *Hund!*" he exclaimed.

"He will look even uglier," von Lehr broke in viciously, "when I am through with him—and this overrated *spion*, Knight, too."

"There's no time to waste on that now," snapped Hiede. "Take them into my office," he added, with a curt gesture to the senior brown-shirt. "Moltke, have preparations made at once to go on with the orders. Have the Northrop plane refueled and made ready for the London trip. That move is timed for shortly after the Paris action."

Robard spoke up, white-lipped.

"There will be a special Hell for you, *Herr* Hiede, if you go through with this!"

"You speak like a child," said the gaunt Nazi, contemptuously. "But you French were ever childish."

He jerked his head, and the prisoners were hurried into a hall which ended in a paneled room. An enormous wall map of Europe hung directly opposite a large desk, and colored lights were lit at various points. A radio amplifier was plugged into a connection on another wall. Knight saw a red leather book and a photostat of a chart on the desk on which several numbers and letters were checked in colored crayon.

Robard stared from the map to the photostat, and the last vestige of blood fled his cheeks, leaving them the color of old parchment.

"You fiend!" he whispered. "Then you were not lying!"

For the first time, Knight heard Hiede laugh. It was like the croak of a vulture.

"So you thought it was a trick, my popinjay Frenchman? You blind fool, by midnight all Europe will be plunged into war!"

# CHAPTER V
## Test-Stand of Death

**F**OR A space of ten seconds, there was only the tense breathing of the men in the room. Robard stood like a statue, eyes riveted on the light-dotted map. Hiede saw the staring brown-shirts, turned fiercely to the senior man.

"Tie the prisoners' hands and leave them here!"

The Nazis hastily obeyed, left the room. Hiede closed the door, looked strangely at von Lehr.

"It is time you knew. But first, are you sure everything is right in Paris—that this affair with the *Amerikaner* will not upset the arrangements?"

"There is no danger of that. No one could trace my agents, and the green light shows they are waiting."

"Excellent," grated Hiede. "Then my plan cannot fail."

"*Your* plan?" von Lehr said hoarsely. He looked at the gaunt general in horror. "But I thought you said *der Fuehrer—*"

"He waits too long!" Hiede said with a sudden fury. "The *Generalstab* waits—everyone puts off the day, afraid we are not quite ready. And all the time England is arming at twice our rate—with all her resources building against us. And France—never will she be less organized—more ready for the slaughter!"

Von Lehr backed away as though he stood before a madman.

"But, *Gott im Himmel,* when *der Fuehrer* finds out—we will all be shot!"

"Not if we show them the way to victory!" A fanatical glow shone in Hiede's sunken eyes. "With France blazing before dawn, and England's capital also in flames, the war will be half-won. Plan Four will be carried out to the smallest detail—every available ship and pilot and our mechanized forces will be thrown into the surprise attack. France will be beaten before noon tomorrow—paralyzed to point of surrender. And London will clamor for a peace-pact when they realize they would stand alone."

Perspiration ran down von Lehr's face.

"But even now, Hitler and Goering may know—may be on the way. The *Gestapo* may be here any second to arrest us—"

"You whimpering coward!" thundered Hiede. "I offer you a chance to gain immortal glory—but you cringe at the slightest risk. Don't worry about *der Fuehrer* and Goering. There is no chance of their learning in time to stop us. I've been waiting months for this opportunity—a time when they'd be off at some remote spot—and tonight they're at the old château in Mecklenburg, holding a secret conference with *Il Duce's* representative from Rome. I've arranged so that their powerline will be cut and the bridge at Ansheim has been blocked by an 'accident' so they can't return that way. As you know, there are no telephones to the château—and without power the radio will be useless. There is no way they could learn."

"A plane could fly over—drop a message," mumbled von Lehr.

"But no one will know anything is wrong," insisted Hiede. "I've shifted the emergency signal control to this circuit for eight hours. At Berlin they will think, when the action starts, that this is the explanation of Hitler's sudden disappearance—that he is controlling the attack from here. I have already given the stand-by signal for all our agents in England and France. And all our pilots have been recalled secretly from leave; I saw to that, making next week's maneuvers the excuse.

"Then as soon as the first air phase is started, I'll flash word to all our mechanized units and the *Unterseeboats*. Everything will go like clockwork—air, sea, land, and sabotage in the enemy lines. Once it is started, not even Hitler himself can stop our war machine from going forward."

"You're stark mad!" Robard broke in. "You'll never beat France!"

"*Nein?*" sneered the gaunt German. "Perhaps this will

interest you. In that first Dewoitine was enough arsenic-base gas to spread over an area two kilometers square. Unfortunately, the ship was too high when it exploded for the gas to take effect—it expands rapidly, and it lost its power by the time the diluted mixture settled to the ground. But the next ship will crash as intended, before the gas is released, and everyone along the Quai d'Orsay and a kilometer on both sides of the Seine will be dead or dying in less than fifteen minutes!"

"The defense interceptors and the anti-aircraft will destroy the ship before it can hit Paris," Robard said desperately.

"I think not," said Hiede. "We will use that Dewoitine which von Lehr equipped with one of our special radioguide sets. Your pilots and gunners will not be sure enough that it is the stolen one. In any event they would be afraid you are still in it, a prisoner. And with that low ceiling they will not have much time to decide. An automatic transmitter will be switched on in a certain room at the Chamber of Deputies, where I happen to know there is a struggle going on tonight against Daladier's government. The Dewoitine will follow the signal like a homing pigeon, will destroy your Deputies and the War Ministry—and France will be left without leaders at the moment our attack begins!"

"That chimes signal!" Robard said hoarsely. "So this is the answer!"

**THE GERMAN** replied with a malignant grin. "We have a score of those sets. Some are in Paris, others at vital points such as your defense squadron fields around the city, and your main industrial plants for war material. There are several in London, also. As soon as we receive word that the first one has struck Paris and the panic has begun, we will send the others at one-minute intervals. Meantime, the Northrop plane will be equipped with a control-relay box and then loaded with as much arsenic-gas as it can carry, along with explosive and incendiary bombs as were in the first Dewoitine. That load of hell will be aimed at Number Ten Downing Street, and if I know the English every important man from the Premier to the heads of their Intelligence will be caught there as they await further news from Paris. In short, England, too, will be left without leaders."

"But why wait, *Excellenz*," von Lehr interrupted nervously, "for the Northrop to be equipped when our Junkers are ready?"

"Because we could not get English motors for them," snapped Hiede. "This Northrop was expected at Croydon tonight—Moltke told me he heard this man Knight inform them he was changing his course to go to Paris, so they would not report him lost in the Channel. We will make him flash a message that he has changed his mind, and thus the Northrop will not be questioned when it crosses London. The radioguided Junkers will follow while London is disrupted by the first shock, and our regular ships will race in according to the schedule, the same as in France."

"If only there is no slip!" von Lehr muttered.

"What could happen?" snorted the general. "Every detail has been figured out, all movements at sea and on land dove-tailed. *Ach*, I have waited and lived for this moment! Ever since 1918, when those devils ruined the Father-land, I have waited for vengeance. I was only an *Unter-Leutnant* when they drove us back, and crushed us with their damned Armistice terms—but I knew then it was my mission to avenge Germany. And my hour has come!"

The germ of a wild hope had sprung up in Knight's mind as he saw the fear in von Lehr's eyes and the mad gleam in those of Hiede. When the gaunt German flung out the last words, Knight threw a swift, warning look at Robard and then burst into uproarious laughter.

"It worked, *capitaine!*" he shouted. "They swallowed it, the fools!"

Robard, after a split-second stare of amazement, took the cue and joined in Knight's laughter. Hiede's jaw dropped, and von Lehr looked at the two men in sudden alarm.

"Silence!" roared Hiede. He gripped Knight's arm with bony fingers. "What in the *Teufel's* name is the meaning of your cackling?"

"You and your smart spy!" Knight jeered. "You thought it was an accident that the Northrop was circling around the Eiffel Tower when that Dewoitine came over! You never wondered why Robard happened to be in that next room! The whole thing was planned, my brilliant general."

Hiede whirled on von Lehr with a snarl.

"If they knew—it was through you!"

"He's lying!" von Lehr cried wildly. "Remember that Robard was astonished when he heard the explanation of the chimes."

The Frenchman laughed in his face.

"Blockhead of an *Allemand!* That was to delay you two from warning your spy-ring in Paris before my men could round them up and seize those sets. Weeks ago, *Monsieur* Knight caught your first test-signals and sent us word through American Intelligence. He followed your supposedly secret flights with his Northrop—night after night. Send your hell-ships across! They'll be guided back here into Germany—against your own cities, by our own ships carrying those chimes-sets!"

**THERE WAS** froth on Hiede's lips, and his eyes blazed like hot coals. "Thick-witted fool!" he screamed at von Lehr. "If this is true, I'll hang you with my own hands!"

"It can't be!" von Lehr moaned. "They're trying to trick you to gain time—I swear I was never followed."

"We'll soon know!" snarled Hiede. He jabbed a button on the desk; and Moltke hurried in. "Is the Dewoitine ready?"

"Almost, *Herr General*," Moltke answered, with a startled look at Hiede's white face. "What is wrong?"

"Perhaps everything—but we will be ready if they were lying. Start the Dewoitine's motors—have all the Junkers started and detonators set. Then return here and give the stand-by signal to *all forces!*"

Moltke's fingers were shaking as he picked up the keys Hiede threw on the desk. The general strode to the door, bellowed an order, and returned with two brown-shirts. Then with Hiede and von Lehr following, Knight and the other prisoners were hustled down the hall, through the shop-section of the secret hangar, and finally into an engine testing-room where a Mercedes-Benz motor with a steel propeller stood on the block. Close by was a movable work-stand—a platform erected on rollers so that mechanics could adjust the chain tackle for lifting the motor and moving it out on an overhead track.

In an adjoining space was a pile of oil-cans, several petrol drums, and an opened packing-case. Five or six wax dummies were scattered around the floor, evidently left-overs from the ones which had been used to look like the passengers of the big Dewoitine when it was sent over Paris. Hiede closed the door, pointed at Knight.

"Tie him face up on that work-stand, with his head hanging over the edge."

An icy chill ran up Knight's spine as he realized Hiede's intention. Von Lehr laughed harshly.

"Now you see where that crazy lie brings you, *Herr* Q-Agent!"

"Wait!" Robard said in a choked voice. "General Hiede—you cannot do this horrible thing!"

"You French use the guillotine—we have our own methods!" snapped Hiede. He wheeled to one of the brown-shirts as they finished tying Knight to the platform of the work-stand. "*Schnell!* Start the engine!"

A starting-motor growled, and with a sputter the Mercedes-Benz whirled into life. Doyle, unable to follow the conversation because it had been in French, began a furious struggle to free himself and aid Knight as he realized Hiede's purpose. But von Lehr and a brown-shirt hauled him back, and the thunder of the engine drowned his frenzied voice.

The work-stand jerked, moved forward a foot or so, as

Hiede signaled for the remaining storm-trooper to push it. A cold horror raced over Knight. The flashing steel blades were less than a foot from his face. Another foot, and he would be decapitated!

# CHAPTER VI
## Song of Doom

**H**IEDE MADE a peremptory gesture, and the brown-shirt held the stand where it was. Pistol in hand, the gaunt German mounted half-way up the steps and bent over Knight, while the trooper-mechanic idled the engine.

"Are you ready to tell the truth?" he rasped.

Knight tried to speak, but his tongue stuck to the roof of his mouth. Hiede shouted a profane command to the trooper, and the stand moved an inch or two closer to the bright disk that meant hideous death. Knight closed his eyes and lay there in a frozen agony, with the suction from the blades pulling at his hair. Hiede shook him savagely until he opened his eyes.

"I give you a last chance!" the general shouted above the roar of the engine. "Answer me or into the blades you go!"

The pound of his fist shook the work-stand. Knight rolled his frantic eyes toward the gun in Hiede's hand, helplessly moved his head in surrender. Hiede's eyes narrowed, and his teeth showed in a wolfish grin.

"*Nein, Herr* Knight, you will not have the chance to seize this pistol. Your intentions are a little too obvious—but I suppose fear makes even such a clever man stupid."

Knight held his breath, hardly daring to hope his prayer would be answered. Hiede motioned to the Nazi who had started the engine.

"Untie his feet first. If you free his hands he will try to get my Luger, and I do not wish to shoot him—yet."

Down below, von Lehr and the other brown-shirt had herded Doyle and Robard into a corner, were holding them at gun-point. Both prisoners still had their hands tied behind them. Knight fought off a sudden faintness which followed the shock of his near approach to death. The Nazi mechanic clambered up on the steps beside Hiede, crawled on to the platform, and untied the rope which held Knight's feet to the boards.

The secret agent let himself go limp, eyes fixed glassily on Hiede. If only the brown-shirt came forward on the side toward the general....

He felt the ropes slaken on his feet. The mechanic twisted around, taking care not to jar the work-stand and move it on its casters. He crawled forward between Knight and Hiede, was unfastening the agent's wrists when the general bellowed something at him, and took a step farther up the ladder to keep Knight covered. The brown-shirt turned around at Hiede's shout, and with a desperate effort Knight jerked his feet up from the boards.

His kick sent the mechanic tumbling over on Hiede, and their combined weight threw the stand sidewise. It slid from under on its casters, whipped sidewise with a crash that threw Knight squarely upon the trooper. He jerked his hands from the already half-loosened rope just as Hiede slammed the trooper aside and lifted his Luger.

Knight's dive and the muffled crash of the gun came as one. He felt the slug sear along his left shoulder, but his hands were now on the gun, tearing it from the general's bony hands before Hiede could fire again.

Then from across the room flame jetted as von Lehr took wild aim and fired.

The bullet from von Lehr's gun smashed against the wall, and Doyle hurtled against him with head lowered like a bull before he could trigger a second shot. The spy fell, breath knocked from his body, and Robard tramped on his outstretched gun-hand. The brownshirt who had covered the Frenchman had whirled to fire at Doyle. Knight pumped a shot into the man, and he doubled over, dropping his pistol.

The Nazi mechanic dived for the fallen gun. Robard lashed out with a booted foot and kicked him away. Then Knight rammed his gun into Hiede's ribs, drove him back against the wall, then stepped out of reach.

"Stand up!" he shouted at the man Robard had kicked.

**DAZED, HIS** bruised face showing the force of the Frenchman's blow, the man obeyed. Doyle was still on top of von Lehr, trying to get his hands loose before the spy recovered his breath.

"Untie him!" Knight flung at the Nazi mechanic. "Keep on his right side while you're doing it!"

All the fight had gone out of the man. He unfastened Doyle's wrists, then staggered over to Robard, and untied his bonds without even a word from Knight. Hiede cursed him foully, but the grim look on Knight's face kept him from making a move. Doyle snatched up von Lehr's automatic, covered the gasping spy while Robard took the gun the dead German had dropped.

"At least, we die fighting," the Frenchman said tautly.

"We may get out of this yet," Knight answered. He stepped back, keeping Hiede covered, and looked swiftly around the room. "Doyle, you and Robard bring two of those dummies over here. I'll watch these men."

"What's the idea?" said Doyle, when he and the Frenchman had brought over two of the wax figures.

"Take off your coats—put them on the dummies in place of the ones they have. And you, General Hiede—I'll trouble you for your uniform blouse."

"*Schweinhund!*" Hiede spat at him. "I'll burn you alive for this!"

"The blouse!" snapped Knight, with a jab of his gun that brought an oath from the gaunt German. As Hiede furiously unbuttoned the uniform, Knight motioned to the stormtrooper. "That shirt and swastika will come in handy. Take them off!"

The Mercedes-Benz was still idling, its droning thunder echoing through the test-chamber. Knight stood where he could see the door. The sound of the engine had drowned the shots, he knew, but at any moment some of the Nazis might appear. And there was no way of barring the door from the inside.

"All set," Doyle reported, laying down the dummy on which he had put his coat. "Now what?"

"Put on that trooper's shirt and the swastika. Captain Robard, you're almost as tall as Hiede—you take his blouse and his cap, too."

"You fools!" von Lehr snarled from the floor. "You'll never get a hundred feet before you're recognized!"

"So you've recovered your voice?" said Knight. "Suppose you line up here with your friends and keep still."

Von Lehr got to his feet, his face a sickly color, and leaned against the wall. Knight was about to continue his instructions to Doyle and Robard when a light flashed on the wall beside a telephone. Hiede tensed for a leap, but Knight swung his Luger instantly.

"Not so fast, *Herr* General. Doyle, watch his *Excellenz* while I see what this is."

He lifted the phone, barked a gruff *"Ja?"* in as near an imitation of Hiede's voice as he could achieve, relying on the roar of the motor to hide any discrepancy.

"General Hiede?" came Moltke's anxious query. "The Dewoitine is ready for launching."

"I have made a change in plans," Knight grated. "Start the Northrop and put it first in line and two Messerschmitts behind it."

"But, *Herr General*," expostulated Moltke, "the Dewoitine is up against the door, and one of the Junkers is next. It will take twenty minutes to move—"

"Open the door, and taxi the Dewoitine outside, then," Knight harshly interrupted. "If you have to move the first Junkers outside, do that also. But I want the Northrop and the two fighters ready in five minutes. Information we just forced from these *verdammt* swine has made a sudden change necessary. We will be there by the time you are ready—and be sure to dim the lights in the hangar when you open the door."

He slammed down the phone, wheeled to Doyle and Robard.

"Here's my plan. You two will go out of here, walking those dummies, as though they're prisoners. With the lights dim, the chances will be ten times better—and most of the men will be up near the entrance. Get as close to the Northrop as you can before you drop the dummies. Let the heads hang forward—the Germans will think the prisoners have been beaten and are about to collapse. Unless you have bad luck, you ought to get near enough to the ship to make the break."

"What about you?" demanded Doyle.

"I'll take one of the Messerschmitts—and if either of you gets separated, make for the other fighter. I'll stay here, to be sure our friends don't break out and give the alarm, until you're part way to the Northrop. Don't worry—I've figured out my escape."

**DOYLE BEGAN** another protest, but Knight cut him short. Carrying one of the dummies, Doyle opened the door cautiously. The rumble of motors added itself to that of the Mercedes-Benz, and with quick relief Knight saw that the lights had already been dimmed so that no glow would shine from the second entrance. He kept the three Germans covered until Doyle and Robard had disappeared in the gloom, then herded the prisoners into a corner.

"I'm going to be just outside that door," he said grimly. "I'll stay there until that Northrop starts—and the first man that pokes his head outside will get a bullet in it."

None of the trio answered, but Hiede's gaunt face was purple with fury. Knight swiftly backed to the door, opened it, and stepped outside. There was no lock. He moved to one side, where he could watch the door and also look toward the entrance of the base. He could dimly see the wings of a huge Junkers moving through the entrance, and mechanics and pilots swarming around like wraiths in the gloom. The base was so dark he could not tell one figure from another, even when the exhaust of the motor momentarily flared up in the shadows.

Knight started as the roar from the Mercedes-Benz rose deafeningly in the test-room. He reached out toward the door, then stopped. Revving up that motor might be a desperate hope that some of the Nazis would investigate, but it was unlikely they would think of interfering with Hiede. It was more likely that Hiede and von Lehr expected him to open the door, which would give them a chance to jump him, or knock him out with a barrage of tools from three directions.

The engine was now wide open, shaking the walls of the test-room with its fierce vibration. And still no sign of action near the entrance. Doyle and Robard must be waiting for a chance—perhaps the Northrop was not even started....

Then Knight went rigid. Two men had just appeared around a ship less than a hundred feet away. He could vaguely distinguish a plump figure, and in a second realized the one on the right was Moltke. He sprang back into the shadows, gun lifted.

Without warning, the door and part of the test-room wall burst open with a terrific crash. A drum of fuel suspended in a looped chain sailed out into the hangar on the overhead track. Moltke gave a yell, and the other man hastily switched on a flashlight. Knight had hurled himself back, the drum missing him by only a foot or so, and now the beam of light fell upon him. At the same moment the roar of the engine broke, and Hiede's voice rose furiously from within the room.

"The prisoners have escaped! Close the main door!"

Moltke had clawed for his gun at the moment Knight was revealed. As his pistol flicked up, Knight blasted a shot at the flashlight, and the colonel's bullet ploughed into the shattered wall. Knight ducked under the still-moving fuel drum and ran between two ships, while the frenzied voice of Hiede rang behind him. He was near the center-aisle between the fighters and the bombers when a pistol spat flame near the entrance. A commotion instantly arose, and guns began to spurt from two or three directions. Above the tumult, a bell clanged, and lights abruptly went on.

The Northrop was directly in line with the entrance, motor idling, and Knight saw Doyle darting toward the ship.

In front of it, where the fight was centered, Robard was crouched over in the cockpit of a Messerschmitt which blocked the Northrop's way. A huge Nazi leaped at the Frenchman, rifle lifted. Robard flung up his hand, hurled his empty pistol into the man's face. The German fell back, and Robard threw himself down at the controls. The Messerschmitt roared out onto the smooth floor of the valley, amid a flurry of wild shots.

Knight, unobserved by the men at front, reached the side of the Northrop as Doyle halted, looking around desperately. A bellow from the rear brought a dozen Nazis dashing back, as Hiede caught sight of the two Americans. With a whoop of relief, at sight of Knight, Doyle vaulted into the rear pit and Knight made the front one in a frantic leap. He seized the throttle, but as he pushed it ahead his heart leaped into his throat.

The huge door was starting to descend!

Knight rammed the throttle full on, and the propeller blast blew Hiede and their other pursuers back in a heap on the floor. At one side, an automatic rifle stuttered above the roar of the Wasp, but Knight never moved his head. For a fateful second, he thought the door would trap them in a headlong crash. Then the Northrop whirled past underneath, with its prop clearing by inches.

**OFF TO** one side, a remote-control radio set had been wheeled out for dispatching the robot-ships. An officer at the switches had sprung up, was staring wildly at the Northrop and Robard's ship. Knight kicked around into the wind, and in the same moment a machine-gun near the entrance whirled to rake the ship. In his hasty swing of the weapon, the gunner overshot, and the Nazi radioman fell over his set, riddled. The Dewoitine, idling a hundred yards away, instantly began to move. By the time Knight had the two-seater at flying-speed, the death-laden airliner was fifty feet above the trees and climbing into the darkness.

"We've got to stop that ship!" he shouted back at Doyle. "Give it a burst!"

"My guns are empty!" Doyle yelled back. "You'll have—look out, here comes a Messerschmitt!"

Knight jerked his head, saw not one but two of the black fighters dart out of the secret hangar. The door had been lifted again, and in that hasty glance he could see another fighter being pushed out for starting. The first Messerschmitt raced through the glare of light from within, and he recognized the half-clad figure of General Hiede. A black shadow pitched out of the night, and Robard dived steeply at the Nazi general. Ground-guns met him with a fierce defense, and he was driven into a hurried zoom. The fighter behind Hiede pulled up in a tight climb, guns warming in short bursts as it drilled after the Northrop.

Knight groaned as he remembered that the retracting-gear was useless. At their reduced speed, and with rear-guns empty, they would be easy meat for the infuriated Germans. He banked hastily in the hope of escaping into the darkness, but the pilot of the second fighter drove him back with a venomous barrage. Tracers and slugs thudded into the Northrop's left wing. He whipped around as tightly as he could turn, tripped the cowl 30s. The Messerschmitt leaped sidewise out of the blast, and for an instant he saw von Lehr's face through the fighter's cockpit enclosure.

With a swift bank, von Lehr cut inside of Knight's turn. Flame streaked from his four guns. But in the split-second when Knight gave up hope, another blast of flame drilled the sky and Robard dropped on von Lehr like a black-winged hawk. The Frenchman's bullets struck into the side of the German ship, and like a blazing, giant saw, cut the fuselage in two.

The front half of the ship plunged into the ground, and fire plumed up, hiding the spot where von Lehr's body was burning. Robard made a frantic gesture to Knight, pointing off toward the west where the Dewoitine had disappeared, then whirled back to engage Hiede's ship. Knight shook his head—with the wheels down, they could never hope to overtake the fast-cruising deathship.

Then a grim inspiration struck him. He switched on the radio, setting it at the wave-length where the chimes signal had been heard. Something electric seemed to fire his blood as he heard the harmony of that ominous signal.

He snatched up the hand-mike, pressed the transmitter switch, and let the microphone dangle out through the shattered enclosure—in the full roar of the motor.

Robard was fighting a losing battle between Hiede and the ground guns, diving at the hangar entrance between each brief lunge at the German. Wide open, at more than three hundred miles an hour, the two black ships plunged toward each other, then-overshot, whirling off into the semi-gloom before either pilot could turn.

Another Messerschmitt was now swiftly taxiing out. Knight nosed down, held his ship in a screaming dive until the German was straight in line with his guns. His fingers shifted to the master-button, pressed hard.

Bright lines shot from the Northrop's nose, into the taxiing ship. The black fighter yawed, crashed into the side of the hill, and rolled back in a ball of crumpled metal. Doyle gave a yell of warning as Knight zoomed, and a cold hand seemed to touch the Q-Agent's heart. He had used his last belt on the ship below—and Hiede was plunging in like a madman, with Robard too far away to come to their rescue.

**HOPING AGAINST** hope, Knight renversed, but the Messerschmitt followed through. Hiede's guns blasted. His tracers were curling in for the deathstroke, when out of the night came the bomb-laden Dewoitine, diving head-on at the Northrop.

With a frenzied turn, Hiede whipped around to flee. Knight spun the Northrop in a violent split, dived after the terrified general. Over his shoulder he saw the Dewoitine plunge down on his tail. Doyle had sprung up in his seat, was staring white-faced at the pilotless liner which was now answering to the Northrop's set as though attracted by a great magnet.

Hiede's mad turn had thrown the Messerschmitt out of control. He caught it, two hundred feet above the valley, with the entrance to the secret hangar almost directly beyond.

Knight shoved the stick forward, took the transmitter switch in his ice-cold fingers. Down roared the Northrop, straight at the hidden base, straight at the zooming Messerschmitt. Hiede flung around, his gaunt face a mask of horror. In that moment, Knight flipped the switch and jerked the stick back to his belt.

One hundred feet from the great door, the Northrop-lured Dewoitine struck. Flame shot up, scorching the side of the hill, and a terrific concussion shook the sky. A vast spout of fire shot out from the hillside, and the black fighter of General Hiede was gone like a moth in the flame.

A minute or two afterward, with Robard cruising close by, Knight stared down from four thousand feet, waiting. Suddenly a titanic eruption split the hillside beneath, as fire reached the massed ships inside and set off their bombs. When it was over, only the flames lived there in hell's hangar.

Knight, abruptly conscious of the throbbing wound in his shoulder, drew a long breath, looked back at Doyle.

"Guess you'd better take over, Lothario," he mumbled through the interphone. "Follow Robard—he'll clear things up by radio before we land."

Doyle took the dual controls, his homely face still pale.

"I thought we were goners, Dick," he said.

"So did I," said Knight. Then he realized that the automatic chimes-beacon signal was still sounding in the receiver. He looked down at the amplifier. But for that little box, a

Nazi fanatic would have plunged Europe into war. But Fate had doomed Hiede and his madman's scheme. Mars was still hooded, and the peace of Europe was saved for yet a while.

It was an ironic end for the madman's scheme. For Hiede had written that music for Death to play—and now he had paid the Piper.

Slowly, Knight reached down for the receiver switch. There was a click, and the music of Death was stilled.

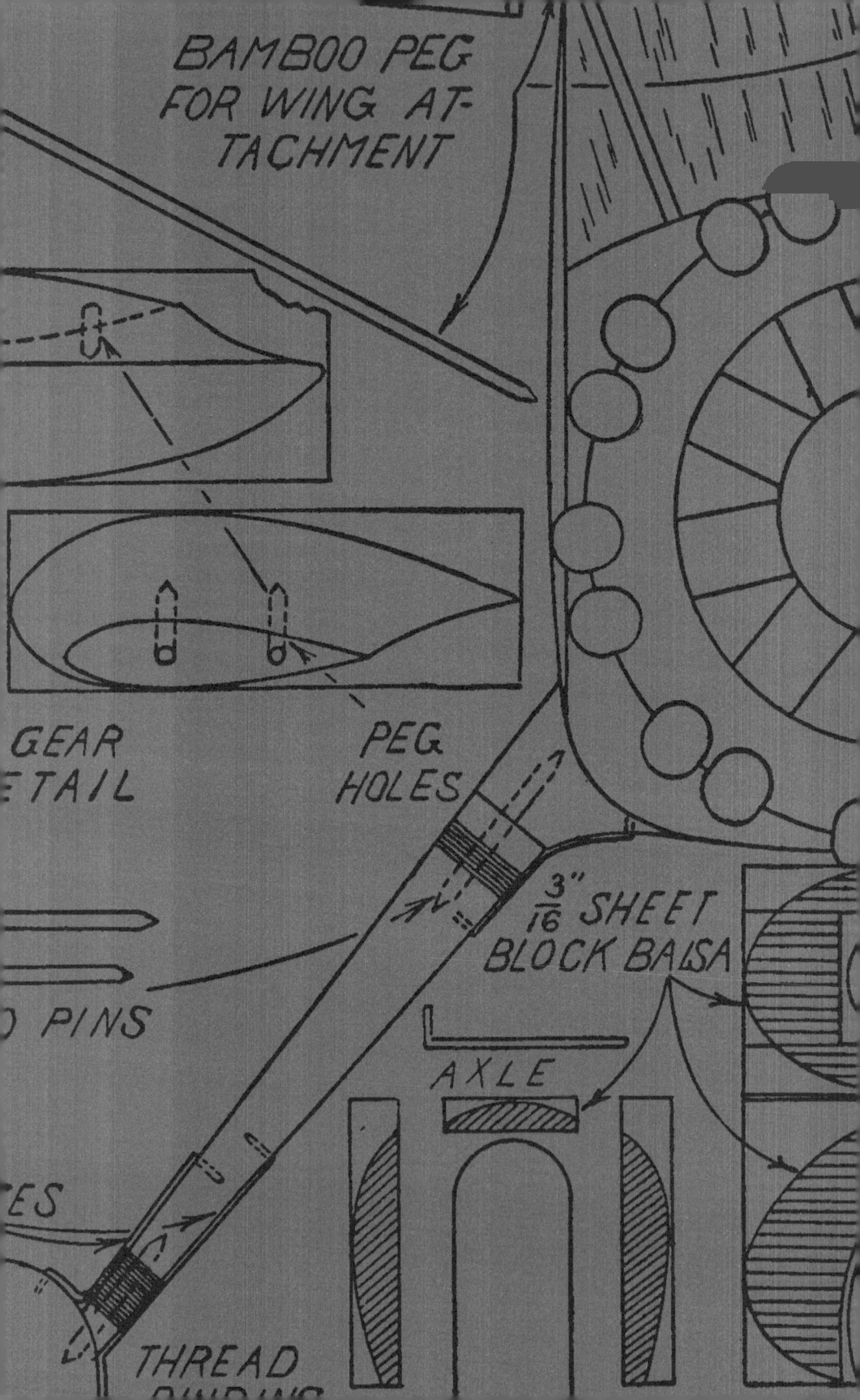

BAMBOO PEG FOR WING ATTACHMENT

GEAR ETAIL

PEG HOLES

3"/16 SHEET BLOCK BALSA

O PINS

AXLE

ES

THREAD

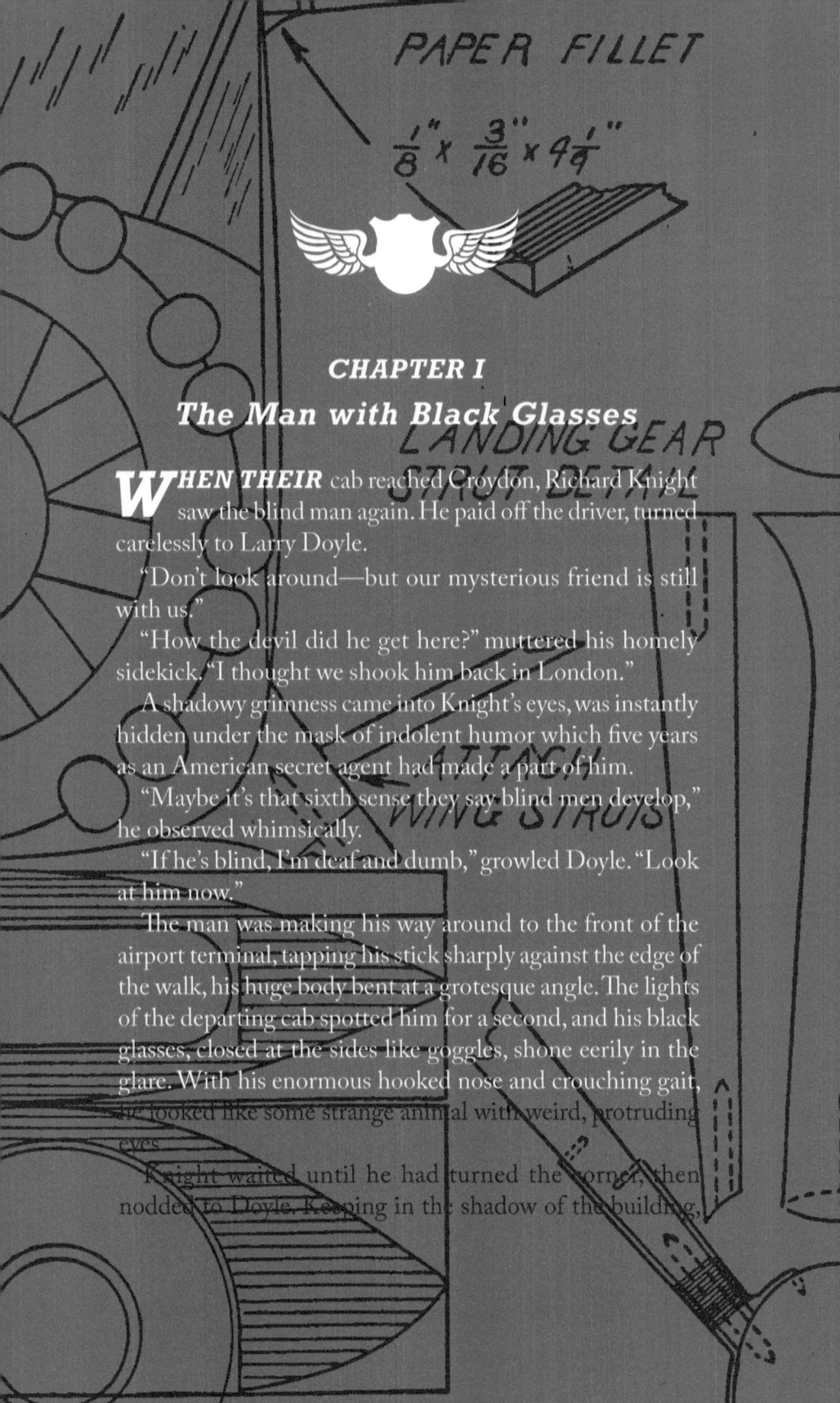

## CHAPTER I
## *The Man with Black Glasses*

**WHEN THEIR** cab reached Croydon, Richard Knight saw the blind man again. He paid off the driver, turned carelessly to Larry Doyle.

"Don't look around—but our mysterious friend is still with us."

"How the devil did he get here?" muttered his homely sidekick. "I thought we shook him back in London."

A shadowy grimness came into Knight's eyes, was instantly hidden under the mask of indolent humor which five years as an American secret agent had made a part of him.

"Maybe it's that sixth sense they say blind men develop," he observed whimsically.

"If he's blind, I'm deaf and dumb," growled Doyle. "Look at him now."

The man was making his way around to the front of the airport terminal, tapping his stick sharply against the edge of the walk, his huge body bent at a grotesque angle. The lights of the departing cab spotted him for a second, and his black glasses, closed at the sides like goggles, shone eerily in the glare. With his enormous hooked nose and crouching gait, he looked like some strange animal with weird, protruding eyes.

Knight waited until he had turned the corner, then nodded to Doyle. Keeping in the shadow of the building,

Knight whirled his plane, triggered a hail of tracers in desperation. Then he went rigid. For a gigantic arc of white fire suddenly blazed down the sky, and caught in that seething inferno, three Hawkers burst into flame.

they followed the stooped figure to the space at the front. Suddenly Knight caught his companion's arm.

"Our ugly friend isn't the only queer thing around here," he said in an undertone. "Most of the lights are out, and there aren't any ships coming in or taking off."

"That's funny," whispered Doyle. "There's usually three or four planes about now, and a crowd hanging around."

"If those men over by the embarking gates aren't Scotland Yard dicks, I'm a Chinaman." Knight's practiced eyes made a swift survey of the scene. "Look down by that second hangar—see the tails of those ships sticking out behind that A.W. transport?"

Doyle peered into the gloom. "Supermarine Spitfires! But what are military jobs doing at a civil airport?"

Before Knight could answer, a gruff voice broke in:

" 'Ere now, what are you blokes up to?"

A uniformed constable had come up from the nearest gate, followed by a lanky Englishman almost as tall as Knight, with a monocle screwed in one eye. Knight nodded pleasantly to the dour constable.

"I think Captain Haldane will vouch for me."

The monocle dropped from the tall man's eye. "Dick Knight!" he exclaimed, in a tone half-way between dismay and relief. Then, as though realizing his voice might have carried too far, he added hastily, "I say, Wright old chap, it's jolly to see you again. Quite a surprise, eh what?"

Knight saw the blind man turn his head, as though listening. Haldane followed his quick glance, screwed his monocle into place and turned to the staring constable.

"It's quite all right, Higgins. Major Wright—old friend of mine—you can get back to your post. Ah—better see what the gentleman over there wants. Tell him all flights canceled, passage fares refunded—th' routine, y'know."

Higgins saluted, strode over to the hunched figure. Haldane gripped Knight's arm, hurriedly led him back into the shadows, with a questioning glance at Doyle.

"He's one of us," Knight said. "Larry Doyle, Captain Peter Haldane. And, Pete, you can drop that musical-comedy Britisher act now and tell us just what the mystery is."

"Then you don't know?" Haldane said tensely. "They didn't send you here because—"

**HE STOPPED** short, as a drone of motors sounded. Knight turned, saw a searchlight flicker up from a truck near the third hangar. The beam probed the low-hanging clouds, circled and caught the wing of a speeding fighter. Another ship showed dimly beyond it, and Knight could hear the roar of others somewhere near.

"Hawker Hurricanes, eh? What's up, Pete—are you expecting war to break out tonight?"

"You're sure you don't know—about the warning?" Haldane said hoarsely. "Or what happened at St. Wendel and Brumath?"

Knight shook his head. "All I know is that we've rush orders to be in Washington tomorrow noon. Our papers are clear—and we ought to be taking off right now. Our ship's down in Hangar Two."

Haldane looked at him desperately, then called to Higgins. When the constable came, the captain gestured to Doyle.

"Take this gentleman to Hangar Two. The men are to give him any help he needs starting his motor."

"Yessir," said Higgins. He looked dubiously at the man with the dark glasses, lumbered away with Doyle at his heels. Haldane spoke up the moment they were out of earshot.

"In Heaven's name, Dick, if you know anything about this—"

"I'm telling you the truth," cut in Knight. "Why, what's happened? Let's have it."

"I—I can't tell you." Haldane turned abruptly, haggard eyes watching the searchlight's slow circle. As the beam shifted, Knight saw trucks backing out between the second and third hangars. The shiny muzzles of multiple pom pom guns reflected briefly in the glow. Haldane flicked a look at his wrist-watch, swore half under his breath. Down at the second hangar, the booming thunder of the Northrop's engine sounded. The man with the black glasses jerked around, his head cocked on one side.

Five minutes later, as the Northrop taxied up in front of the terminal, he came tapping his way along the walk.

"Speak up!" his voice snarled above the drone of the Wasp. "Where's the senior official here? I demand to talk with the senior man."

Before Knight had time to whisper his suspicions, Haldane answered, "I'm in charge. What do you want?"

"I want my rights!" rasped the misshapen man with the glasses. "I chartered a plane—a Miles Peregrine—and paid the pilot for a flight to Berlin tonight. Some one just told me all flights were canceled—but he was lying! I can hear a plane out there somewhere—"

"Just a minute," Haldane interrupted. "That is an American Government pl— an American plane," he corrected himself hastily. "We have no authority to hold it here. But all British commercial and private planes are temporarily grounded."

The other man raised his cane with a furious gesture. "If you're lying to me, I'll sue you! I'll sue every man in Imperial Airways. I've got to reach Berlin—it's a matter of life or death."

"I'm sorry," Haldane said firmly, "but all trips to and from the Continent have been stopped by official command. If you wish to wait until midnight, the ban may be lifted by then."

The man with the black glasses subsided, muttering to himself. Knight had watched him with a hawklike glance, but the man's fury now seemed to be lost in his profane mumbling. Haldane beckoned to Knight as the Northrop rolled to a stop beyond the nearest gate. Constable Higgins had returned, replacing one of the plain-clothesmen who had been at the gate, and as Doyle shoved open the Plexiglas enclosure he turned and crisply saluted.

"Ready for the other gentleman, Captain."

The British Intelligence officer went through the gate with Knight, halted near the somewhat battered spyship.

"Good luck, Dick," he said, and held out his hand. His face was oddly white as he added, "Better get underway, old man—don't circle near here to get altitude—strike out for your course at once."

Knight looked at him, puzzled, then took his hand.

"Thanks, Pete—and I'm sorry I didn't know anything to help you."

He was turning to climb onto the step when above the Wasp's thunder he heard a faint report. As he whirled, he saw Higgins tumble to the ground. The man with the black glasses, no longer crouched over, but now a giant figure, was dashing for Haldane with a smoking gun in his hand.

"Get into that ship!" he snarled at the Englishman. "And you—get your hands up!"

**HALDANE LEAPED** forward, one hand stretched out for the pistol. The man jumped aside, struck him a blow that hurled him back against the ship. Knight's right hand was inside his coat, fingers on the butt of a shoulder-harness gun. The impostor spun with incredible speed, pistol lifted for a point-blank shot. But before he could pull the trigger, Doyle's one hundred and eighty pounds hurtled from the rear cockpit and threw him to the ground.

His gun blasted, but the shot went into the ground. Knight sprang to disarm him, but with an amazing strength the man threw Doyle off and jumped toward the Northrop. Haldane had staggered against the trailing-edge of the wing. The impostor rammed his gun into the Englishman's ribs, screamed a frenzied command. Then, as though realizing his plan was hopeless, he whirled for a final shot at Knight.

Haldane was so close that Knight dared not fire. With a

desperate plunge, he dived at the killer's feet, and the man's shot blazed harmlessly over his head. Haldane clawed out at the smoking weapon, and knocked it from the giant's hand. By now, a dozen plainclothesmen were charging toward the ship. With a furious oath, the impostor kicked free from Knight's grasp and leaped onto the wing. Something fell beside Knight as he scrambled to his feet, then he saw that the black glasses no longer hid the giant's eyes. As he glimpsed the man's now fully revealed face, a sudden rage swept over him.

"Serloff! You murdering rat!"

He raised his gun, but the giant's hand struck the throttle before he could fire. The Northrop lurched ahead with a blast that hurled Knight to the ground. Through the thin eddy of dust he could see the man trying to pull himself into the cockpit. The boom of the motor lessened for a second, and the giant sprang into the front seat. Guns were barking from a dozen directions as he opened the motor again. But the Northrop swiftly gained speed and lifted into the gloom.

Knight raced up to Haldane, who was surrounded by three or four excited inspectors.

"Pete, we've got to stop that devil! That's the international spy, Vladimir Serloff—the worst cut-throat in Europe. Unfortunately, you can never tell whom he represents. He always sells to the highest bidder."

"Serloff?" gasped the Englishman. "Good Lord, I thought he was dead."

"So did I—that's why I failed to recognize him. Give me a ship—or send one of your men after him before he gets away."

A machine-gun was already clattering from a small truck which had been rushed out onto the field. Two more joined in as the Northrop pulled up into a chandelle. Haldane flung an order at an R.A.F. non-com who had joined the crowd, and the man darted back toward the hangar where Knight had seen the Spitfires.

"It'll be too late," said the Englishman. "Even though the engines have been kept warmed up, they'll never get them started in time to—"

He broke off with a groan—for the Northrop had plunged back, guns blasting at the crowd. In a panic, the men fled in every direction. Tracers struck into their midst, smoked into the ground, leaped ahead and into the backs of the nearest men. Five or six wilted to the ground. Knight saw one mechanic, only a boy, topple in a heap, his uniform coat torn with a dozen bullets.

"The dirty butcher!" he moaned. "Pete, give me one of those ships!"

"Go ahead—I'll follow as soon as I flash word to the Hurricane flight commander!" Haldane ran toward the buildings, and Knight dashed for the second hangar. Doyle caught up with him, a flight-lieutenant at his heels. Mechanics were already starting the motors of the Spitfires, and pilots were tugging on helmets and goggles. At the lieutenant's hasty relay of Haldane's command, two pilots jumped down, and Knight and Doyle sprang into the empty cockpits.

**KNIGHT JERKED** his enclosure shut, snapped his belt, and sent the sleek-lined fighter rolling out of the hangar. The instant he was clear, he raced the Rolls-Royce Merlin up to take-off speed. A swift glance showed the gun belts were full. He lifted the fighter in a thundering climb, quickly retracted the wheels. Tracers were flaming up from two machine-gun trucks, and he saw the Northrop twisting out of their fire. With his thumb on the gun-control button, he whipped his Spitfire into a sharp turn.

For an instant his hand refused to clench—to fire on the old Northrop was like stabbing a faithful friend. In that split-second of hesitation, the Northrop's nose flicked down again, cowl-guns blazing. And nearby, Doyle was zooming into the fight, wings bright in a searchlight beam. Knight's thumb tightened suddenly on the button, as Serloff's tracers shot toward Doyle's cockpit. The Spitfire's guns throbbed savagely, and a bullet-track leaped slantwise over the Northrop's tail. As the slugs hammered into the fuselage behind him, Serloff kicked out frantically. The Spitfire's blast missed him by less than six feet, and he renversed to flee for darkness.

A crossfire from the machine-gunners below sent him whirling back in a tight chandelle. Doyle, now almost at the Russian's altitude, drilled in with Vickers spouting. Serloff whirled desperately, and in the searchlights' glare Knight saw his face. It was stark white, distorted with terror. But he was not looking at either Spitfire. His head was turned, and he was glaring over his shoulder.

Knight followed his eyes, but saw nothing. The lights shifted in the next second before he could range the man with his guns. Doyle pounded another burst at the two-seater, and Serloff shot into a furious zoom. Knight crashed out a fusillade, raked the swift-climbing ship. The Northrop flung into a vertical bank, and he thought he had scored. But with a skillful twist around a darting light-beam, Serloff leveled out and raced into the gloom. As Knight plunged after him, he caught the flash of wings across the sky.

Two Hawker Hurricanes were racing down out of the lowering clouds, and back of them he saw still more of the flight. As the seven ships came into the partly-lighted sky, they drew into tight formation. Knight was fumbling for his radio switch, planning to guide the Hawker flight-leader after the now-vanished Northrop, when above the drone of his motor came a strange, blasting thunder.

He jerked around. For the sound seemed to come from somewhere close behind. But there was nothing near him, save Doyle's Spitfire. Then suddenly, a blinding light flooded Doyle's ship. Knight whirled his plane, fired a hail of tracers in desperation. Then he went rigid.

A gigantic arc of white flame was streaking out of the clouds!

Like a bolt of lightning, the deadly arc blazed down the

sky. And caught in that seething inferno, three Hawkers burst into flames, and were gone!

# CHAPTER II
## White Doom

**H**ORROR STRICKEN, Knight saw one Englishman charge blindly into the blaze and vanish. Half-blinded himself, he thrust one hand before his face as the heat swept into his cockpit. The sky was now a white glare, lit by the stabbing doom from the clouds. Dimly, he saw three of the Hurricanes whirl to flee. But the blazing arc leaped after the twisting ships, and the nearest was aflame before the mystery fire even touched its wings.

As Knight whirled away from the blinding light, he saw the Northrop again. Revealed in the glare, the two-seater was climbing frenziedly. Doyle, racing away from the deadly white flame, abruptly saw the Northrop, and a burst from his guns drove Serloff into a turn. Knight saw the huge Russian pawing at his eyes, then to his consternation the Northrop hurtled straight at him. He tripped his guns, then skidded aside as he saw he was too late. Serloff banked away from the glare, pitched a torrent of Browning slugs at the banking fighter. Knight crouched, almost completely blinded, trying to feel his way out of that deadly sky-trap.

An inferno of heat drove him to one side, away from the roaring white arc. Something whipped past him, and he faintly made out Serloff's ship, with Doyle blasting at the Russian.

For ten seconds, he kept his eyes closed. Then sensing that the heat was gone, he opened them and saw Croydon Airport beneath him, brightly lit. Men were running frantically about the great terminal, and the blazing wreckage of two planes lay upon the field.

Doyle was circling down, one hand before his eyes. The Northrop had disappeared, and the terrible white arc had dimmed. A searchlight, until then a pale luminance in the glare, swung toward the boiling cloud from which the weird beam came. Instantly the arc blazed forth with a new fury.

Like a colossal, flaming sword it whirled down and across the field. The searchlight truck went up in a blast of exploded gasoline, and a trail of flame on the ground marked the path of the swift-moving arc.

Knight fell over the stick, gasping for breath as the heat wilted his strength. With a desperate effort, he turned the Spitfire away, reached up and pushed the enclosure partly open. The cool air struck in at him, drove the numbness from his brain. He was lowering the wheels, gliding toward the far end of the airport, when the fire-beam suddenly lanced in his direction.

He rammed the throttle full open, and the Spitfire's wild lunge hurled him back into his seat. The needle shot past the three hundred mark, but in despair he saw that the flaming arc was closing the gap. Once again, the scorching heat seemed about to engulf him. The roaring rose once more above the Merlin's thunder, and for one horrible instant he gave himself up for lost.

Then the arc flicked back toward Croydon.

Dazed, Knight stared over his shoulder and saw what had saved his life. Pom-pom and machine-gunners were firing into the clouds near the mystery-beam. As the blazing arc swept back at them, all but one crew fled. There was a blinding flash—and the pom-pom truck was a mass of flame. Then as suddenly as it had appeared the great arc vanished.

One second it was streaking across the field; the next there was only a weird, whitish smoke in the sky. In a moment this dissolved, and only the chaos below remained to prove that the arc had ever existed.

Knight landed by the glare from one of the burning trucks. Doyle's ship was already on the ground, surrounded by a dozen men. As Knight switched off his engine and shakily crawled from the cockpit, Haldane came running over, pale as death.

"Dick! What in heaven's name was it?" he moaned.

"Don't know," Knight mumbled. "Tried to see—but the light blinded me."

"Thank the Lord you and Doyle didn't get—" Haldane's eyes rested on the smoldering wreckage of the two Hurricanes which had fallen onto the field. "Poor devils! And *I* sent them up there—*I* killed them!"

Knight put his hand on the Englishman's shoulder.

"No, Pete," he said grimly. "It wasn't you—it was the fiend who invented that damned thing."

"But I was warned. I thought this way we'd learn the secret." Haldane's tortured glance jerked away from the burned planes and the still flaming gun and searchlight trucks. "Come inside—and bring Doyle with you. Maybe you can help, some way."

**A MINUTE** later, when the Intelligence captain had restored a semblance of order among his men, Knight and Doyle followed him into an isolated office.

"And you couldn't see anything, either?" Haldane said to Doyle.

"Did you try looking straight at that blaze?" Doyle said bluntly.

Haldane nodded helplessly. "I know. But I thought perhaps when it shifted away—"

"Even then, it still blinds you," said Doyle. "You can't see anything for half a minute afterwards."

"It's obvious now why Serloff was wearing those black goggles," interrupted Knight. "They weren't just a disguise, as I thought at first."

Haldane reached into his pocket and brought out the black glasses. He held them up to the light, handed them to Knight.

"Almost opaque," muttered the secret agent. "Now if I'd have had these, maybe I'd have learned something."

The Intelligence captain pressed a button, and in a moment a young R.A.F. lieutenant entered. He had a sick look.

"What's the latest?" said Haldane.

"Only two of the flight escaped," said the lieutenant huskily. "And at least thirty-five ground men were killed. Eleven others have been taken to hospitals. Most of them are burned so badly they can't live."

For a moment, Haldane was speechless. Then like a man grasping at a straw he said, "This may help us." And he gave the young pilot the black glasses. "See if you can find any dark glass like this. If you can, get some glass-cutters and have two or three men cut sections to cement in behind the lenses of regular goggles. Do this as quick as you can."

The lieutenant hurried out. Haldane closed the door, filled his pipe with unsteady fingers.

"I'm going to give you the whole story and see what you make of it. The first inkling we had was when our agents in Germany reported something odd going on near St. Wendel. An observation squadron and a fighter outfit were moving into a war base near there. Since that's not far from the French border, we began to worry, what with this mid-Europe crisis and all. Then we also got wind of a peculiar letter received by the French War Ministry. It was posted in Paris, and it said a demonstration of a device for control of the air would be given at Brumath in twenty-four hours. Price of the device and all equipment would be one hundred million francs—payable in jewels and gold, to be delivered at an assigned spot, at sea."

"One hundred million francs!" whistled Doyle. "Whoever they are, they're not pikers."

Haldane shook his head.

"The secret of what we saw tonight is worth ten times that—if we could get it exclusively. It would mean exactly what was promised—control of the air. But the French thought some crackbrain was back of it, and ignored the whole thing. That night, a mechanized battalion on the road near Brumath was practically destroyed. Only five men survived, and three of them were stark mad. All the others could say was that 'fire had come out of the sky'."

"And St. Wendel?" queried Knight quickly.

"The same thing happened to the Nazi squadrons," replied Haldane. "Apparently they'd had a similar letter, but took it more seriously. They lost all but seven pilots and four observers, according to our secret reports. The Germans have clamped down the lid on the story—as have the French. Paris is obviously trying to make a deal with the owners of the secret, but they won't tell us a word.

"Just one day after the Brumath affair, we received a letter similar to the French one, mailed in London. It also said that after the demonstration—at Croydon—negotiations would be made through a certain British Intelligence officer. I made a thorough check, but could find no one who knew anything about it."

"Naturally," said Knight. "Since you were the one."

"What?" said Haldane, startled. A flush came into his cheeks. "See here, Dick—"

"Serloff meant to kidnap you, force you to act as intermediary," Knight cut in. "He expected to use the Miles Peregrine and trick you into it. When that slipped up, he tried that stunt with the Northrop."

"You're right!" exclaimed the Englishman. "With all this horrible business, I'd almost forgotten about that. Serloff links the thing definitely with the Soviet, of course."

"I don't know," Knight said slowly. "The Soviet could use the money, of course—but they'd never consider selling a secret like that. I've a hunch there's something else. And by the way, how long before that flaming arc appeared did you hear the roaring sound?"

"About twenty seconds. Why?"

"I'm wondering why it was so long between the first roar and the appearance of the flame. Did you have sound-rangers listening?"

"At a dozen points. Nothing was heard but our own ships—until the roaring started. But what have you got in mind?"

**BEFORE KNIGHT** could answer, there came a rap at the door. Haldane admitted an airport attendant, took a sealed envelope from his hand. He tore it open, glanced at the contents, then turned to Knight.

"This is for you, Dick. Sorry, but I've been instructed to examine every radio coming here that might be a code—and this is obviously in cipher."

Knight ran his eyes swiftly over the words. There was no change in his expression when he looked up.

"Pete, can you let us have a two-seater? I'll sign an official voucher to cover you."

"What's back of this?" demanded Haldane.

"I don't know," said Knight. "Doyle and I have been instructed to be at a certain place. And now that the Northrop is gone, we've got to have a ship."

"Is it connected with this other business?" Haldane persisted.

Knight hesitated.

"It may be. But nothing is explained—only directions for this contact."

Haldane stared at the code message in Knight's hand.

"I'll give you a ship on one condition: That if you get any clue to the secret, you'll flash word to me."

"If you were in my place, would you bind your government to such an agreement, not knowing the situation?" Knight asked quietly.

The Englishman's pale face flushed.

"Sorry, Dick—this thing has made me desperate. I'll arrange for a plane. The best I can do is a Fairey Monofox. We've taken one of the models designed for Belgium and converted it into a two-seater. She does about 240 at 14,000 feet. But her range is only three hours—maybe that won't be enough?"

"That will be all right," Knight said calmly, aware of Haldane's intent gaze.

"Good," said Haldane. "I'll see that it's made ready at once." And he went out.

But just as he left, Knight had made a warning gesture, seeing that Doyle was about to speak, and the ex-Marine was now staring at him, puzzled.

"What's the matter?" whispered Doyle. "You don't think he's mixed up in this?"

"No," Knight replied in an undertone. "But the code said to let no one know where we're going. I'll explain later."

**HALDANE WAS** absent about five minutes. When he returned, he was wearing a helmet and a flying-suit. "I've been ordered to Paris," he said hurriedly. "Going to put pressure on them—see if I can get a lead to work on. Your ship will be ready in about ten minutes."

"Thanks," said Knight. And he and Doyle followed the Englishman out to the hangar where Haldane's Spitfire was idling. All the lights had been put out, and the fires were only smoldering embers. Haldane's face held an odd expression as he turned for a quick farewell.

"You'll find new goggles in the Monofox," he said almost curtly, and climbed into the Spitfire before either Doyle or Knight could answer. The fighter taxied out, roared away.

"What did he mean by that?" demanded Doyle.

Knight went over to the Fairey biplane, where mechanics were about to start the motor. Both of the coupé tops had been opened, and hanging on each throttle was a pair of goggles with dark glass sections cemented behind the lenses.

"Fast work," Doyle grunted.

"Made 'em out of old wine bottles," vouchsafed one of the mechanics. "The curves fit almost perfect."

Knight took one pair of goggles, beckoned Doyle a little distance from the ship.

"I'd better warn you now," he said in a low tone. "Don't start shooting if you see a ship near us."

"You mean—Haldane?" blurted Doyle.

"Right. He thinks I'm holding back, and that we'll lead

him to the solution of this business. We'll have to shake him off, or he's liable to get drowned."

"Drowned? Don't tell me we're going out to sea with only three hours' gas?"

"It's nearer four. Pete was trying to figure out where we're going when he said three. But that ship of his won't be able to make it."

"Well, where in hell *are* we going?" Doyle insisted. "Or is it so secret even I'm not supposed to know?"

"We're to make contact with the *Enterprise*—and land on her flight-deck," said Knight.

"The *Enterprise?* I thought she was still on her trial runs."

"No, she finished those three weeks ago. But what she's doing over here I haven't the slightest idea. She's heading due East at Latitude 59, and she was at 11 West Longitude at six o'clock. We ought to intercept her due North of Scotland, about fifty miles from the Orkney Islands."

"That's all the message said?" Doyle asked dubiously.

"No, it also said to avoid all other planes, including American."

"The whole thing sounds screwy to me," muttered Doyle. "I only hope the *Enterprise* is where they think she is. We'll have just about twenty minutes gas left when we get out over that spot."

"Well, that's enough for a jump to the Orkneys. Come on, they're ready with the ship."

**THE HISPANO-SUIZA** "Y" motor was turning over briskly, and in a minute or two the mechanic at the controls climbed out. Knight took the front pit, gazed over the instruments, checked the controls and also the guns, two of which were mounted high in the upper wing outside the propeller arc. Doyle climbed into the rear, tilted the swivel gun aft, and closed the coupé top.

"Okay," he grunted.

Knight closed his cockpit cover, sent the Monofox trundling out into the gloom. The red embers of a wrecked

Hurricane were a gruesome reminder of the thing which had happened, and his face was hard as he lifted the roaring two-seater up into the darkness.

Few men had ever seen that granite look. Now and then, keen observers had caught the veiled steeliness behind his indolent humor. More than one foe had been dismayed to find Richard Knight a sharp blade sheathed in velvet. But no man had ever entirely lifted the mask. For Knight had played many roles, from wealthy air sportsman and Washington man-about-town, to the grim part of spy-hunter in a dozen lands and under as many names. Roles that went from the suave politeness of diplomatic intrigue, to the blood and crashing guns of deadly sky battles.

Each role had left its subtle mark, and in Knight's eyes was always the shadow of violent, sudden death. In the playing of each role he had absorbed some part, so that he was not one man but a dozen—each ready with some grim reminder that kept him forever on guard, swift hands prepared to strike first, and fast!

Five years of this life had left him keenly alert, sensitive to danger. But there was more than danger in the air tonight. His flesh crawled as into his mind there came again the horrible picture of the doomed Hawker pilots. What fiendish mind had contrived that frightful thing—that man-made lightning? And Serloff....

As though he had spoken aloud, Doyle's voice cut abruptly through the rumble of the Hispano.

"Dick, where does that devil Serloff fit in? I thought the Soviet stood him against a wall back in 1937."

"That must have been a faked report released as a counter move to stop the agents of certain interested nations from looking for him," Knight answered. "Too many countries were after Serloff. He once passed himself off as an air explorer for the U.S.S.R., and in America he fooled G-2 and the O.N.I. for a while. Then he made the mistake of killing a Naval Intelligence officer and trying to pin it on an old

Chinese in San Francisco. It just happened I knew old Mott Ling, and I couldn't believe he was a murderer. I managed to clear him and expose Serloff. Though Serloff got away, he's hated me ever since—and I might add that it's mutual."

"He's an ugly customer," said Doyle. "I'd just as soon tangle with a gorilla."

Knight suddenly looked up through the coupé top, then partly throttled the motor. Faint purplish red flashes showed above and slightly to one side.

"There's Haldane," he said quickly to Doyle. "Watch his exhaust—I'm going to try to lose him."

He opened up the motor, climbed steeply. In a few seconds they were boring into the low-hanging clouds. He changed course, flew for ten minutes due West, then climbed again. At ten thousand feet, still in clouds, he settled on a course of 318 degrees. He held this for another ten minutes, then climbed until they broke through into clear air. There was no moon, but the stars twinkled brightly.

"No sign of your Limey friend," observed Doyle.

"I guess we've shaken him," said Knight. "Break out your sextant. We'll have to do some accurate navigating to make this contact."

Doyle opened a compartment under his seat.

"I wonder what the devil they've got cooked up for us," he growled as he took out the sextant.

"In about three hours," said Knight, "we ought to know."

# CHAPTER III
## Behind the Flame

*IN A* long power glide, the Monofox droned down over the open waters of The Minch, with the ragged coast of northwest Scotland thirty miles behind. Knight shot a glance at the clock, peered down into the darkness.

"We ought to be picking up Tolsta Head, on Lewis Island," he said to Doyle.

"We're down to 500 feet," Doyle growled. "Better turn on the lights—or we're liable to pick it up with a bang."

Knight grinned, switched on the landing-lights. At first, only the gloomy sea was visible. Then a dark headland appeared, well on the left.

"That must be Tolsta," he said. "We're just about on course. We ought to meet the *Enterprise* in about twenty minutes at this speed."

He turned off the light, started to climb. Then Doyle gave a sudden exclamation: "Look—over to the northeast! A light just flashed on. That must be the carrier."

"If it is, she's not where the code said she'd be." Knight watched the light blink on and off, then bent over the radio switch. As he plugged in the phones, he caught the end of a message in some unfamiliar code. He waited, but it was not repeated. He shifted the dial, but nothing came in on the other frequencies. The light was flashing again, as he cut off the receiver.

"Why don't you give the *Enterprise* a call?" queried Doyle.

"Too risky," said Knight. "I doubt if they'd answer, anyway, after all the trouble they've taken to keep this under cover."

He banked toward the blinking light, climbing at almost full motor.

"Can't be more than twenty-five miles away," he told Doyle. "We've enough gas for a look, anyway."

"Yeah," said Doyle. "And it'd be embarrassing to skip it—and then find later it was the carrier after all."

The Monofox had covered about half the distance when the light stopped blinking and burned steadily. Almost on the instant, a sinister roar rose above the Hispano's rumble, then a blinding white flame split the sky.

For a second, Knight thought they had been trapped. But as he whirled the Monofox around he saw that the blazing white arc was not directed at them. Like a colossal flaming blade, it was sweeping down at a freighter abruptly revealed in the glare.

Knight snatched at his special goggles, fastened them in place. The dazzling light was at once dimmed, and through the ovals of black glass he saw a startling sight.

A gigantic flying-boat was plunging down toward the freighter. And fully a hundred feet beneath it was the deadly flaming arc, apparently with nothing to connect them.

"That's no European ship!" bellowed Doyle. "It's one of those new Boeing 314s!"

Knight had already recognized the outlines of the huge trans-Atlantic skyliner, but the horror of the scene for the moment blotted out this new puzzle. On the deck of the freighter, frantic figures were now visible. He saw a dozen men leap into the sea, but their frenzied attempts to escape were in vain. With a jerk, the swordlike flame whipped over the freighter's deck, and on into the water.

Fire and steam whirled up, half hiding the stricken vessel. The huge Boeing circled, and now through the black glasses Knight dimly made out some kind of nozzle protruding through a trap in the aft-section of the flying-boat's hull. As the nozzle turned, the flaming arc changed direction also, and then he realized that a stream of chemicals, almost invisible, led to that deadly curved beam.

By now, the freighter was on fire from bow to stern, and a pool of flame surrounded it. There was no trace of the men who had jumped overboard. Knight had swung into a circle, in the shadowy edge of the lighted area. He was banking swiftly, to escape before the Boeing crew could spot the two-seater, when two thin, fiery lines drilled into the ship's left wing.

Doyle's rear-pit gun clattered furiously as Knight flung clear of the burst. A wing reflected in the glare, and with a start Knight saw the Northrop, with Serloff still at its controls, diving to get under their blind spot. He rammed the nose down, tripped the wing-guns. The Northrop's rear cockpit-enclosure vanished under the burst, but Serloff whirled away before Knight could shift his tracers.

The Northrop's lights went on blinking—faint spots seen through Knight's black glasses. With a sudden presentiment, he hurled the two-seater aside. The flaming arc lifted viciously, shot through the space where the Monofox had been. But before it could cut them off, Knight dived after the Northrop. If they could keep close enough to Serloff, they might escape that frightful blazing death.

The Northrop's lights went out, and Serloff whipped off to the right to shake off the Monofox. Doyle threw a quick blast after him.

"Hold it!" shouted Knight. "If we finish him, they'll get us with the arc!"

**AS THOUGH** he abruptly realized this situation, Serloff shot into a tight turn, charging back at the British ship. Knight kicked away, darting from side to side in the desperate attempt to evade Serloff's furious bursts. The Boeing 314 was trying to close in from the east. The fiery arc had diminished until there was only a sputtering blaze, about fifty feet from the projector-nozzle.

Knight shoved up the black goggles in order to see in the resulting semidarkness.

Then the top of the Boeing's entrance-hatch opened without warning and a machine-gun pounded across at the Monofox. Knight slammed the stick hard back, corkscrewed out of the cross fire from both ships. The Boeing gunner tilted his weapon, but Doyle stopped him with a savage barrage. Dropping his gun, the man tumbled back down the hatch. Knight spun the two seater at the top of its zoom, pitched back with all four guns throbbing. Over the pointed nose of the Monofox he saw his tracers rip into the Boeing's hull. He pressed the rudder, sent the torrent of smoking lead straight for the airliner's bridge.

The snout of a sub-machine gun poked through one of the cabin windows, and a hail of cupro-slugs tore through the two-seater's lower wing. Knight ruddered back, drove a murderous answer through the side of the airliner. The sub-machine gun ceased to spout, but another man snatched it up. And simultaneously Serloff charged in, with the Northrop's wing-root fifties fiercely grinding.

Almost boxed, Knight booted the tail around to give Doyle a chance at Serloff. As the nose lunged past the bridge of the Boeing, he cut loose again at the pilots. Three gunners were now blasting at the British ship. He crouched as one burst of tracers smoked overhead and across the cowl. He was almost on top of the Boeing now. Over the cowl, he saw his bullets crash into the airliner's bridge. The huge ship swerved, and he had to skid madly to avert collision.

The skid dropped him below the giant Boeing. In a flash the death-dealing nozzle jerked toward the Monofox. He jammed the stick to the instrument board, and for one frozen instant his heart stood still.

A hideous, white flame shot through the sky—but his frenzied plunge had been too swift for the man at the nozzle to follow. Before they could swing the torrent of fire, the two-seater was a mile underneath and safely out of range.

Knight pulled up, drew a shuddering breath. When he looked over his shoulder, Doyle gave him a ghastly grin.

"I thought it was curtains that time!"

"So did I," Knight said hoarsely. He started to draw the black goggles back over his eyes, but the white flame died out abruptly. Only the lurid glow from the blazing freighter remained to light the darkness, and it was now at least ten miles distant.

The giant Boeing was speeding eastward, almost swallowed up in the shadows. Knight swiftly started after it, checked its course as 85.

"Look out!" Doyle suddenly yelled. "There's Serloff!"

The Northrop plunged from the gloom, and livid streaks stabbed from its cowl-guns. Knight renversed and the other ship overshot. In a twinkling, Knight was diving on the spy. As Serloff pulled out, a blast from the Monofox's wing-guns pounded the Northrop's tail. The stolen ship lurched, but Serloff regained control and plunged toward the sea. Knight lost him in the darkness, spent a minute hurriedly searching before he started to climb.

"That's not the course to the *Enterprise!*" Doyle howled.

"I'm going after that Boeing," Knight retorted grimly.

"Are you crazy?" Doyle shouted. "We just got away by the skin of our teeth as it was."

"We won't get that close again," Knight replied. "But we've got to find out what's up. It's obvious now that the *Enterprise* business has something to do with the Boeing."

"But how did Serloff's mob ever get hold of that ship in the first place?" demanded the other man.

"Your guess is as good as mine," said Knight, probing the gloom with anxious eyes as he swung the Monofox eastward. "But we've half an hour's gas left, and if they're hiding that ship where I think they are, we may be able to find it."

Doyle bent over a map, switched on a tiny shielded lamp. "This course leads straight to Leningrad! A fat chance we've got of going there in half an hour."

"Even so, I believe Serloff is carefully avoiding Russia," said Knight. "Did you notice the flag on that freighter?"

"No. What was it?"

"Soviet. I think Serloff and his friends are playing a lone hand."

The Hispano began to sputter. Knight switched to the reserve tank, breathed a little freer when the engine picked up again.

"What about the *Enterprise?*" Doyle said uneasily. "We'd better flash her a warning about this—just in case."

"I thought of that," said Knight. "Unfortunately, a few of Serloff's bullets went through the radio."

"That's swell," Doyle said gloomily. "I was just thinking maybe they'd send a couple of squadrons to help us."

"At the worst," Knight reassured him, "we can stall in on one of the inhabited islands and then get word over to the mainland for them to relay to Haldane."

**DOYLE LAPSED** into silence and for the next twenty minutes Knight held the course, keeping the Monofox at an altitude of five thousand feet.

"We've got about ten minutes to find one of those inhabited islands of yours," Doyle finally observed morosely. "Right now, I wouldn't care if there wasn't even an ant-hill on it—just so it was land,"

Knight stared down anxiously into the dark. "We must be over the coast by now. I guess we'll have to give up the other idea—I was hoping we'd spot the Boeing by its exhaust flashes."

He started a power glide, released a flare at three thousand feet. A rugged cliff, with waves breaking at the base, showed directly beneath. Piles of rock extended eastward, sloping onto flat, barren ground. To the south was another island, separated by a narrow firth.

"We're farther north than I thought," muttered Knight. "I'm going to climb up and drop the other flare. We might see another island within gliding distance. This one obviously is uninhabited."

He eased the throttle open, climbing southward, but keeping the barren stretch in gliding range. The Monofox, built for fast climbing, was at six thousand feet in less than a minute. He was about to release the other flare when a huge wing slid into view a thousand feet below and to the north. It was the Boeing 314!

The giant airliner was gliding toward a long, narrow inlet

which pierced the western cliffs and which curved slightly so that most of its surface was hidden from anyone at sea. Apparently the crew had not seen the Monofox.

"They must think Serloff dropped the flare!" exclaimed Knight. "I believe we've found their hide-out!"

He turned, still climbing, and watched the Boeing swing out to sea to approach for a landing. Then without the slightest warning, the stolen Northrop pitched headlong out of the blackness above.

Knight's only warning was the first flash of Serloff's tracers past the nose of the Monofox. He jammed the rudder hard to the left, and the blasting fire of the Northrop's guns whipped off through space, missing them by inches. Doyle was already clawing at the rear pit gun, trying to train it on the diving ship. Serloff made a desperate effort to rake the Monofox before he overshot, then hurtled past, twisting away toward the shadows. Knight rammed the nose down, tripped a long burst at the fleeing Russian. But the Northrop was out of range before he could score a hit.

The Boeing's landing lights had been turned on, but as Serloff attacked the British ship, the twin beams lanced upward and away from the inlet. Knight kept the two-seater in its plunge, with the throttle wide open. Wings screeching, the Monofox drilled down the flare-lit sky, and the broad hull of the airliner swam under his guns. He cut loose with all four, and in a surge of exultation saw his tracers smoke into the huge tail-group.

If he could only wreck the controls.

Then from somewhere down by the inlet, a machine-gun blazed into action. Knight set his jaw, hurled the Monofox through the thin ribbons of fire which lanced up through the wings. A hundred yards from the first gun, another one started to fire. Doyle swiveled his weapon, poured a furious barrage down at the nearest gunner. But in the same moment, sub-machine guns blasted from one of the Boeing's windows and a trap in the top of the bridge.

For a last tense moment, Knight held to his suicide dive, with bullets gouging and smoking through the biplane's wings. Then with a final burst, aimed straight at the bridge, he hauled the stick back. Tracers sparkling on all sides, the Monofox screamed back up into the night. It was a thousand feet above the Boeing when a parachute flare blossomed still higher and left them starkly revealed.

Knight whirled to one side, expecting instant attack from Serloff. But to his astonishment a Spitfire came streaking down under the torch.

"Hell's bells!" shouted Doyle. "It's Haldane!"

**THE ENGLISHMAN'S** ship flashed past them, guns spurting at the airliner. The Boeing was now climbing at full speed, trying to escape from the lighted space. Haldane's bullets stabbed through the tangle of tracers from below, struck near one engine. Smoke suddenly poured from the nacelle, and the monster ship nosed down.

But before Haldane could re-align his guns. Serloff charged furiously to the defense. Knight, already diving back to aid Haldane, ruddered to catch Serloff in his sights.

The Hispano's deafening roar broke sharply. Knight groaned as the fast-diving ship sucked the last drop of gas through the engine. If he had had only one more minute....

But the prop was still turning—his guns could still be fired! He tripped the cowl-Vickers, stood the ship on its nose. Serloff was too far away—but the Boeing was now squarely beneath him. Through the shriek of the wings he thought he heard Doyle bellow something, but there was no time to look back. His taut fingers flipped the gun-control switch, and the wing-mount Vickers joined in with a throbbing snarl. Over the wing of the Boeing whirled the smoking torrent, as Knight made one last try at the man who held the controls.

With a muffled pounding, bright bullet tracks ripped into the cowling before him. Instinctively, he booted the rudder—and the lethal charge of his guns spent itself in thin air. As he pulled up, with the ragged top of the cliff two hundred feet below, he saw a machine-gun nest which had been concealed among the rocks. It was this which had wrecked his last chance to destroy the giant Boeing.

He also saw that Serloff and Haldane were battling fiercely two thousand feet above. But now he had to point the Monofox toward the level ground. The riddled ship dropped swiftly, and he shouted a hasty warning to Doyle as the ground leaped up. The wheels hit, and the landing-gear crunched ominously. But it held and they came to a bumpy stop.

"I tried to warn you about that gun," Doyle said unhappily.

"I know—I shouldn't have tried that last dive," Knight told him. "But I thought if we got the Boeing, we'd have only Serloff and a few of his cutthroats to deal with."

He took a hurried look about him as he climbed out. The only thing which broke the barren expanse to the east was an ancient-looking round tower, a hundred yards away, with what appeared to be a pit beside it. The tower was about sixty feet in diameter, made of roughly shaped stone, and was not more than twenty feet high. The flare which Haldane had dropped still brightly lit the scene, but he could find no break in the precipitous rocks behind the stone tower. Apparently there was no path leading to the shore of the inlet.

He turned and followed Doyle's gaze toward the fight between Serloff and Haldane. The two ships were in a fast-tightening circle, each man's guns just missing the other's tail.

"Burn him down, Limey!" yelled Doyle.

Knight stood with his fingernails digging into his palms as the two ships thundered overhead. For an instant he thought Haldane had won—for the Spitfire's tracers seemed to be shooting straight into Serloff's cockpit. But with a furious twist the Russian dodged out of that fateful blast, and before Haldane could turn back, the Northrop's guns were raking him from one side. A puff of oily smoke whipped from the Spitfire's cowl. It spread into a black pall, then a tumbling figure appeared. Hardly a second after Haldane jumped, a plume of fire shot through the smoke, and the Spitfire dived earthward in a mass of flame.

Above the plummeting ship, Haldane's parachute bloomed whitely. The Northrop swung in toward it.

"That damned fiend is going to drill him!" groaned Doyle.

"No," said Knight. "He's forcing him to slip the chute so he'll land over this way."

Then the implication of his own words hit him with sudden force. He spun around, then froze in consternation. He was staring into the muzzle of a sub-machine gun!

# CHAPTER IV
## Traitor Crew

**F**IVE MEN, four of them armed with pistols, had stolen up behind them, and two more were running from the direction of the pit by the round tower. The leader, a squat, black-browed figure, held the machine-gun ominously poised as Knight whirled.

At Knight's startled exclamation, Doyle also turned, his hand jerking toward his coat. The muzzle of the machine-gun twitched toward him, and the man behind it cursed him in Russian. Doyle sullenly lifted his hands in disgust.

*"Ne dvee'gatsa!"* snarled the Russian, glaring from him to Knight.

Knight had no intention of moving. But he let a blank look come into his face to convince the man he did not understand the language.

*"Peestale't!"* the Russian snapped, looking hard at Knight. *"Dah'ite mne."*

The secret agent made no move to surrender his gun, and the leader growled a command to his men. The two Americans were seized and quickly disarmed. While their pockets were being searched, the two who had arrived last were sent out to capture Haldane. The Englishman was within three hundred feet of the ground, and Serloff was leveling off to land.

Haldane dropped to the ground not far from the round tower. His chute started to drag him, then collapsed at the rim of the pit. Before the Englishman could get to his feet, the two Russians were on him. Meantime, the Northrop had rolled to a stop near the Monofox. Serloff cut off the motor, swung his huge body to the ground, and strode toward the two Americans and their guards. There was a murderous snarl on his face, and the man with the machine-gun hopefully lifted his weapon.

"Not now," Serloff said harshly in Russian. "Unfortunately, I have need of them."

"They have been searched," said the other man. "This may have some importance."

He held out the code message which had been taken from Knight, Serloff scowled at the words, turned and thrust the message under Knight's nose.

"What does it say?" he grated.

"Sorry," said Knight, "I left my code-book at home and I can't remember a thing."

The blood rushed into Serloff's dark face. He made a motion as though to snatch out his gun, then his lips twisted into a sneer.

"I'll find a way to refresh your memory. But first we'll see what the Englishman has to say."

Haldane's captors marched him up before the big Russian, arms twisted behind his back. Serloff's ugly grin deepened.

"So you decided to accept my invitation after all. If you had climbed into that Northrop, you would have saved yourself a lot of trouble."

"But I wouldn't have had my chance to kill you," Haldane said coolly. "Too bad I muffed it."

"You won't have another, I promise you that!" Serloff glared from him to Knight and Doyle. "I'll not waste words with you. You've seen a demonstration of what I have to sell. Whether you live or not depends on how much your governments offer me. So far, Hitler is the highest bidder—but he is trying to trick me, and I hate the Nazis, anyway."

He paused a moment, then went on: "For ten million dollars I will deliver the Boeing and the liquid-fire projector, together with the formula for the chemicals used."

Haldane's eyes narrowed.

"What proof can I give my government that you will live up to such an agreement?"

"My terms will cover that," Serloff retorted sharply. "You agree, then, to act as intermediary?"

"He'll only trick you, Pete!" Knight broke in.

"Hold your tongue!" snarled Serloff, and two of the Russians viciously jabbed Knight with their pistols.

"I agree to act as agent," Haldane muttered, "on condition you prove your statements." He met Knight's eyes, flushed. "This is no time for personal feelings—I've got to think of England alone. With that weapon in our hands, we could force Hitler to back down on all his demands. The crisis in Central Europe may lead to war at any moment—and we're sure to be drawn in. But with that ship, we could either block the war—or win it quickly."

"You are a sensible man," Serloff said in a jeering tone. He fixed his dark eyes on Knight. "Perhaps the United States would like to offer a higher price?"

"Where did you get that Boeing?" Knight said bluntly.

"We borrowed it," Serloff mocked him. "It was the only way, after my men learned that the big Douglas and the Martin our high minded comrades bought could not lift the equipment. So we planted a few men at the factory, and three of them were on board when the ship made its test-flight. There was a little argument—but it did not last long. So now, Mr. Knight, you know the story of the vanished airliner."

"I didn't even know it was missing," said Knight. "And I'm not an agent for any dirty deal with you."

Serloff was holding his temper by an obvious effort. "Don't lie to me!" he rasped. "I know you're the senior secret agent of the United States. You were sent to try to recover the plane—or buy it back."

Knight masked his satisfaction at learning that Serloff knew nothing of the *Enterprise*. But Doyle gave him a side glance which the big Russian caught.

"So there *is* something I have not learned!" he said shrewdly. He stared at the code message again, then deliberately drew the pistol with which he had killed the British constable. Knight stiffened as Serloff's sardonic gaze went from him to Doyle.

"I have already heard of this Damon and Pythias friendship," Serloff said with a curl of his lip. "It would be unfortunate if I had to end it."

He raised the gun, took cool aim at Doyle.

"Wait!" Knight said hastily. "What is it you want?"

"The truth!" snarled the Russian. "What were you doing in London? What does this code message say?"

"I was trying to find you," Knight lied grimly. "Our attaches lost your trail in Paris, and I was told to look for you in England. The message is an order to return to Paris and cooperate with the French Second Bureau. Evidently my superiors thought you had returned to France."

"How did you manage to follow me from Croydon?" Serloff shot at him.

Haldane spoke before Knight could open his mouth.

"I arranged that. Sound-rangers plotted your course from Croydon and relayed it to us by radio. If you had been really clever, you would have avoided flying a straight line."

"I think you're both lying," Serloff said furiously. He wheeled to the leader of the armed group. "Take the prisoners down below. I'll soon get the truth out of them."

**KNIGHT AND** the others were herded toward the old round tower. As they neared the pit, Knight saw an opening which led into the base of the tower. One of the Russians switched on a flashlight and illuminated a dank, subterranean room, from which steps led down to a larger room at a lower level.

"I thought as much when I saw the *broch* tower," Haldane muttered to Knight. "This is a *weem*—one of the underground shelters built here in ancient times."

"I wish we'd known about it," Knight said glumly. "We might have arranged matters so we wouldn't have been captured so easily."

One of their captors swore at him in Russian, and made an angry gesture for him to keep still.

"Let the fools talk," Serloff interrupted in the same

language. "The looser their tongues, the better chance I have of learning what I want."

There were two more levels before they reached the shore of the inlet. The last tier of the underground rooms had been converted into quarters for Serloff's men. A number of bunks, obviously removed from a ship, lined the walls of two rooms, and a third had been equipped with tables and benches from a galley. Supplies, blankets, and miscellaneous equipment were strewn around in varying degrees of disorder.

There was no one in the rooms, but as the prisoners were marched out onto the beach Knight saw at least twenty men working feverishly about the big Boeing, which had been taxied up close to the shore. A portable floodlight revealed three hoses which ran along a crude pontoon bridge to the hull of the airliner. One hose was connected with an ordinary fuel pump and gasoline drums. The others were painted red and blue, and were connected with two large tanks, similarly painted and separated by a distance of a hundred feet. Mechanics were working on the engine which had caught fire.

Serloff looked startled as he saw the frenzy of activity. He stopped short, sent a bellow toward a blue-uniformed figure by the side hatch.

"Borzna! What's the meaning of this?"

The other man hurried ashore, his broad face damp with perspiration. He shot a look at the prisoners, spoke in hasty Russian.

"We must take off at once! An American aircraft carrier is steaming directly this way!"

Serloff turned white. "Impossible! How could they know?"

"One of the men they caught at Seattle must have betrayed us. The carrier is holding a course directly for this island."

"Then why didn't you attack?" raged Serloff.

"We used the rest of the chemicals on the freighter," Borzna retorted. "I told you we should have filled the tanks."

"When did you see the carrier?" Serloff demanded. "How far out was it?"

"She is about a hundred miles from here," Borzna said nervously. "We made an error in estimating the wind and were too far at sea when we first looked for the freighter. Then suddenly the carrier's lights were turned on, illuminating her deck. She was about thirty miles west of us at that time. They must have heard our motors, even though they were muffled; I think they were about to send off some planes—"

"No!" snarled Serloff. "They were expecting these two!" He flung a murderous look at Knight and Doyle. "I see the whole thing now. We found a code message on the man Knight. It was from either the carrier or some official in Washington, ordering them to meet the vessel and help recover the Boeing. I'll make him regret—"

"We've no time to waste on him now," Borzna broke in. "Why not shoot all of them and be rid of them?"

"You fool, they're the intermediaries I've been trying to get! The Englishman has already agreed to arrange terms with his government."

"If that carrier isn't destroyed quickly, the Americans will be setting the terms—with bullets!"

"We've still enough time," snapped the beak-nosed Russian. "But wait, what about Karnsky?"

**AT THIS** question, Borzna brought his voice to a whisper. "He still believes the Soviet is at war," he said, with a glance over his shoulder at the Boeing. "I decoyed him up to the bridge while we got rid of the freighter, and he thinks it was one of the Soviet's 'enemies'."

"After we finish the carrier, I'll get the formula out of him if I have to kill him," muttered Serloff.

"Be careful," warned Borzna. "He's a true fanatic. He'd die before he'd talk—if he ever guessed the truth."

"I'll handle him carefully," promised Serloff. He turned to the men who were guarding the prisoners. "Take them back to the middle tier rooms—no, put them on board, in the tail compartment, and tie them up securely."

"Why not leave them here?" Borzna said quickly.

"Because I don't intend to lose them," Serloff grated. He looked significantly toward the listening guards, then finished his explanation in French. "Suppose some of the American pilots take off before we strike at the carrier, and bomb this place?"

Borzna's face began to perspire again.

"We had better hurry. We have enough fuel and chemicals on board now."

"Very well," said Serloff. "Have the hose-lines brought ashore, then send some men to refuel that British plane the Americans flew. They can siphon some petrol from the Northrop's tanks—there is enough for both."

"We need no escort," said Borzna.

"No, but if the Americans on the carrier are expecting a Northrop, they are more likely to light their deck when they hear its motor. They will be doubly on their guard after having heard your motors and not having seen any plane."

The conversation had been in Russian, except for the few words in French with which Serloff had avoided alarming his guards. Knight had kept his face expressionless, hoping for some bit of information which might be of aid later. It was clear now that neither suspected he knew the language. With a curt nod, Serloff motioned Borzna to carry out his orders, then wheeled savagely to Knight.

"So the code message was an order sending you to Paris?" he said harshly, in English.

"That's right," Knight said shortly.

"You lie!" snarled Serloff. "I know all about the aircraft carrier."

Doyle's start was sufficient answer to his charge. Serloff's smoldering eyes darted from Doyle back to the senior agent.

"I'll give you one chance. If you fail, I'll have both of you burned alive!"

# CHAPTER V
## Karnsky

**K**NIGHT WAITED, dry-lipped. Serloff, after a brief hesitation, gruffly ordered Doyle and Haldane taken aboard the Boeing. As soon as they were out of earshot, he turned back to Knight.

"America is a rich nation—much richer than England. What do you offer?"

"I've no authority to deal with you," Knight muttered.

The Russian's dark eyes blazed.

"Do you take me for a child? Your country can't afford to have that Boeing discovered over here—much less mixed up in attacks on other nations. After putting out that story of the plane having been lost at sea, it would be an international scandal."

Knight stared at him a moment.

"If you'll agree not to destroy the carrier, I'll send a message to Washington."

Serloff laughed sarcastically.

"And warn the carrier crew while you're doing it—so we'd have gunners with black glasses firing on us."

He turned, snapped an order to the guards.

"Wait," Knight said desperately, "you can't kill all those men! You'll only inflame the United States—defeat your own purpose!"

"They'll listen more carefully," retorted Serloff, "when they hear you describe how I destroyed one of their prize vessels."

Knight was dragged away before he could say another word. Two of the Russians hustled him along the pontoon-bridge to a floating platform, from which a gangway led up to the hatch in the top of the hull. He could see numerous bullet-holes in the dural, where the guns of the Monofox had connected. But he paid scant attention to these. For the first time, he was close enough to see the deadly flame projector, and he made a hasty survey as he was marched up the gangway.

The trap through which the projector had appeared was now closed, but the device itself was still visible, linked with the interior by two large flexible-metal tubes. These were connected with the projector itself, which he saw was not one but two nozzles, rigidly secured to maintain the correct angle between them. It was evident that the two streams of chemicals ignited by spontaneous combustion when they met, at a safe distance from the hull. Cables running through watertight plugs were fastened to the projector so that it could be pointed in various directions, or drawn up under the tail, as it was now. Braided copper wires linked the tips of the projector nozzles, and connected with another thick wire leading inside the hull. Knight surmised that this was to ground the nozzles and discharge any static caused by the swift flow of chemicals.

Inside the hatchway there was blood on the stairs, a grim reminder of the battle they had fought. As the guards pushed him down the ladder, a fierce, high-pitched voice sounded and he saw a strange figure confronting Doyle and his captors. At first, he thought it was an old man, for his head was totally bald and there were dark splotches on his face. His bent shoulders added to the appearance of age, but as he came closer Knight saw that the splotches were burns from chemicals, and that his eyes held a vigorous flame.

"Prisoners!" he cried shrilly. "The fools! What do they want of prisoners! Take them ashore and shoot them!"

"But, Comrade Karnsky," one of the men said uneasily, "it is Agent Serloff's order. I think these men have some secret information he wishes to get."

"But why bring them on board?" insisted Karnsky. "He can attend to them ashore."

Two of the guards exchanged surreptitious glances.

"I don't know, Comrade," said one of them. "But it was the order. All three are to be tied up in the tail compartment."

Karnsky's eyes narrowed in a look of suspicion. "There is something being kept from me! I can see it in your faces."

"No, Comrade—we know nothing." One of the guards shoved Doyle past, and Knight was hurried into the passage. He had a lightning glimpse of a huge compartment, made by the removal of a partition. Four large tanks, two red, and two of them blue, were connected through valves to the flexible tubes of the projector. Beyond was a board with gauges and several instruments, but he was given no time for a second glance. The two men who held his arms gave him a push and he sprawled headlong on the floor of the de luxe compartment just forward of the tail-planes.

**ONE OF** the men went out, returned with coils of rope, and in a few minutes the three prisoners were tightly and separately bound. The door slammed, a key grated, and they were left alone. Haldane twisted his head around, looked wryly at Knight.

"Too bad we didn't combine forces, old man. We might have done better than this."

"I didn't know anything about this place," Knight said dispiritedly. "We had orders to meet the *Enterprise,* and that's all."

"Thank the Lord we didn't!" Doyle said, and for a moment there was a grim silence.

"There must be some way," Knight said huskily. "We can't let Serloff burn those poor devils like rats."

He tugged at his bonds, but the tight-drawn ropes only cut-deeper into his arms and legs. Doyle and Haldane, after similar attempts, gave up hopelessly.

After a minute's silence, the Englishman looked uncertainly at Knight. "There's a chance we might buy off that devil, if we combined on an offer."

"That wouldn't stop him from burning the carrier," Knight muttered. "You couldn't trust him no matter what he said. It's pretty clear that he's double-crossed the Soviet."

"I guessed that much," Haldane agreed. "The freighter

must have been the ship which brought their supplies here. I'd say that the Soviet was planning a few tests of this fire-projector and didn't want it linked with them officially. That would explain their picking this out-of-the-way base."

"Either that, or else Serloff picked it himself," said Knight. "I've an idea that the Soviet intended him to work from the freighter, using it as a tender from some spot well off the ship-lanes. He probably found which men would go in with him on this deal, and tricked the rest of them into sailing on the freighter. That would keep the secret from getting back to Moscow, and cut down the number with whom he'd have to split when he sells the ship."

"The dirty rat will probably bump off everybody but Borzna when it comes to the split," growled Doyle. "And maybe Borzna, too. Even if we worked a deal for him, he'd finish us off after he collected."

A muted rumble sounded, as one of the Boeing's motors was started. In a few minutes all four motors were smoothly idling, still warm from the flight just ended. The eyes of the three men met as the ship began to move through the water.

"We've got to do something!" Doyle said hoarsely.

"I'm afraid we're sunk," Haldane said in a helpless voice.

Knight gazed desperately at the bulkhead separating their compartment from the one with the chemical tanks. The airliner was lifting from the waves that slapped against the hull when he suddenly jerked his head around toward Doyle and Haldane.

"Karnsky!" he exclaimed. "He's the only weak link."

"What do you mean?" said Haldane.

"Start a row with me—we're fighting over whose government is to get the secret. Doyle, you'll have to pretend to be a Nazi agent—you know a few German cusswords and you can throw them in when the thing gets hot."

"But what—?" said Haldane, bewildered.

"No time to explain!" Knight raised himself as well as he could on one elbow, shouted toward the partition. "Damn the British Government! I say the ship belongs to the United States—and that gives us first claim to the invention!"

"I've already agreed to buy the secret!" roared Haldane. "Keep out of this, Yankee—if you value your life!"

*"Gott im Himmel!"* bellowed Doyle. "Alreaddy vun million marks haff I paid this Serloff swine! Vat you tink I—"

**VOICES ABRUPTLY** sounded outside, and the door was flung open a second later. Karnsky and a scowling Russian mechanic came into the compartment, the inventor with a pistol gripped in his hand.

*"Kamerad!"* howled Doyle. "Tell these *Schweinhunds*—"

*"Malchee'te*—hold your tongue!" Karnsky said in a furious voice.

"Pay no attention to the Nazi pig!" Knight shouted in Russian. "I will pay you a million rubles extra to influence Serloff so he will sell to America instead of Germany or England!"

Karnsky's face went ashen-white.

"What—what is that you said?" he whispered.

"One million rubles!" said Knight. "All you have to do is get Serloff to take America's offer for the fire-projector and the formula. We will pay double—"

A strangling sound came from Karnsky's throat. He whirled toward the other Russian, and at the look in his eyes the mechanic turned pale, cried: "He lies, Comrade! He lies!"

"I have proof!" Knight broke in, still pretending to misunderstand Karnsky's emotion. "Sewed in the lining of my vest is authority from Washington to pay—" he stopped, a cold chill racing up his spine, as Karnsky's livid face twitched toward him. For a second he thought he had overplayed the part, that the man was going to kill him. But the gun in Karnsky's hand finally lowered.

"Untie him!" he croaked at the mechanic. "I will soon know if he lies."

"But, Comrade, shouldn't we call Agent Serloff?" moaned the other man.

*"Untie him!"* Karnsky said in a terrible voice, and the mechanic fell to his knees beside Knight, began with shaking fingers to unfasten the secret agent's bonds.

There was only one rope. It had been tied about Knight's ankles, then about his wrists, and finally looped tightly about his arms. He held his breath as the mechanic set to work. If the man untied only the upper part, then his desperate plan would fail. But the Russian, terrified by Karnsky's blazing eyes, had no thought but to obey orders in full as quickly as possible.

In a few seconds Knight's ankles were free. But he made no motion to get up, for Karnsky's gun was pointed straight at his middle. The mechanic fumbled with the knot at his wrists, finally got it loose.

As the ropes were unwound from Knight's arms, Karnsky stepped closer. The secret agent felt his heart pound as the man bent over him. And both Doyle and Haldane looked on, white faced.

"Take off your vest!" ordered the bald Russian.

Knight sat up, began to fumble with the buttons. With Karnsky's eyes glaring over the pistol at him, it was not hard to assume a look of terror to forward his plan. The man's finger was trembling on the trigger.

*"Faster!"* Karnsky raged.

"I'm hurrying," Knight cried. He jerked at the vest, tore off two buttons, and hastily pulled his right arm out of the arm-hole. At Karnsky's command, the mechanic leaned down to take the vest.

Knight reached across as though to free the other arm— then hurtled into the mechanic's legs. Knocked off balance, the man stumbled against Karnsky.

## CHAPTER VI
## *Rendezvous With Fate*

**THE REPORT** of Karnsky's gun roared in the closed compartment, and the mechanic toppled to the floor. It was only a second that the man blocked Karnsky's aim at Knight, but it was enough. Before Karnsky could fire again, Knight sprang up and seized his wrist with both hands. Karnsky jumped back, stumbled over the dead man and fell.

Knight was on him with a tigerish leap. Karnsky tried to lift the gun, but Knight's fist crashed on his jaw. The impact made a fierce smack, and Karnsky sprawled limply under the secret agent.

There was a sound of excited voices outside the door. Knight snatched up the gun, jumped to his feet. The door burst open, and two mechanics appeared. The first one had a gun in his hand. Knight whipped his own pistol down at the Russian's head, and he dropped with a muffled groan. The other man sprang back, frantically raised his hands.

"Don't kill me!" he cried. "I am unarmed!"

Knight threw a hasty look along the passage. The door at the end was closed, and apparently no one else had heard the shot.

"Untie those two men!" he rapped at the frightened mechanic. While the man obeyed, Knight picked up the weapon the other Russian had dropped, keeping watch on the passage door. In a minute both Doyle and Haldane were freed. Knight handed Doyle the other gun.

"Watch that mechanic—bring him into the projector compartment."

"What are you going to do?" exclaimed Haldane.

"Get rid of those chemicals—if possible," Knight clipped back. "Without the fire-projector, Serloff will be at the mercy of the *Enterprise* pilots."

He opened the door to the projector compartment, looked around swiftly. There were machine-guns mounted at port and starboard windows. Under them were stacked half a dozen parachutes. The water-tight hatch was still closed, but the "dogs" around the edge had been turned for opening. A map had been fastened on the instrument board, and a pointer was tracing a line with red ink. Above the board was a compass, an air-speed meter, a drift-indicator, and an altimeter.

"That cross must be the position where they estimated they'd meet the carrier!" said Haldane. "They're flying wide-open—we'll have only eighteen minutes at that speed!"

Knight wheeled to the prisoner. "If one of those main valves is opened alone, what happens?"

The man's face held a mixture of fear and hate.

"The—the fuel is blown out under pressure," he mumbled.

"Swing open the trap," commanded Knight. "Pete, be ready to open that red valve. If we empty one set of tanks, we'll draw Serloff's fangs. Doyle, watch the door—be ready to grab anybody that comes through. Don't shoot if you can help it."

The trap was speedily opened, and under the threat of Knight's gun the prisoner maneuvered the projector down from its position under the tail. As it was descending, Knight looked anxiously at the clock.

"Pete, fasten on one of those chutes. You, too, Doyle."

"What's the idea?" Doyle said, as he and Haldane obeyed.

"The carrier pilots probably have orders to shoot down the Boeing unless Serloff surrenders. We won't be able to explain—so we'd better be ready to bail out. If we have luck, the *Enterprise* will pick us up."

"Yeah—if we have luck," Doyle said gloomily. Then his eyes glinted. "Say, what's that?"

Something had flitted near the faint light from the open trap.

"It's the Spitfire!" Haldane said tautly. "Better turn out the lights—the pilot may be able to see into here."

Knight sprang to the switch, and in a moment there

was only the faint glow from the instrument-board lights. Haldane was starting to open the red valve when a buzzer sounded sharply.

"What's that?" Knight flung at the mechanic.

"The telephone to the bridge," muttered the prisoner.

Knight lifted the receiver.

"What is it?" he said in a high-pitched imitation of Karnsky's voice.

"Why have you lowered the projector?" Serloff fumed. "I told you it cuts down our speed."

"By the map, it is only fourteen minutes," Knight answered in a guttural tone.

"Five minutes would have been time enough!" Serloff hung up with a savage click, and Knight whirled to Haldane.

"Hurry up, Pete! We've got to empty those tanks!"

**HALDANE GRASPED** the red valve, gave it a turn. There was a dull hiss half-lost in the moan of the wings, and a transparent stream shot from one of the projector nozzles into the darkness. Intent on watching this, Knight almost failed to see a crawling figure emerge from the shadows. He whirled with an oath, and in the same moment Karnsky swayed to his feet and clawed at one side of the instrument board.

"Stop him!" screamed the mechanic. "He'll kill us all!"

Knight hurled himself forward. Karnsky swung around, made a frenzied leap at him. Knight jumped aside and the inventor fell to the floor. Doyle rammed his gun against the man's head, and he lay there, panting.

"What was he after?" Knight demanded of the other prisoner.

"The ground-wire to the nozzles," gasped the mechanic. "The fuel from the red tank is partly hydrogen. If the ground-wire were broken, static would set it off by a spark—we'd all be killed!"

Knight made a hasty examination, but the braided wire was still firmly grounded to the hull. Haldane had closed the valve, but now he opened it again and the hydrogen-fuel streamed down into the gloom. Both he and Doyle had put on parachutes, and while Doyle watched the two prisoners, Knight started to fasten on a harness.

But just as he was snapping the last buckle, Haldane gave a yell. "Look out, Dick! Back of you!"

Knight tried to spring aside, but the cold muzzle of a pistol rammed against the back of his neck.

"Drop that gun!" came Serloff's furious voice.

Helpless, Knight let the weapon fall. Doyle had jerked around, trying to watch the prisoners and also see the doorway. A gun roared from the direction of the doorway, and Doyle's pistol fell from his hand as a bullet creased his forearm. A man in the uniform of a freighter captain jumped past Knight, turned off the red valve, and scooped up Doyle's gun.

"Don't kill him!" ordered Serloff. "Keep him and the Englishman covered."

He stepped around Knight, keeping his gun pointed at the secret agent. "Are you hurt, Comrade Karnsky?" he said anxiously.

Karnsky slowly got to his feet, his eyes fixed on Serloff's face.

"You devil!" he cried. "You've lied to me—you've betrayed the Soviet."

Serloff started, but quickly covered his dismay.

"Are you mad?" he demanded. "I have risked my life a hundred times in the Service—no man loves the Soviet more than Vladimar Serloff!"

"But these men—I heard them fighting. The tall American said you were trying to sell the secret to our foes!"

"A trick to deceive you!" Serloff retorted. "They are enemy spies. I had them on board only so I might force them to tell how much their countries have learned about our plans."

"If I thought you were lying, I would kill you!" Karnsky said grimly.

"You can question the prisoners yourself—when we have

finished with the American airplane carrier. That should be proof in itself—would I destroy an American vessel if I were preparing to deal with them?"

The uncertainty faded from Karnsky's eyes, and Serloff turned hurriedly to the freighter captain and the mechanic.

"Lock them up in the tail compartment again. It is almost time to start the attack."

He reached up to draw a pair of black goggles down over his eyes, and Karnsky started across to switch on the compartment lights. The mechanic, armed with the gun Knight had dropped, began to herd Haldane and Doyle toward the doorway. Blood was dripping from Doyle's arm, and his face had lost its color. Knight stepped forward to help him as he stumbled to the passage door.

"Get back!" said the freighter captain. "And keep your hands up."

Knight helplessly obeyed. He was following Doyle, with the freighter captain close behind, when the Boeing abruptly nosed down. Doyle slipped and fell and Knight heard the man behind him thud against the bulkhead. By a desperate leap, he reached the machine-gun swiveled in the port window.

"Watch out—the American!" Karnsky screamed from the switchboard.

**THE MECHANIC'S** pistol roared, and a slug drilled the hull close to Knight's head. He clamped the release-catch, whipped the gun loose from its swivel. Haldane hurtled against the mechanic and knocked him to the floor just as he fired again. But by now the freighter captain had recovered his balance and was whirling for a shot. Knight's finger closed on the trigger just as the man aimed. The clattering blast of the machine-gun filled the room, and the Russian fell, almost cut in two.

The lights flashed on, and Karnsky dived frenziedly for the pistol the man had dropped. Serloff, pawing wildly to lift his black goggles, jumped forward at the same moment and they collided. With a shriek, Karnsky plunged headlong through the open trap and vanished.

The collision had left Serloff sprawled on the floor. He tried to get up, then saw the machine-gun in Richard Knight's hands.

"Don't shoot!" he cried. "I surrender!"

"Turn over—onto your face!" rasped Knight.

As Serloff obeyed, there came a chorus of shouts from the passage. Knight sprang past Haldane, who was struggling fiercely with the mechanic. Four or five of the crew were racing aft, each with a pistol. Knight triggered the heavy gun, and three of the men fell, riddled. A fourth doubled over screaming, and collapsed as the last man made his escape.

A bright light from somewhere below flashed over the trap as Knight whirled back. It was followed by an explosion near the starboard wing.

"Anti-aircraft!" bawled Haldane. He staggered to his feet, his smoking pistol testifying to the mechanic's end. "The carrier's firing on us!"

Through the trap, Knight glimpsed the lighted deck of the *Enterprise*, less than five miles ahead. He sprang to the switchboard, turned off the lights, and ran his hand along the edge of the board, fumbling with something in the darkness. Then:

"Jump!" he shouted at Haldane. "Try to alight on the water near the carrier!"

Serloff raised his head, cringed as Haldane took a step forward, leveled his pistol. Knight dropped the machine-gun, shoved the Englishman's pistol hand aside. "No time for that," he cried. "You've got to get out."

"What about Doyle?" queried Haldane.

"I'll get him out! Jump!"

Knight's shove sent Haldane halfway through the trap. Anti-aircraft shells were bursting on both sides as the Englishman disappeared. Doyle had crawled close to the opening. Knight threw his pistol across the compartment, and flung his arms tightly about the wounded man. Serloff lunged up with a furious oath, but Knight dived through the trap before the Russian could get his hands on a weapon.

The dangling projector shot past with only a few feet to spare. Knight gripped Doyle's rip-cord, gave it a fierce pull. There was a violent jerk, and Doyle was snatched from his hands. He waited a moment, pulled his own cord.

His chute opened with a jolt, and as it jerked him upright he saw Haldane drifting down the sky, half a mile away. The Northrop was falling in flames, and the Spitfire was desperately twisting out of the searchlight beams and anti-aircraft fire from the *Enterprise*.

**THE BOEING** had pulled up. It seemed on the point of fleeing, but suddenly it whirled back toward the carrier. The fire-projector swung aft at a sharp angle, and as Knight stared upward he saw a faint grayish stream emerge from one of the nozzles. Icy horror gripped Knight as a second stream shot from the other nozzle.

His scheme had failed—and both Doyle and he would be caught by that blazing arc!

Fire spurted as the two streams met, and above the glare Knight saw a black-goggled figure staring down through the trap. The horrible white arc leaped down the sky....

With a terrific roar, flame split the night. Deafened by the explosion, Knight stared up and saw a hurtling inferno. Blazing from nose to tail, with one wing blown clear off, the Boeing fell toward the sea. A thousand feet above the water, there came another deafening blast—and when the flame died out the Boeing was gone. Knight's jerk at the ground-wire of the fearful device had been successful!

Searchlights from the *Enterprise* tilted past Knight, and with a thankful heart he saw that both Haldane and Doyle had escaped the flames. Both men were slipping their chutes to land near the vessel, and in a moment Knight saw that a boat was being lowered. He pulled on the shrouds, let the chute fill again when he saw that he would drop near the boat.

As he unfastened his harness, to be ready when he struck, he looked across the water. There was a faint chance that Serloff might have jumped at the first sign of disaster....

But only a sullen red smoke drifted upon the sea.